THE HELLION'S HEART

CLAIRE DELACROIX

DEBORAH A. COOKE

The Hellion's Heart
The Ladies' Essential Guide to the Art of Seduction #4
By Claire Delacroix

THE LADIES' ESSENTIAL GUIDE TO THE ART OF SEDUCTION

REGENCY ROMANCES

The Ladies' Essential Guide to the Art of Seduction is a series of Regency romances. In each story, a marriage in dire straits is rescued by the lady's consultation of Miss Esmeralda Ballantyne's incomparable volume of amorous advice. Over the course of the series, Esmeralda matches wits (and more) with the resolute Duke of Haynesdale, who is determined to stop her endeavor, no matter the price.

1. The Christmas Conquest

2. The Masquerade of the Marchioness

3. The Widow's Wager

4. The Hellion's Heart

5. The Bluestocking's Bargain

~

THE HELLION'S HEART

DEAR READER

Dear Reader –

Welcome to Joshua and Helena's story, which hadn't orig- inally been part of the plan for this series. Helena fascinated me when she walked onto the pages of The Widow's Wager, and it quickly became clear that she would need her own book—and exactly the right hero. I think Joshua is that man. It doesn't hurt that he falls with just one look, though Helena has to learn to look beyond superficial appearances to find her hero. I hope you enjoy their story.

*The story of the duke's ancestors, Bartholomew and Anna, that Joshua shares at one point is told in my medieval romance, **The Crusader's Kiss**.*

*Next up in the series will be **The Bluestocking's Bar- gain**. You might remember Catherine's sister mucking up the books in their father's bookshop in **The Widow's Wager**. Arthur Beckham subsequently discovered, upon arrival in Venice, that instead of a lending copy of Childe Harolde, he has Harris' List of Covent Garden Ladies. How scandalous! He attributes this to mischief on the part of one of the younger sisters at Carruthers & Carruthers and resolves to investigate on his return to London.*

By the time he arrives in town, Patience has a scheme of her own to recover the book and proposes a bargain with the dashing young rake. She wants to publish Mrs. Oliver's guide of amorous advice for women, but needs a man's help to arrange publication. Intrigued by this bluestocking who determined to rewrite the rules of society, Arthur proposes a marriage of convenience as the basis of their alliance and Patience accepts. But this business arrangement quickly whets appetites for more – Arthur is a rake, after all, and he already enjoys surprising Patience. I'm curious to see whether it will be Arthur or Patience who suggests that Mrs. Oliver's advice be put to the test. Will it be a dare? Who will fall in love first? Who will admit it first?

This one is going to be fun to write since both will get more than expected from the bargain! I'm planning for **The Bluestocking's Bargain** to be published in October 2024.

As you know, we have the story of Esmeralda and the Duke of Haynesdale that continues throughout the series. You might have noticed that they had fewer scenes in **The Hellion's Heart** – that's because they tried to completely take over the book. To keep the focus on Helena and Joshua, I removed most of those scenes, leaving just a hint of Esmeralda and the duke's activities.

Esmeralda and the duke will have their own book, coming next spring, and you'll be able to read the full version of their story. **The Duke's Desire** will be book seven in the series – book six will be published in January.

I never cease to be surprised by how often – and how effectively – characters can turn everything around!

I plan also to write the story of the duke's ward, but that will come after **The Duke's Desire**.

Now you know the entire plan! Thank you for reading my books. :-)

Until next time, all my best—
Claire

~

CHAPTER 1

Addersley Manor, Nottinghamshire, England - April, 1817

It has often been said that those who eavesdrop seldom hear good of themselves. Joshua Hargood, seventh Viscount of Addersley, had never believed as much until this day.

Of course, he was not inclined to eavesdrop. In this particular instance, he overheard the comments of his servants entirely by accident. He was seeking his butler, Fairfax, to communicate that he would assume his late father's habit of dining in the library when alone. Enough of the lonely sound of one set of silverware on the china, echoing in that vast chilly space. Bachelor and viscount, Joshua could do as he chose. Perhaps he would become eccentric early.

The fact was that solitude chafed upon him. It had been easy to keep his vow to his father when there was a task that had consumed him utterly. The end of the war meant the end of that labor, though. He missed analyzing messages from spies and covert individuals, seeking the patterns and aiding in the crown's strategies. Tending his hereditary responsibilities at Addersley Manor simply could not compare.

Joshua was haunted by that season in London, its revels and pleasures. Though he had no desire to return to such reckless abandon, he tired of a staid and predictable life. Surely, there was some middle ground, one that would not require breaking his promise to his father.

He had need of a quest, but had yet to discover one of merit.

Joshua slowed on the stairs at the sound of voices in the kitchen, then halted entirely when he heard his own name.

"'Tis a right shame, it is, his lordship being such a good man but nary an inclination to marry," his cook, Mrs. Baird, said with a heavy sigh. "'Tis unnatural. There shall never be any wee bairns in this house, if matters continue as they are."

Joshua could readily imagine the stocky older woman shaking her head.

"It is admirable for his lordship to forgo matrimony after the loss of his betrothed," Fairfax said with authority.

"But it has been a decade!" Reed, Joshua's valet, protested.

"And that marriage was arranged, as I heard it," Mrs. Baird said grimly. "With the old lord dead and buried, there is no one to arrange another match."

Fairfax, the butler, cleared his throat pointedly. "His lordship might choose a bride himself."

Reed chuckled. "Oh, and the pretty ladies will fall over their feet to accept a man said to have ice in his veins."

Joshua looked down at the floor. If that was said of him, it was not without justification. He took pride in keeping his thoughts to himself.

"He has a title and enough wealth to keep a wife content," Fairfax said. "If young ladies were not so frivolous, they might see the merit of that."

"I do not see a line at the door," Reed said with his usual irreverence. "Not even ambitious mamas consider him a good prospect."

"If ever he left Addersley, he might catch the eye of one of them," Mrs. Baird said.

"His lordship is in mourning," Fairfax said severely. "Surely, you have better things to do than speculate endlessly and achieve nothing."

Joshua turned away, considering the notion. Could he arrange a match for himself? He would have to mingle more in society, but perhaps a wife would resolve his restlessness. It would provide him with a task, to be sure, and perhaps a much-needed sense of purpose.

"Oh, how these halls used to ring with laughter and mischief when first I came to this house," Fairfax said. "So much changed at Addersley with the untimely demise of the viscountess." The deep tones of the butler were as unmistakable, as was that man's philosophical tone. "An enchanting woman, gracious, beautiful, and always cheerful. I never met a lady so like a welcome beam of sunlight."

Joshua was startled by this markedly poetic compliment from his staid butler.

"Died when his lordship was six years of age, did she not?" Reed asked, for he had not been at Addersley that long.

"And Master Gerald only five," Fairfax intoned. "There were those as said she had the boys too closely together, but even I knew how she yearned for a houseful of children. The old viscount could deny her nothing." Fairfax dropped his voice. "'Twas whispered that she was with child when she caught that illness."

Mrs. Baird clicked her tongue. "Two lost at once then. 'Tis a pity."

"Indeed. His lordship was never the same after her demise, even though Master Gerald was so like her. Perhaps it broke the old viscount's heart to see so much of his lady in that boy."

Joshua's frown deepened. It was true. Gerald had shared their mother's nature. No wonder the house seemed dark and dreary in the absence of both of them.

If he took ever a wife, she should be lively.

Mrs. Baird chuckled. "A proper scamp Master Gerald was, but one with charm to spare. No one could remain angry with that boy, no matter what he did. And now he's dead and gone, along with the old viscount, and there is only quiet as his lordship seems to prefer. Addersley Manor might as well be a tomb!"

Joshua could only agree. But what price to change matters? Could he endure a season in London, even to find a bride? He feared his resolve might crumble in the face of so many temptations. He could not return to the life of a wastrel and break his vow.

"Such doings in London, that wicked place, but it must be ever so lively." Mrs. Baird sighed again, her words unwittingly echoing Joshua's own thoughts. "I suppose there is no chance of ever seeing it with my own eyes."

"I believe his lordship intends to sell the London house," Fairfax said, which was entirely true.

Mrs. Baird and Reed sighed as one at the opportunities lost with that potential transaction. "Tell us of that last time in London again," Mrs. Baird urged, undoubtedly speaking to Reed. "I wish I could have seen the argument between those two boys myself."

"I saw only a part of it and could not hear it all, but you would not have recognized his lordship," Reed said, ignoring how Fairfax cleared his throat in disapproval.

"He was as a man possessed. Such fire and fury! I have never seen him thus, and there were hot words between they two, for the first time I ever heard. Of course, Master Gerald was unrepentant, and the old lord was livid with them both."

"Curious," Fairfax said. "One must wonder at the cause."

"There is no cause to wonder," Reed said. "'Twas always about a woman with Master Gerald."

Mrs. Baird laughed. "Ah, he would have had a dozen children in these halls by now if he had been the heir."

"His lordship is a good man and a better viscount than his younger brother would ever have been," Fairfax chastised her. "We might have found ourselves in the street with no more than a crust of bread if positions had been reversed and Mister Gerald had inherited the title."

Joshua turned away. All of their lives, the brothers had been compared, and save for his father and apparently his butler, Joshua was always judged to be inferior to Gerald. A better companion, a better guest, better with a jest and in coaxing a lady's smile, Gerald had possessed more charm in his smallest finger than Joshua in his entire body.

Gerald had lived every minute of every day. He lit a room when he entered it. His smile prompted even the most surly curmudgeon to soften. And the women. Joshua shook his head. Women had fallen at Gerald's feet wherever he went.

The two brothers, to be sure, could not have been more opposite in nature. Yet despite that and all that had passed between them, he missed his younger brother.

Joshua returned to his library, no longer caring where he dined. Oh, Gerald would have enjoyed every moment of having the title and the modest Hargood fortune. It might have taken him a fortnight to rid himself of every last shilling. He would have laughed when it was done, unburdened by regret—then charmed some heiress and spent her legacy, too.

In contrast, Joshua was committed to keeping the estate solvent for the rest of his life. It was true that the house seemed to brood in silence in these days, the shadowy corners filled with ghosts. Fairfax was right. Once, these halls had been lively. Once there had been guests and parties, even the occasional ball. Christmas had been magical. But the merriment had ended with his mother's death.

Addersley Manor had need of a viscountess.

Where would he find a bride?

Of greater import, what kind of wife would suit him best?

Joshua began to compose a list, for every task was more readily achieved with a clear objective. First and foremost, the lady should be vivacious. He yearned for his home to echo with laughter again. She should be of a health and age that allowed for the bearing of children., so their laughter might join her own. He would not mind if she were lovely, though he was more interested in her nature than her appearance. Was it wrong to wish for a wife who snared his attention, who surprised him on occasion, who might match wits with him or share in the pleasure of good books? Joshua thought not. Such a woman could not fail to stir his blood.

Beyond that, he had few requirements. If she could not ride, he could teach her. If she knew little of managing a household like Addersley Manor, he would be content for her to learn at her own pace, even if she made mistakes. He did not care whether she had a dowry either, for he was comfortable in his own right.

He reviewed his list then added one more item. It

would be best, in his view, if the lady bore no resemblance to Miss Charlotte Havilland, his betrothed who had died. People would make much of it and though he cared little for gossip and rumor, the lady might be wounded by such idle speculation. If a lady accepted his suit and became his wife, she would be beneath his protection and Joshua would not allow her to be injured in any way.

Dark hair then, or chestnut tresses. Anything but blonde the hue of honey. She should not be tall and willowy like Charlotte. In truth, he had a fondness for petite women. There was something delightful about sweeping a woman off her feet and into his arms. He recalled carrying off a courtesan in those London days, much to their mutual satisfaction—although that happy result had not solely been due to his carrying her to the bed.

Was it wrong to consider the appeal of marriage's physical delights? Joshua thought not. Indeed, he had been solitary too long and sons were not conceived by will alone.

He had a list then, and an objective. What remained was to create a plan, ideally one that did not require his return to London for the season.

Were there any ladies in the vicinity of Addersley that fulfilled his list?

He could not say.

Joshua frowned at his desk and picked up the letters that had been delivered that morning. There were a few tradesman's bills, anticipated and of little interest, and one letter.

He noted the unkempt state of the paper. Had this missive been dragged through the mud before its delivery? Frowning, Joshua held it with distaste as he opened it, then stared at the single line within.

You must pay for your brother's crime.

JOSHUA TURNED THE MISSIVE OVER, finding neither return address nor postmark, nor indeed, any other distinguishing mark. Had it been delivered by hand? He would ask Fairfax but could already guess what the reply might be. Someone had gone to some trouble to deliver this message without detection.

Just like the last one.

The other had not been so filthy, but it had also been without any identifying marks or signature. The message had been the identical.

His brother's crime. Joshua could think of a thousand insults and misdemeanors committed by Gerald, pranks and jests every one, but a crime? The notion was preposterous, which was why he had burned the first note, thinking it a tasteless joke.

Why *had* their father bought Gerald that commission? Had there been a specific impetus? Joshua had not been privy to that interview but had only been told of it in the briefest of terms after Gerald's departure. He had never liked the lost opportunity of seeing Gerald off, or of reconciling after that one bitter fight.

His father's arrangements had meant the brothers had never spoken again, let alone reconciled. Had that been the plan? Joshua looked across the library, to the chair favored by his father, wishing the old man's ghost might appear to answer his queries.

But then, his father had answered few questions while alive, and a habit of such discretion refined over a lifetime was unlikely to change, even in death.

Who was sending these notes? The threat was clear, though vague. Joshua reasoned that his best chance of solving this riddle was with the assistance of the Duke of Haynesdale. He had been away from Addersley and Nottinghamshire too long to hazard any guesses himself.

He knew that Haynesdale was not in residence at his country house, but perhaps that gentleman's mother knew her son's plans. It could not hurt to ask the dowager duchess, not just about the plans of her son but possibly the availability of local ladies. His estate manager, Mr. Newson, was expecting him at four but it was only just past one.

A ride to Haynesdale House would fill Joshua's afternoon most admirably.

~

THE ONE THING CONSTANCE DEVRIES, the Dowager Duchess of Haynesdale, could not abide was an ambitious female.

It was one matter to have reconciled—to some extent—with Lady Frances Dalhousie, her long-time social adversary, but quite another to further that woman's obvious aspirations to secure Haynesdale for her niece.

Yet Constance had been fool enough to send the coach to collect aunt and niece for tea. She had not initially considered what hay would be made of a gesture she saw as merely courteous, not until the coach was out of earshot.

Since then, she had fumed in anticipation of Fanny's gloating. The woman could be insufferable!

The friction between them had begun in their debut season, when Constance had caught the eye of the heir to Haynesdale, who subsequently became her husband. Though the two young woman had initially been amiable, Fanny had been vexed with Constance ever since Luke's preference had become evident. In recent weeks, they had reached a more friendly balance again, mostly due to Frances' nephew marrying Constance's daughter. Nicholas and Eliza were a very happy couple.

To Constance's thinking, her former rival should have been content. But the interest of Fanny's young niece in the graces of Haynesdale had been unmistakable, never mind her apparent fascination with Damien, Constance's sole surviving son and the duke.

Constance had once remarked upon Fanny's tenacity and it seemed that some matters did not change with time. Having failed to secure Haynesdale herself, Fanny would undoubtedly seek to see her niece graced with the coronet. Miss Helena Emerson appeared to have the identical objective in mind.

If only Damien had seen fit to wed in a timely fashion.

If only Damien had seen fit to wed at all.

Constance did not doubt that her son waited for love, as she and his father had done, but still. It was absurdly inconvenient for him to be an unattached duke with Fanny's niece in the vicinity, her ambitious gaze fixed firmly on strawberry leaves. How far would Helena go to win Damien's attention and his ring? Constance could not guess, but the girl had been raised by Fanny, which was no good portent. Doubtless they two would ally together to win their goal.

If only men were not so often foolish about pretty girls.

If only Helena were not so very, very lovely. Truly, the girl was an incomparable beauty, which was the worst possible luck.

Damien, Constance well knew, would be unshakable once he settled upon a bride, no matter how unsuitable the lady in question might be. She knew the obstinacy of her son well. It would be prudent to resolve Helena's match before Damien returned to Haynesdale, whenever that might prove to be.

Indeed, that had been the impetus behind hosting a ball in less than a fortnight's time—it would be a sensible investment with the objective of seeing Helena matched before Damien's return—yet Constance had not been able to secure the appearances of more than a handful of eligible young men.

None of them could hold a candle to Damien, either in looks or fortune.

She was not an overly proud mama: she was honest.

And she was vexed.

Constance was considering her own limited possibilities for ensuring a happy outcome when a caller was announced. She rose as Viscount Addersley stepped into the room and bowed to her, and found herself smiling in genuine welcome. How she liked this young man, who was not so young anymore. She calculated quickly. He was several years older than her daughter Eliza, but much younger than her son Damien. Why, he must have seen thirty summers by now.

She blinked in realization of a simple truth. Joshua Hargood was of an eligible age, possessed of a fortune and a title, tall and handsome and not without assets of his own. In her view, his character was one of the best. His dark brown hair had a wave to it, his eyes were green and thickly lashed, his profile such that he could have been used as a model for a statue of Adonis.

He had been his father's pride and joy.

She could only admire a man who had surrendered, along with his brother, to the temptations of London yet managed to extricate himself to establish a respectable life. There had been, of course, the tragedy, but Constance knew many men whose path would not have been altered about it.

Of course, the viscount was not a garrulous man.

Indeed, he could sit in silence for longer than she found reasonable. He was not a fool, though, his gaze sharp and incisive, and she doubted he missed many details.

Pretty girls seldom had their wits about them, though, when they considered suitors. Too many of them were seduced by charm or lavish spending, empty compliments and promises. The viscount might take time to make a pledge, but once it was made, he would keep it at any price.

It was curious that Joshua and his younger brother had been so very different. Lady Haynesdale's sons had possessed marked similarities, all resembling their father in one way or another. But that had not been the case with the viscount's sons. While Joshua had every honorable trait of nature, being noble, steadfast and thorough in the fulfillment of his duties, his younger brother, Gerald, had possessed an unholy measure of charm and vivacity.

To her thinking, Gerald's beguiling manner had disguised a selfish nature and an obsession with his own pleasures. She thought him reckless. The man could not have kept his word to save his life, but those undiscerning females had adored him. Joshua had often been overlooked in his brother's company, to be sure.

It was a shame for such a fine young man to be unwed.

But then, Miss Emerson and her aunt were expected momentarily, at her own invitation. Perhaps the meeting of the two younger persons was meant to be. Perhaps Constance could ensure a most suitable match, one that would eliminate any threat to Damien. Truly, for a viscount to wed the niece of a viscount would be entirely suitable.

"Lady Haynesdale, I thank you for seeing me without announcement on this day," the viscount said, accepting a cup of tea. "I had hoped that the duke might be in residence as well."

"Alas, Damien departed from London over a week ago. I fear I do not know either his destination or the date of his planned return." The viscount said nothing, his expression inscrutable. "Might I be of assistance?"

"I fear not, madame. I wished to consult him on a private matter." He stared into his cup as if he would conjure conversation from its depths. "I will not trouble you any longer…" he began.

Constance hastened to fill the cup again. "I did not realize you were in the country,"

He nodded as he settled back in his seat. "Father wished to be buried at Addersley Manor, as is traditional in the family. We returned two months ago, in his final illness."

"I must extent my condolences, as well."

The viscount nodded acceptance and sipped his tea with troubling purpose.

"And all is well at Addersley Manor?" she asked.

"Quite well, thank you."

He would put his cup aside and leave.

Trust Fanny to be late on this occasion!

Constance would simply have to chatter and detain him somehow, hoping his manners were sufficient that he would not rise while she was speaking.

She took a breath and began, not intending to fall silent before Fanny and her ward arrived.

JOSHUA HAD FORGOTTEN how some women felt compelled to fill a silence with idle chatter. He had not expected Lady Haynesdale to do as much but perhaps she was lonely in the absence of her son. She began to speak hurriedly, and he listened with some reluctance. He could not cause offense, though he wondered whether there was a way to guide the discussion.

Truly, the dowager duchess spoke with the fury of a spring river and he doubted anything could change the course of whatever she desired to say.

"It is so long since our paths have crossed," she said with a smile. Truly, she must have been a beauty in her youth and still she was an attractive woman. "Perhaps you are unaware that my daughter, Eliza, recently wed Captain Nicholas Emerson, who served alongside Damien in Spain? Were you at all acquainted with him when he lived at Southpoint as a boy?"

Joshua shook his head. "Only slightly."

"Well then, you may not recall his skill with horses," she said. "Captain Emerson always had a touch with horses, my son has assured me as much."

"I do." Joshua strove to make some contribution to the conversation. "He had a fine stallion, I recall, of stock from Haynesdale perhaps?"

"Yes! He has begun to breed horses at Southpoint, with Damien's encouragement, and perhaps that will be of interest to you. Gentlemen are so often interested in horses and knowing of good stock."

Joshua nodded politely.

"I am hoping that you will take pity upon me, sir," the dowager said with another charming smile. "I have been in town of late and am desperate for local news. I do not suppose you might indulge me?"

What was this? "How so, Lady Haynesdale?"

Her smile broadened. "I do have weddings in mind this spring, to be sure, given my daughter's recent and happy union. May I be so bold as to ask whether you have become betrothed since we last met?"

Perhaps assistance for his plan was closer than Joshua had realized. "Not I."

"Even though you have inherited the title?"

"It has been less than two months, Lady Haynesdale."

"Of course, you are still in mourning, and there must be many details to attend."

Joshua nodded.

She smiled again. "Dare I ask if a particular lady has claimed your attention?"

Joshua smiled. "Do you mean to contrive a match for me, Lady Haynesdale?"

"I would not be so bold, of course." She smiled at him and he was not convinced of her claim. "Your arrival is most timely this day as I would like to ask for your assistance."

He inclined his head. "I am at your service."

"Lord Addersley, you almost make me wish I had another daughter of eligible age."

"You are kind, Lady Haynesdale."

"An acquaintance of mine has recently arrived in the area and will be visiting today. I fear that her niece, who is Captain Emerson's younger sister and my friend's ward, must be disappointed in Haynesdale after the activities of London. To that end, I am planning a ball in less than a fortnight and do hope you will attend."

Joshua felt his brows rise. "A ball to entertain the ward of a friend? That is most generous, Lady Haynesdale." Who was this young lady and why did the duchess wish to see her attached? Joshua was intrigued.

His hostess leaned forward, and he watched her cheeks flush slightly, as if she had been caught. "But the young lady is lovely. I must ensure that her dance card is full, lest she find my hospitality lacking, yet I had forgotten how few gentlemen there are in the vicinity who dance well."

"I do not dance, Lady Constance." He spoke firmly

and set down the cup. His pledge to his father was uppermost in his thoughts and he would not break it so readily as this.

"Nonsense! I recall your tutor well." She shook a finger at him, her tone teasing, not allowing him a chance to speak. "I will not have your refusal, sir," she said, pretending to be stern. "Will you not at least meet Miss Emerson before you decide?"

Joshua blinked. "You *do* strive to make a match, Lady Constance," he accused softly, guessing the reason was less about his own prospects than those of the duke. "Does this young lady have a *tendre* for your son?"

The dowager's cheeks flamed. "I could not speak as to her interest," she began, though Joshua sensed that was not the case. The young lady aspired to wed Haynesdale but his mother did not approve. Why not?

Did it matter? He would not welcome Haynesdale's leavings, simply to suit the dowager duchess's plans. He could be insulted by being deemed to be merely useful and set down his cup, mustering his refusal.

But there was an audible flurry of activity from the foyer, much to his hostess' visible relief. "Why, they have arrived and you can make their acquaintance in advance of the ball. How perfect an opportunity!"

Joshua stood and spoke with resolve. "Lady Constance, I remind you that your son is most capable in evading the aspirations of even the most ambitious of young ladies." He reached for his hat. Why did some women persist in striving to orchestrate the situations of others? It was a kind of meddling Joshua could not admire...

The door was opened in that moment and the newly arrived guests announced. Joshua glanced up, then could only stare in silence.

If he had believed in kismet, fate or other such frippery, Joshua might have concluded his alliance with this young lady was meant to be. No sooner had he realized he had need of a bride and despaired of finding one without returning to London, than the perfect young lady stepped into his presence.

Her hair was as dark as a raven's wing and her eyes were blue. They sparkled with an enthusiasm for life that could not be disguised and her step was spritely. She wore a white gown with blue embroidery upon the hem and a wide ribbon of sapphire blue at the high waist. Her spencer was black velvet, and altogether she was a most appealing sight. She was so delicately built that he could have easily carried her all the way back to Addersley Manor. Better yet, she bore absolutely no resemblance to Charlotte Havilland.

He might have conjured her by will.

He blinked, averted his gaze with an effort, and cast Lady Haynesdale a glance.

The dowager smiled at him, triumphant.

But her success was not yet complete. What trait was lacking in the lady? Was she witless or foolish? Joshua watched her gaze rove over the drawing room, as if she had plans to change it all, and guessed that her ambitions were as suspected. What made her unsuitable for Haynesdale in his mother's view? Was it only her open ambition?

Joshua put down his hat, determined to find out.

"Oh, but Constance, you have a guest!" the older lady protested.

"Of course, you cannot have met. Our neighbor, Lord Addersley, seventh Viscount of Addersley," Lady Haynesdale said. "My lord, Lady Dalhousie and her niece, Miss Helena Emerson."

"Ladies," Joshua Hargood said smoothly and bowed as he took Helena's hand. She was as tiny and perfect as a fairy maiden.

Joshua saw absolutely no reason to depart from Haynesdale House with haste.

There was a riddle to solve.

Of course, he would have another cup of tea.

CHAPTER 2

*H*elena Emerson could not imagine a worse fate than her own. Not only had she been compelled to leave the marvels of London for the desolation of Nottinghamshire, but every soul in the vicinity was hovering at death's door due to advanced age.

Even the maid employed by her aunt was older than she.

One day soon, Helena was convinced, they would all contract some illness—possibly a cold, this coming autumn—and expire in unison, abandoning her in this remote backwater, like an orphan in a novel.

She entertained herself briefly with the possibility of the Duke of Haynesdale himself nursing her back to health. She had asked her brother, Nicholas, about the duke's inclination to heal the sick, since they were both friends and former comrades, and Nicholas had laughed so hard that tears had leaked from his eyes. He said that the duke was more likely to order a person to get on with it and keep up the pace. It was clear that her older brother, despite being recently wed, had no proper sense of romance.

Helena could only hope the duke returned home

soon. No one seemed to have any notion where he had gone, how long he would be there and when he would arrive at Haynesdale.

Worse, no one seemed to care.

Helena could make no sense of it. Perhaps senility addled their wits. The duke was the most important person in the vicinity, but everyone acted as if he was of no relevance whatsoever. His mother was planning a ball, which Helena had been certain must be intended to herald the duke's return, but that lady had laughed when asked as much. Damien, the dowager had confided, did much as he wished, regardless of her thoughts upon the matter. Even if her son was in residence on the date of the ball, there was no guarantee he would attend. He might, his mother had assured Helena, simply sit in his library and brood in privacy. Lady Haynesdale seemed to find this prospect amusing.

Helena would never permit that to happen.

At least on this day, she would finally escape the prison known as Bramble Cottage. Her aunt had no horse and no carriage, not so much as a cart, and the walk to the village was ridiculously long. Helena had realized within hours of her arrival that she was doomed to die of boredom there, forgotten by all the world.

Her aunt would be too busy choosing draperies and cushions to even notice her ward's demise.

Further, it had rained for three entire days, making it impossible to even wander through the gardens of the cottage—such as they were. Her aunt was full of plans for clearing the weeds and planting perennials, even wretched roses, to the point that Helena almost began to wish her death would occur soon.

Matters improved with Lady Haynesdale's invitation of this day. The dowager duchess had invited Helena and her aunt to tea and had even sent a coach to

Bramble Cottage for them. Helena could not disguise her admiration of the vehicle, running her hands over the upholstery and bouncing against the cushions. It was not the largest or the best coach owned by the duke, but it was the finest she had ever ridden in. The four horses pulling it were as white as snow and perfectly matched, like they had drawn it out of a fairy tale palace.

Soon it might be her own to request!

She waved to all and sundry from the windows with such enthusiasm that Aunt Fanny chastised her. Helena did not care. This sign of the dowager's favor could only be a hint of alliances to come! She blew a kiss in the direction of Southpoint when they passed that house, even though there was no sign of Nicholas or Eliza to witness her triumph.

Helena's first glimpse of Haynesdale House, however, was somewhat of a disappointment. While the house was large, it sprawled in every direction, burdened by additions and a woeful lack of symmetry. It was beyond ancient and though Aunt Fanny thought it glorious, Helena knew it would need considerable improvement to be suitable. She did not doubt that the chimneys smoked and that there were too few of them. The roof must leak in some areas, and the floors were undoubtedly in need of repair. Goodness only knew how many creatures had taken refuge within its walls and cupboards over the years. Clearly, the place was in need of the governing hand of a young duchess like herself.

Upon arrival, they were informed that Lady Haynesdale was reviewing the plans for the replanting of the rose garden. Helena watched a familiar gleam light in Aunt Fanny's eyes and groaned silently. The discussion and dispute between the two older women about roses was seemingly endless. Her aunt followed the butler to the drawing room with purpose as Helena strove to resign herself to yet more interminable discussion about the plants in question.

Perhaps when she was duchess, she would have the roses removed from the gardens of Haynesdale House and a terrace created instead. There could be columns and a reflecting pool, and no one need ever talk about roses again.

It was a most admirable notion and one that might allow her to tolerate the inevitable discussion topic of the afternoon. She considered the proportions of the foyer with appreciation, noting that a lighter hue on the walls might favor the space better. Oh, she would see every detail changed to her satisfaction! She could not wait to begin.

To Helena's surprise, there was a gentleman already with Lady Haynesdale. Introductions were made and Aunt Fanny positively preened when she learned that the other guest was Joshua Hargood, the Seventh Viscount of Addersley.

Helena smiled politely, if only to prove to the dowager duchess that she had sufficient grace to become the duke's bride.

She stole a look at the gentleman through her lashes and caught her breath. He was certainly not as venerable as others she had met in Haynesdale. He might even be younger than her brother, Nicholas. He appeared, Helena had to admit, markedly more youthful and vigorous than the duke, who used a cane and often looked disgruntled.

Even with due consideration, she could not imagine how he might be more handsome.

The viscount's expression was polite but calm, as if he was in the habit of hiding his thoughts. (Perhaps he had none at all.) His hair was chestnut brown and wavy, and he was tall. His boots were polished to a gleam and his jacket of dark green was perfectly tailored. His cravat was not as flamboyantly large as Mr. Melbourne's had been, but it was tied with precision. He wore no gem in it and no flower in his buttonhole; there was only one ring on his smallest finger and no other ornament about his attire. Helena ceded that his valet was skilled but found herself reluctant to give more credit to the man himself.

It was a tragedy his father had not anticipated that his son would need a higher rank to wed well.

The viscount bowed to Aunt Fanny then to Helena, but offered only a minimal greeting before returning his attention to his tea. Helena imagined she might have a more enthusiastic discussion with one of the statues in a London park.

Perhaps he suffered from the liability of being dull.

"It is a delight to meet you, sir," Aunt Fanny said, settling onto her chair with purpose.

"My pleasure, Lady Dalhousie," he said, his voice lovely and deep. It was a little rough in a most appealing way. Truly, the sound of it made Helena feel a little shivery, in a very good way. She stole another glance at him, only to find him watching her. What was he thinking?

There were shortbread, which thrilled Aunt Fanny, though Helena accepted only a small one and did not eat it.

She dared not become plump in the duke's absence.

"And is your wife in London or in the country?" Aunt Fanny asked the viscount, so direct that Helena nearly winced.

"Lord Addersley is unwed," Lady Haynesdale interjected quickly, though Helena wished she had not. She would have liked to hear the viscount's delicious deep voice again. "It is not yet two months since he inherited the title. We all miss his father a great deal."

"You have our sincere condolences, sir," Aunt Fanny said.

The man in question nodded agreement. His gaze flicked to Helena and lingered.

His eyes were green, his chin square with a cleft in the middle. He would be utterly dashing if he had a dimple. Or perhaps if he smiled at all.

On impulse, she smiled at him.

For a heartbeat, something flared in his eyes that made him look too dangerous and disreputable to be sipping tea in Haynesdale House. There was suddenly a vitality about him and Helena had a thrilling sense of power held in restraint. She envisioned him outdoors, perhaps striding to the stables, or riding to hunt. No, he would be fighting a duel at midnight, defeating his opponent with confidence and skill. His cravat would be loosened, his jacket discarded, his hair tousled, his hat lost.

Oh. Yes. Helena caught her breath, feeling a flush right to her toes. The viscount, apparently unaffected, averted his gaze and the moment, if it had existed, was gone.

He was as inscrutable as earlier. Had Helena glimpsed his truth though a chink in his armor? Or had she had seen more than was present? Perhaps her hopes of adventure tinted her view of her mundane surroundings. Perhaps her imagination ran rampant.

She sighed and sipped her tea.

The viscount did not speak again but neither did he leave. The two older women filled any deficiency with their chattering, and Helena had heard it all before.

"Mr. Marchand is quite adamant that the Great Maiden's Blush roses will not flourish in the position we had assigned to them," Lady Haynesdale said to Aunt Fanny.

Helena barely refrained from grimacing. The viscount examined the pattern on his saucer with apparent fascination.

Perhaps they had *something* in common.

"But they must!" her aunt insisted. "I had mine in just such a position at Hexham and they were the subject of considerable admiration."

"Perhaps the air is cooler there," Lady Haynesdale suggested. "As Hexham is further north."

"Not so much as that," Aunt Fanny replied and partook of her tea for fortification. Her tone hardened. "We are in Nottingham, after all. Remind me—how long has Mr. Marchand been tending to roses?"

"Twenty years!"

Aunt Fanny shook her head sagely. "Yet he is *mistaken.*"

Lady Haynesdale caught her breath, her indignation clear.

Aunt Fanny did not so much as blink.

The air crackled between them, as so often it did.

For that moment, even Helena did not dare to breathe. She noticed that the viscount looked between the older women with the barest curiosity, then Lady Haynesdale swept to her feet and gestured imperiously to a large table on the far side of the room. Those wretched garden plans were spread across its surface.

"Perhaps we might review the plan," she invited in a tone like steel.

"Perhaps I can divine your gardener's unfortunate error," Aunt Fanny countered. Lady Haynesdale's eyes flashed and the pair turned to march toward the table in unison, spines rigid.

When they were out of earshot, Helena could not keep silent. "They will argue for hours," she confided quietly to the viscount. "It might be prudent to make your excuses. I, alas, am doomed to remain until the final foray."

His eyes were a vibrant hue of green when his gaze fixed upon her. "But it would be unchivalrous to abandon you, Miss Emerson."

Oh, that voice!

Helena wanted to hear more.

No, she wanted him to whisper scandalous suggestions into her ear, at midnight on the heath, immediately before fighting that duel. She smiled at the unlikelihood of that, given his advanced age. Undoubtedly such an elderly man would be in bed alone with his hot brick by nine each night.

"Alas, I am accustomed to it," she said when the silence grew long. "The ride from London seemed twice as long as it was in truth, for all the discussion of roses and soil. This rose and that rose, this hue and that, shade and sun and *terroir*." She shrugged and sipped her tea.

The viscount nodded, his gaze unswerving. Did the man even blink?

The silence set Helena's teeth on edge.

"You have no fondness for gardening?" he asked finally.

Perhaps it was because of the splendor of the duke's abode – or the feminine décor—that he was so quiet. Helena felt obliged to prove herself a good guest and make conversation.

After all, Lady Haynesdale might tell the duke of it.

She shook her head with a smile. "Perhaps in my dotage, I will find it more interesting. I do like flowers. My aunt says that I have a gift for arranging them, and I enjoy that task. Not that we have so many flowers as yet at Bramble Cottage." He gave the slightest nod of acknowledgement. "Are you interested in gardening, Lord Addersley?"

He lifted one brow, which made him look diabolical

for the barest moment—then he was impassive again. "I am not yet in my dotage, Miss Emerson."

"Oh, but you are so old! You must be nearly thirty, if not more."

Were his eyes twinkling? She could not be certain for he looked across the room. "I *am* thirty," he acknowledged in a low rumble that made her shiver, then set aside his tea.

She had no notion why it should amuse him to be so very old, much less why she should be so affected by a few words from a man who should be utterly lacking in appeal. It must be his voice, so rich and dangerous, it seemed at odds with his composed manner. Her imagination made too much of little. Again. "And are you plagued by many ailments?"

The viscount shook his head, once more, he was solemn and watchful.

She dared to lean closer, dropping her voice in confidence. "You need not be proud with me, sir. I am only curious. One day, I may reach your advanced age and it would be better to be prepared for the challenges that beset me in my infirmity."

"Or you might not reach such an advanced age at all," he countered. "Which I can hardly believe is a preferable alternative."

It took Helena a moment to understand his meaning, then she gasped, feeling her cheeks flush. "But I am in the most robust health, sir!"

"You do appear to be. But future prospects, Miss Emerson, have a way of being unpredictable."

What a grim prognosis. He turned then to watch the two older ladies and Helena missed his attention just a little.

She cleared her throat slightly. "Is Addersley in the vicinity of Haynesdale, sir? I confess that I know little of the neighborhood."

"I understand you have recently come from London."

"Well, yes." His silence invited her to continue. "It is the wrong time of year to leave, you know. We should be *going* to London for the season instead of lingering here. But Aunt is most content at Bramble Cottage." He neither concurred with this nor showed any empathy for her situation. "Do you know it?"

He nodded. "It has been vacant for some time."

"Well, not any longer, thanks to my brother. Perhaps you know him? Captain Emerson, who now resides at Southpoint."

The viscount nodded again. "With his new bride, the duke's sister."

"Precisely. Nicholas has let the cottage to Aunt Fanny. She is my guardian, so we are there together." She pursed her lips, aware that she was chattering but unable to stop. "Do you like small dogs?"

"Not particularly." He lifted a brow. "Do you?"

"I don't know. I've never had a dog, but Aunt seems resolved to get a small dog, perhaps to see me entertained." She grimaced. "I am not certain I should like to have a dog at all." She studied him, then. "Why do you not like small dogs?"

"It is my understanding that they are inclined to bite."

"But you are not certain?"

He shook his head. "Large dogs are all I have ever known. They are even of temper, every one of them."

"Truly?" she asked. "How large?"

The viscount held out a hand. If he had been standing, it would have been at his hip.

"So big as that?"

He nodded. If her brother had made the claim, Helena would have thought he teased her. Such a dog would be almost as large as a pony. But the viscount's gaze was steady and his manner sincere, an indication that he told the truth.

There was something to be said of a man whose word could be trusted.

She would not remember her folly over Mr. Ethan Melbourne, a man whose every declaration had been a deception. He had been fulsome, all the time, a marked contrast to the viscount.

Hmm.

"Goodness. They must eat a lot," she said.

The viscount chuckled then, surprised into it, and amusement transformed him utterly.

Helena smiled at his pleasure, savoring the sight. If he looked like this all the time, she might have been unable to resist him, duke or not. If he had been outside, doing some purposeful deed, she might have lost her wits over him. If he had possessed a dimple, well, her heart would be captive. She could envision a man with just such a small confident smile fording a stream in a storm, the water surging around him but unable to slow his progress, to pluck a lost child from the churning waters.

Or climbing a tower, oh yes, to free a maiden locked in its highest room. Storm clouds would churn behind him, waves of the sea would crash against the rocky shore, the wind would snatch at his cloak, but he would be undeterred in pursuit of his goal. Oh, yes, he would be the silent hero, upon whom everyone could rely.

He sobered as he studied her, his gaze falling to her lips with such concentration that she caught her breath. She watched his eyes darken in a way that reminded her suddenly of that forbidden passage she had read in Eliza's letters.

What had it said? Something about the signs of a man's interest in a lady, how it might be revealed by a quick inhalation or the darkening of his eyes. Helena had thought it must be nonsense but as she held the viscount's gaze, she wondered.

In his youth, the viscount must have been most alluring.

Suddenly, as if shutters closed against the sunlight, his expression became composed again, his very soul seemingly hidden from view. The viscount looked again into the depths of his tea, as if he had forgotten her.

Helena was irked by the change.

On impulse, she abandoned her seat and moved to sit beside him. The viscount did not retreat or visibly disapprove. He simply flicked a glance at her, as if she were unpredictable.

Truly, his wariness made her feel bolder than was even her custom. "I must ask you, sir, since you abide near Haynesdale, if there are any highwaymen in the region?" The question fell from her lips unplanned, but made a kind of sense, given her impression of him as a man of daring. The viscount might, in fact, make a good highwayman, if he could abandon his reserved manner for longer intervals than he had thus far.

She wondered whether it was possible to provoke him to do as much.

She was tempted to try.

"Of course not," he replied stiffly and Helena almost sighed in despair.

"Aunt said that Robin Hood was believed to have lived in Nottinghamshire, and there are highwaymen everywhere else. Why should there not be any in these particular region, especially if tradition supports it?"

"Because any such person would be swiftly made to face justice," he replied, his tone crisp. "You may be confident, Miss Emerson, of your safety in Nottinghamshire."

"But safety is dull, is it not? Even at your age, you must yearn for a little adventure."

His tone was stern when he continued. "Miss Emerson, you cannot wish to encounter a renegade, outlaw, or other individual pursuing some view of rough justice beyond the measure of the law."

He was so severe that Helena had to defy his expectations.

"Oh, but I would," she assured him. "Next to a duke, a highwayman would be the most enticing of men to encounter, especially one who stole from the rich to give to the poor as Robin Hood was said to do." She sighed. "So dashing and dangerous, but governed by a noble need to ensure the welfare of all. Of course, he would be handsome and reckless, braver than most men."

There was another of those painful silences.

Then the viscount cleared his throat slightly. "If not a nobleman in disguise?" he asked.

If his expression had not been so impassive, she might have thought he teased her.

"Oh! A duke and a highwayman both! That would be best of all!" Helena agreed and he shook his head as he looked down, as if she were a foolish child. His lashes were dark and thick, and Helena wondered whether they were as soft as they looked.

She also wondered what he was thinking.

This time, she waited in silence, though it was a ferocious challenge.

"You would have liked my brother, Gerald," he said finally, his voice husky.

"Is he dead?" she asked in a horrified whisper and he nodded once. How could he insist that he was not ancient when his brother had already passed away? He might himself be at death's door, despite his assurances. "I am sorry," she whispered, knowing she had blundered, and impulsively put her hand on his sleeve. She could feel the tense strength of his forearm beneath the cloth and she thought she heard the viscount inhale sharply.

Just as the pages had noted.

She had no opportunity to see if his eyes had darkened again, for he rose abruptly to his feet.

"I regret that I have an appointment," he said, then bowed to her. Helena offered her hand and he bent over it after a moment's hesitation, then kissed its back. She felt the heat of his lips through her glove, which was inordinately thrilling.

"It has been a delight to meet you, Miss Emerson," he said politely. "Perhaps our paths might cross again."

She knew she should not ask, but she could not help herself. "Will you be attending Lady Haynesdale's ball?" The more gentlemen in attendance, the better, in her view. She hoped to dance for the entire evening.

"Yes, Lord Addersley, will you be?" Lady Haynesdale asked, returning with Aunt Fanny in such a timely manner that Helena knew their conversation had been followed by the two older ladies. "You have not given me your reply."

"I should be delighted, Lady Haynesdale," he said, his tone decisive.

"How wonderful!" Lady Haynesdale enthused. "I am pleased."

"Doubtless you will be overwhelmed with partners," Aunt Fanny said.

He looked a little grim at the prospect. "As mentioned earlier, I do not dance."

Helena was not truly surprised. Perhaps he was too old to dance well. Elderly people could have arthritis and rheumatism. Helena knew this because of her aunt's consistent complaints. Perhaps he had sustained an injury in his youth that precluded such merry doings now that he was so aged. Or perhaps he was going deaf, like Aunt Fanny, and could not hear the music.

Truly, the possibilities of infirmity were sufficient to make a person wish to die young.

"In the meantime, perhaps you might visit Addersley Manor," the viscount said to Aunt Fanny, whose features lit at the unexpected invitation. He granted Helena a polite smile, one that convinced her she had imagined any roguish glint or darkening hue of his eyes. "Miss Emerson may pick a puppy from the new litter in my stables, if she chooses."

"How generous you are, Lord Addersley!" Aunt Fanny cooed, her eyes alight with familiar ambition.

"But I wager it will become a large dog," Helena guessed, hoping to provoke his smile again.

Her effort failed. "Undoubtedly, Miss Emerson. You will be able to see the parents to gauge your expectations." That twinkle did not reappear, much to her disappointment. "Good day, ladies."

Then he was gone and the room seemed to echo with his absence. Helena went to the window, hoping to glimpse his departure, though she told herself that she simply sought a diversion from the topic of roses. The viscount rode a horse alone, a large chestnut hunter, and urged it to a canter as he left the drive. He did make a fine figure as he rode away.

The wind was not wild on this day, but if he had removed his hat, surely his hair would have been tousled in a most satisfactory manner.

He did not look back at the house, which disgruntled Helena a little, if for no good reason.

Evidently life in the country had bored her beyond desperation. She took solace in anyone's companionship and contrived tales to make them more interesting than they were. Perhaps she would descend into madness in such isolation and end her days, confined to some horrible institution, but imagining herself at court.

She returned to her tea, wishing there was a way to convince Aunt Fanny to return to London. Did she wish a large dog? Helena could not be certain, but his offer was generous. And she was curious about Addersley Manor.

Not that it could possibly compare to the rambling dimensions of Haynesdale House. She surveyed the drawing room, thinking that the pink might have to be replaced. A pale green or a sunny yellow might favor her own coloring better.

She hoped the duke returned soon. They would have to be wed almost immediately to have the house ready for the arrival of their first child.

~

Not only was Miss Emerson alluring but her company was delightful. Her whimsy about highwaymen troubled Joshua even as he rode away from Haynesdale House. Her mention of such desire for peril had sent a pang through him, igniting a need to ensure her protection from such ills.

Had he not already lost a lady to folly?

He could not permit such an incident to occur again. Indeed, he must offer for Miss Emerson with all haste, lest she find disaster before their vows were exchanged. He knew full well how rapidly a young lady resolute upon her objectives could find trouble.

Joshua's first task was to ascertain that the way was clear. On the way home to Addersley Manor, he could stop to confer with Nicholas Emerson about the prospects of that man's younger sister.

She might have a suitor, a betrothed or an understanding with another gentleman.

Joshua checked his pocket watch and noted there was yet time before his meeting with Mr. Newson, but clicked his tongue to the horse all the same.

Even he could not fail to notice the change in his perspective. He found himself filled with a welcome purpose, if not a measure of urgency. Clearly, he chose aright in pursuit of this goal.

He need not abandon the promise to his father. He need not gamble, duel, dance, or otherwise waste his advantages in foolish endeavors. He need not return to London and its temptations. He would take a bride and bend his considerable energy upon making her happy.

The lovely Miss Emerson would suit him very well, indeed.

CHAPTER 3

icholas Emerson was whistling to himself in the stables at Southpoint. He was tired, but did not care. He never resented any labor associated with horses and having this small holding for his own was a dream come true. Like so many of his newfound joys, he owed this one to his Eliza. He would happily spend the rest of his life ensuring she had no doubt of his love and admiration.

He had discarded his jacket after his morning ride, and changed to old boots to muck out the stables. The horses nickered to each other contentedly, and he heard them stomping in the straw. Sunlight shone through the open door and the air was warm with the promise of spring. He had hired two grooms to begin working for him shortly, and had already been invited to choose a mare from the stable of a former comrade later in the week. He already had his stallion, Sterling, as well as a mare given to him by Haynesdale and another mare Eliza had brought to the match from Haynesdale's stables. His stable was growing steadily, and it was early days as yet.

It was a day to whistle, for certain.

He looked up when the beam of sunlight was interrupted and a gentleman rode into the barn. The new arrival looked around himself with interest and it wasn't until he dismounted and removed his hat that Nicholas recognized him.

It had been roughly ten years since they had seen each other, after all. That had been in London, and the other man had not appeared so respectable in those days.

"Joshua Hargood," he said with pleasure. There was more than a decade's passing in the change in Hargood's appearance. In London, he had dressed as flamboyantly as his brother, and been almost as reckless in his dares. Now, he stood in Southpoint's stables, dressed precisely and conservatively, his manner inscrutable.

"Captain Emerson," that man said, inclining his head.

"Captain no longer, I fear," Nicholas said readily. "I must offer my condolences on the recent passing of your father."

"I thank you. He was comforted to be at home when he passed."

"I hope he did not suffer too much."

The viscount's lips tightened. "His illness was long."

So, that was what Hargood had been doing since the end of the war. "I heard also that your brother was lost at Waterloo," Nicholas continued. "I am very sorry, Hargood."

"As am I." The viscount's throat worked and his voice became husky. "I thank you."

Clearly, there had been fondness between the brothers, despite the difference in their natures. "I suppose you were curious to see what changes I mean to make to Southpoint. We are nearly neighbors, after all."

"Not precisely," his guest said. "I don't suppose you

know when the Duke of Haynesdale is expected to return?"

"No, but perhaps the dowager duchess knows more."

"I have just called upon her, and she does not." Hargood frowned, hesitating for a moment before he continued. "Your sister and aunt were at tea."

His gaze lifted to Nicholas and Nicholas suspected then that he understood.

"I believe I knew they were invited today, but I had forgotten. My wife, Eliza, did comment that she saw the coach pass. I supposed Lady Haynesdale sent it for them."

Hargood shrugged, then waited, his manner expectant.

Nicholas was content to explain. "Bramble Cottage was in the grant to me, and I offered it to my aunt, who has been my sister's guardian for most of her life." he continued, wagering that Hargood had a keen interest in Helena and her situation. "She was Viscountess of Hexham, but when her husband passed, the estate was entailed and the title fell to a nephew. My aunt resided in London for some time but wished to move to the country. The timing of Haynesdale's gift to me was most opportune."

Hargood betrayed no emotion. "It must be a pleasure to have your family so close."

"Sometimes it is," Nicholas ceded with a smile. "Though I do not doubt that there will be days I wish one side or the other to be a little less readily accessible."

"I was delighted to meet your sister." This was said with a resolve that confirmed Nicholas' suspicions.

"Helena can be very charming."

Hargood cleared his throat. "Having inherited the

title, I feel it is my obligation to take a wife and ensure the future of Addersley."

"Of course." How strange to hear this man who had once run so wild sounding precisely like his father. Of course, the revels had been only for a year, and in Gerald's company—likely at Gerald's instigation. But could there be anyone so opposite in temperament to Helena?

Hargood looked Nicholas in the eye. "And I wondered at your sister's situation."

"Helena has no attachments at this time." Nicholas could not discern whether Hargood was relieved or not, but the other man's manner prompted his warning. "But I am not certain how happy you might make each other."

"But surely Miss Emerson will be content with financial security and a sensible match."

Nicholas laughed. "I suspect that financial security is the last detail that would concern Helena, if she was left to make her match herself."

Hargood frowned, looking into the distance as if he reconsidered his choice. "She did confess her fascination for highwaymen." He looked at Nicholas, as if inviting that man to challenge the assertion which he seemed to find incomprehensible.

Nicholas could not.

"That would be Helena," he agreed easily. "She is often enamored of how matters appear, at the expense of overlooking how they are," Nicholas admitted. "She was, for example, recently courted by a Mr. Ethan Melbourne, who cultivated her affection solely because he thought her an heiress."

"A prudent man might have verified such a detail, if it was key to his suit."

"True enough, but Melbourne did not. He was well-attired and well-mannered, as well as handsome and persistent. He persuaded Helena to leave London in his company."

Hargood's brows rose. "Alone?"

"And unwed, but mercifully in a public carriage. They did not reach Gretna Green before Mr. Melbourne realized his error—my sister has no dowry—and as a result, Helena found his charm diminished both markedly and quickly."

"Has she been cast into disrepute?"

Nicholas thought he could guess the other man's view of that, but Hargood sounded more curious than disapproving. "No, the kindly wife of a solicitor riding in that coach with her own daughter took note of the situation. With Helena's surety that I would pursue her, she took my sister under her protection. I retrieved her from that lady's household and returned her home safely."

"Ah." Hargood nodded. "I did think her impulsive."

"She is."

"Though she is yet young."

Nicholas was not convinced his sister would abandon such tendencies as she aged, but neither did he wish to discourage Hargood. "I would hope her inclinations might change in time, but I am by no means confident of it," he felt obliged to say. Hargood ignored this, as Nicholas had anticipated. "There is nothing that would give me greater happiness than to see Helena betrothed to a suitable gentleman who will treat her well."

Hargood straightened and spoke with precision. "I would be honored to be that man. In terms of practical considerations, I have twenty-five thousand pounds a year, as well as the house here and the one in London."

It was more than sufficient to see Helena kept and Nicholas did not hide his admiration. "I would welcome your success, Hargood." Nicholas felt the need offer one last warning. "You should know that my sister has a fanciful conviction that she might wed the Duke of Haynesdale. My aunt has told me of it."

"I wondered," Hargood mused and Nicholas could only wonder what his sister had said. "Is there an understanding?"

Nicholas shook his head. "None. I am not certain Haynesdale has noticed her at all. I think it a harmless affectation on Helena's behalf, for Haynesdale has no inclination to wed anyone by my understanding. I mention it only as you will have to overcome the appeal of that prospect."

"His grace is not here," Hargood noted.

"True enough."

The other man nodded and took his leave, as if his triumph was inevitable. Nicholas watched him go, wondering what would come of it all.

Perhaps Helena would suddenly develop a measure of good sense.

Nicholas chuckled to himself and turned back to his labor. It would be a cold day in the devil's realm before that happened, but Hargood might prove to be more persuasive than Nicholas believed. He could not have completely forgotten his wild youth, and that might grant him an understanding of Helena that would serve him well.

Nicholas could only hope.

IN MATTERS MARITAL, Joshua's father had always insisted the mind saw more clearly than the heart. That man had valued reason over emotion and Joshua saw little reason to doubt such counsel. His own match with Miss Havilland had been a calculated alliance, negotiated between the two fathers to provide best for their children. It had been arranged, sensible and planned for the benefit of both parties.

And so would this match be.

Even though Joshua arranged it himself, his marriage to Miss Emerson would be such a logical prospect that no person of intelligence could dismiss or decline his suit.

He already had Captain Emerson's agreement.

The aunt would undoubtedly also concur.

Miss Emerson herself was perhaps impulsive, but she was not a witless fool. She had to know that any childish fancy for the Duke of Haynesdale could not come to fulfillment.

She would see sense, Joshua was certain of it.

Surety of his victory made him impatient to see the matter resolved. Of course, he had already invited Lady Dalhousie and her niece to the house, but he would send a written invitation to formalize it. Miss Emerson could come to Addersley Manor on the morrow with her aunt, purportedly to choose a puppy. In truth, she would have an opportunity to see her new home, and he would propose to her. The aunt would undoubtedly wish to assure herself of his prospects and it would only be fitting for Miss Emerson to be chaperoned.

They might wed before the end of May.

By this time next year, he might have an heir.

Joshua was not truly concerned about Haynesdale as a competitor, but it might be better to see Miss Emerson's agreement secured before the duke's return. He would dispatch the invitation as soon as he completed his business with Mr. Newson.

By this hour on the morrow, his future would be resolved.

~

Aunt Fanny, predictably, was in a fluster about the viscount. She practically interrogated Lady Haynesdale about him and his prospects, much to Helena's mortification—but then, Lady Haynesdale seemed almost as anxious to discuss him. Perhaps she, too, tired of the topic of roses.

At any rate, it seemed Lord Addersley was a paragon of virtues, a noble, honorable, honest, reliable man Lady Haynesdale had known from infancy, one who attended to his responsibilities in a timely manner and was unfailingly courteous. His father had been a wonderful man; his mother a delight who passed too soon.

Helena could not suppress her yawn. Clearly, her fleeting impressions had been her own fabrications. He was dull beyond belief. He paid his bills and his taxes. He took care of his tenants and his holdings.

They returned to Bramble Cottage to find an invitation from the man in question to visit Addersley Manor on the following day.

"How gracious of him to formalize his offer," Aunt Fanny said.

"It arrived not half an hour ago, ma'am," Becky, their maid provided. "'Twas his ostler, Hoskins, as brought it."

Helena fairly saw her aunt's realization that Becky had been raised locally.

"What do you know of the viscount, Becky?" Aunt Fanny asked, feigning polite indifference.

"Not much, ma'am, seeing as he has been in London these past ten years. I was but a girl when he left."

London? He had been in London? Helena found her curiosity revived.

"He has a London house, then?" Aunt Fanny asked and Helena knew her aunt would next demand the address to determine its value.

"His father did, ma'am, and his father before him. I forget where it is, ma'am, but Jenny Percival went with the old viscount and his sons as upper housemaid and she says it is ever so fine."

"And what do you know of the new viscount?"

Becky, interestingly enough, shivered, though not with the delight Helena had experienced at the sound of the viscount's low and velvety voice.

"They say as there is no blood in his veins," she provided. "And that if you were to prick him, 'twould be ice water that flowed from the wound. Colder than a winter wind, he is, ma'am, to be sure. A lady would have to disguise herself as a ledger and speak only of sums and tallies to win his attention. That must be why he is unwed as yet." She nodded with enthusiasm. "There was to be a wedding all those years ago, but it never happened. Perhaps the lady found him lacking."

Even Aunt Fanny surrendered her ambitions with that confession and spent the evening frowning at her needlework. She suggested that they might not accept the viscount's invitation, but Helena wanted to see the dogs. How large could they be?

And she would acquaint herself with the duke's neighbors. She knew there could nothing else of interest for her at Addersley Manor.

All the same, she dreamed that night of a taciturn highwayman with eyes of glimmering green.

ADDERSLEY MANOR WAS a complete contrast to Haynesdale House. Helena was astonished by the difference. While Haynesdale House was centuries old, large and of indeterminate design, Addersley Manor could not have been fifty years old. It was so obviously new—tall, broad and relentlessly symmetrical—that it might have been completed the year before. There were no stains or marks of age on the stone walls. The gardens, too, were formal—and to Helena's delight, there was not a rose in sight. The chosen plants offered a soothing composition of green and white, each specimen in its place and mirrored by one in the opposite location. The stairs before the house were broad and even, the doors wide and surrounded by panes of glass that sparkled in the sun.

Helena was certain she had never seen an abode that reflected its owner so well. Every detail was perfectly contrived and organized to reason. She would have liked to have seen a few pink peonies tumbling over themselves to mar the mathematical perfection of the garden or one of those enormous rhododendrons from Bramble Cottage, in full bloom.

"So new," Aunt Fanny clucked before the carriage door was opened. "It probably has every amenity," she said with a disapproval Helena did not share.

"No smoking chimneys," Helena agreed, thinking there was much good to be said for new construction. "No crooked floors and awkward corners. The spiders must have abandoned it in disgust, if ever they took up residence at all."

"Spiders! Do not speak to me of such creatures!"

"I doubt there are any, Aunt. I doubt there is any dust. There cannot be a nook to shelter a mouse, and there will be no bats in the attics for they cannot contrive a means of entry. It looks absolutely pristine."

"It has no character, no soul, no spirit," her aunt complained. "No *history!*" A footman opened the door then and she bit her tongue. She fortified herself with a deep breath, then left the carriage.

Helena was quick to follow her aunt, pausing to appreciate the wide level drive covered with pea gravel. The skies seemed bluer over this house and the sun a bit brighter. Lord Addersley himself emerged from the house to greet them, and his manners left nothing to be desired, according to Aunt Fanny's gracious response.

Helena thought he looked very fine in a navy jacket, buff trousers and his tall gleaming boots. His cravat was as white and crisp as previously, and again, he wore no adornment. He wore no hat and the breeze tousled his hair just enough to make him look less forbidding.

If only he were a little bit wicked. She sighed.

She had hoped that she would have confirmation of his secret side, the dangerous rogue with the glimmer lurking in his eyes, but he was the very heart and soul of indifferent politeness. They might have been strangers for all the warmth in his tone.

Surely the statue could not have been his true nature?

But then, who else would live in such a house?

"I thought we might resolve the question of the puppy first," the viscount said and gestured. "The stables are this way."

"The puppies are in the stables?" Helena asked as he offered Aunt Fanny his arm.

"Of course." He looked at her as if she had responded to him in Greek. "They are hunting dogs."

"Yes, but I thought you would have them in the house, perhaps in your library," Helena explained. "You do have a library?"

"Of course."

"With a grand fireplace?"

He halted. "Would you prefer to see it first?"

"No, but I always imagine a litter of puppies gathered around their mother, before a fire in a library."

He hesitated, a small frown between his brows. "There were dogs in the house when I was a boy, but my father and I have been in London in recent years.

We have only come to Addersley Manor on occasion to hunt. The dogs were better cared for in the stables."

That made sense. "But if you mean to remain in the country, perhaps you should have dogs in the house," Helena said. When he did not reply, she dared to continue. "If I had a dog, I should want it to be with me all the time," she said. "I would expect it to sleep in my room and follow me through the house. I do not hunt, my lord, so there would be no other reason for me to have a dog than companionship. If that is not your expectation, perhaps I need not choose a puppy at all."

"A dog might also defend my niece," Aunt Fanny contributed when the viscount did not argue with her. "When they are part of the family, they are more inclined to be protective."

"Of course, you are correct in all of that," Lord Addersley inclined his head crisply and led them onward. Either he was unconvinced or he had another matter on his mind. He seemed, for a man who hid his thoughts well, to be preoccupied.

They might have crossed the distance in silence, if not for Aunt's chatter. Neither the viscount nor Helena spoke.

His stables were as newly constructed as the house and nearly as fine. The floor was swept clean and the horses were most handsome. Helena knew that Nicholas would have appreciated both the stable and the horses.

A large brown dog emerged from the shadows as they approached and barked a warning. It was indeed as tall as the viscount's hip and Helena gasped in surprise. The ostler came out and patted the dog. "Easy, Rufus," he said. "They're friendly enough." He grinned then inclined his head to Lord Addersley. "You see he recognizes his lordship. That's his bark to greet friends."

"He barks differently depending upon who arrives?" Helena demanded.

"Of course, miss," the ostler said.

The dog came to her, his tail wagging, and she was taken aback by the size of his teeth. He was a shaggy creature with a long rough coat, and it looked as if he had bushy eyebrows and a moustache. Lord Addersley offered his hand and the dog sniffed his fingertips, still wagging, then stepped closer to sniff the viscount's boots and trousers. Lord Addersley then patted the dog's head, his touch both sure and gentle.

The dog certainly appeared to have a calm manner. Helena followed the viscount's example and was delighted by the dog's easy acceptance of her. His fur was stiff but also soft, he was warm and she could feel the strength in his shoulders. He sat down and leaned against her leg, a not inconsiderable weight, tipping his head back with a blissful expression as she rubbed his ears. He began to emit a growl of satisfaction when she rubbed his throat.

"Ah, he likes that," the ostler said with a chuckle. "You'll own his soul in a heartbeat, miss."

Helena laughed, glancing up to find the viscount watching her, his attention so intent that her heart skipped. His eyes were dark again and their gazes locked for a moment during which she could not catch her breath.

"I do not want his soul, just one of his puppies," she said and the ostler chuckled.

The viscount averted his gaze.

"You'll need to know a little of dogs and their barks then, miss. There's his warning bark, when something is amiss or a stranger is coming," the ostler explained. "There's his welcome bark when someone he knows is arriving. There's his growl, which is for trouble that does not yet merit a bark. There's a yip he makes when he's playful."

"Dogs have an entire vocabulary for those who know to listen," Aunt said as if she knew of such matters.

"Goodness," Helena said, laughing when the dog licked her fingers. He gave yet a different bark, a high one that sounded happy. "He sounded as if he was purring when I rubbed his ear."

"Aye, he likes you, miss," the ostler said with satisfaction. "And a good thing that is since his lordship means to let you see the puppies." He turned and walked into the shadowed interior of the stables. "Rufus is as proud a father as ever you saw, miss."

He led them to a stall at the end. There were old blankets piled there and a darker dog of similar size to Rufus lying upon them. The mother was almost black, her fur a little more curly and glossy than that of Rufus. No less than eight tiny puppies scrambled around her, some nursing, some sleeping, some tumbling over their enormous feet. Their fur was silk and shiny, softer than belief, their antics and wagging tails so adorable that Helena was enchanted.

Lord Addersley crouched down beside the bed and she watched him doff his gloves. One puppy flopped against his boot while another nipped at his fingertip. They trusted him, it was clear. He smiled, oblivious to her perusal, and once again, she thought he was wonderfully handsome.

It was unfortunate that his nature was so restrained and quiet. He would be a dreadfully tedious companion once a woman looked beyond the cleft in his chin.

"They nigh all need new homes, miss. We can keep two or three, but Rowena here had a large litter." The female dog oofed, a low sound that might have been born of pride. "Though it is too soon as yet for them to leave their mother."

"Truly?" Helena asked.

"Aye, miss, they are nursing yet. I would not take them from her for another week."

"But you can choose one today," Lord Addersley said.

"Pick of the litter to the lady," Hoskins said with approval.

"There's a fine tribute, Helena," Aunt Fanny said. "You must thank Lord Addersley for that." Helena did as her aunt surveyed the puppies with a critical eye. "You will want the largest female, my dear."

"I will?" Helena knew nothing about dogs, but it was clear her aunt did.

"We had hunting dogs at Hexham, Helena. Do not look at me as if I am mad," Aunt chided.

"I did not know, Aunt. I apologize." Helena curtsied to her aunt, mollifying the older lady. The viscount, she was well aware, watched her keenly.

The ostler nodded approval. "Naught better in the house than a female," he said. "She'll take you all on as her family."

"How lovely!" Helena said. "You do let dogs into the house."

"These hunting dogs run through the muck, miss, for 'tis their job to flush the game, wherever it is to be found. It would be no good for them to be in the house with his lordship in London all the time. But I take Rowena home when she is not with a litter."

Helena smiled at this.

"Miss Emerson's suggestion is a good one, Hoskins. I think I will choose a pup to raise in the house myself. I remember running through the house with a pair of dogs that must have been the forebears of these. Rex and Riley."

Hoskins grinned. "Riley was Rowena's grandfather, sir."

The viscount smiled just a little. "There is a resemblance, to be sure. I remember him as enormous, black and fierce."

"But loyal, as well, sir."

"Indeed."

"But why the biggest female?" Helena asked.

"She will not be shy, nor will her siblings have bullied her," the ostler said. "She will not be timid." Helena watched as one pup growled at another, nudging it away from the mother with a purpose that was not a jest. "'Tis better if the bigger pups have homes first, then in their absence, the smaller ones come into their own."

"Goodness, it sounds complicated."

"They work it out, miss, just as nature intended." The ostler reached down and lifted a glossy black pup, taking her from the nipple with authority. She was as black as midnight with a white bib and half of her face was white. Her eyes were dark and she was as soft as velvet. "This would be the biggest of the girls. Born first she was, this one, and she already knows her mind."

"Look at her paws!" Aunt said.

"She will be as big as her father, I wager," Hoskins said. He set her down beside Helena, who offered her hand to the dog as she had with Rufus. The puppy sniffed her and wagged, then licked her gloved fingertips before pouncing on the toe of her slipper that peeked out beneath the hem of her skirts. Helena squealed and retreated but the puppy followed, stumbling clumsily after her, that tail aloft and wagging.

"Don't you chew my slippers," Helena said, scolding.

The puppy's eyes glinted and her tail wagged. She gave a little bark and jumped toward Helena's other toe. Helena fled a few steps and the pup bounced after her with delight. When she halted, the puppy collapsed over her foot and nuzzled her instep so that it tickled. Helena laughed and the pup gave a joyful bark. The mother barked a summons but the puppy did not return to her, simply looking up at Helena in adoration as she wagged her tail. Her tongue was a lovely shade of pink and her nose black and cold.

By the time Helena had confessed her satisfaction, the puppy had demolished a ribbon rose on one slipper. She attacked the second, moving so quickly that there was no chance to stop her.

"If you had worn your boots, Helena, your slippers would not have been damaged," Aunt Fanny chided.

"But I like these slippers," Helena protested. She leaned down and tapped the puppy's nose. "Naughty girl. You must leave my slippers alone." The puppy wagged her tail as if in agreement and Helena could not remain cross with her.

"She will need a name," Aunt Fanny said, as if the decision was made.

"Mischief," Helena said on impulse, patting the pup's head. "Her name shall be Mischief, for what she has done to my slippers." The pup barked then nipped at her finger, spinning in a circle as if in approval. She then tumbled to the ground as she tripped over her own feet, rolled over and bounced to her feet again. Helena could not help but laugh and the puppy barked.

"That is a happy bark," Helena guessed and the ostler nodded approval.

"That it is, miss. I wager she likes you."

"A good choice then," Lord Addersley said. He picked up the puppy and carried her back to the mother, nestling her back in place. The pup looked back at Helena before suckling again. Helena realized she would be able to identify her, given her size and coloring. It was a case of learning to look at what was before her eyes.

"She doesn't want me to forget her," Helena said.

"She will not forget you," Lord Addersley said with authority. "Nor will Hoskins and I forget that she is your choice. I thank you, Hoskins. Please choose a pup for the house for me."

"I will indeed, sir. The biggest male, sir?"

"Indeed, in the spirit of Riley."

Rufus escorted them from the stables, as if to ensure that they were not taking any of the pups with them.

As they headed back toward the house, Aunt Fanny cleared her throat. "Such a handsome house, my lord, with a fine prospect."

"My father had it built as a wedding gift for my mother," he acknowledged without much interest.

"Was there not a house already?"

"It had burned in my grandfather's time. He and my grandmother preferred to live in town, so he acquired the London house then. My mother preferred the country to town, however, so my father had this house built for her."

"Most generous," Aunt said with approval. "Do you still keep a house in town?" she asked as if she had not learned as much from Becky.

Next she would demand the address. Helena might have wished her aunt would be a little less direct in her inquiries, but the viscount did not seem to mind—and she found herself curious about the answer, as well.

She told herself that she was simply learning about their new neighbors.

"I do," the viscount said. "It is an older house and perhaps in need of improvement, though my father and I found it very comfortable in recent years. It is in Cavendish Square."

Aunt Fanny caught her breath, that gleam appearing

in her eyes again. "When you marry, your wife will have to consider herself very fortunate," she said and Helena could not believe her aunt's presumption.

"I can only hope as much, madame," the viscount said with a force that seemed uncharacteristic.

Aunt Fanny was smiling, looking as smug as a cat who had stolen the cream. Helena could make no sense of this.

Puppies, it was clear, addled the wits of everyone. She hoped there was something good for tea. Aunt was always certain that bachelors could not see a household administered properly and had lamented the prospects of a meagre refreshment all morning long.

CHAPTER 4

Joshua was certain of his success, so did not hasten to the moment of his proposal. He thought Lady Dalhousie's open curiosity about his property was a bit vulgar, but he was content to show her the house that her niece would soon consider her own. Lady Dalhousie would likely continue to live nearby, so he would have to accustom himself to her mannerisms, for better or for worse.

His father had often jested that one could not choose one's family. The aunt's manner was no reflection upon the niece.

Miss Emerson wore a dress of pale pink on this day, festooned with black and pink embroidery, along with that black spencer. The combination was both flattering and elegant. Her cheeks were flushed and her manner with the dogs had been utterly charming.

And truly, he had no issue with Miss Emerson preferring her silk slippers to boots. He had been granted a most admirable view of her ankles when the puppy made trouble, and found himself keenly aware of Miss Emerson's allure.

He would even allow Mischief in the bedroom if that prompted the lady's approval.

Meanwhile, he strolled through the house with his guests, seeing it with new eyes as he showed it to them. The drawing room was found to be most attractive, the library suitable to a gentleman—even with an acceptable fireplace for the comfort of dogs —the dining room a delight and the foyer most commodious. The views from the principal rooms were complimented, the lighting remarked upon, the quality of the furnishings admired. They reviewed the portraits in the foyer, one of each of the six previous viscounts and a large one of his mother. Joshua even imagined that his father beamed down upon them in approval of his matrimonial scheme.

When they sat in the drawing room and he invited Lady Dalhousie to pour the tea, he was certain of her approval. He knew she tested the weight of the teapot and ascertained (correctly) that it was sterling, for he saw her satisfied smile. Miss Emerson, for her part, surveyed the room with an interest that seemed a good omen for his prospects.

"It is so bright and cheerful," she said. "I like the pale yellow very much."

"My mother favored the hue." Joshua could not help but notice how the shade favored Miss Emerson as well. She looked like a flower in the sunlight, and just the sight of his intended in his mother's favorite room made Joshua's chest tighten in a way that was decidedly not rational.

Miss Emerson flushed with pleasure and smiled, which only increased his awareness of her. "She chose the furnishings?"

"Every detail was left to her."

"A most comfortable and elegant house," Lady Dalhousie said with approval, handing him a teacup. "You must always be glad to return to such a refuge."

"Yes," he ceded. "But in the absence of my father and brother, the house seems quiet."

"Of course," Lady Dalhousie agreed. "But when you wed, sir, if I may be so bold as to mention such an eventuality, the house is likely to be filled with the sound of children shortly thereafter."

Miss Emerson blushed and averted her gaze, evidence that they were in agreement about her aunt's commentary.

"I should like nothing better in such circumstance, Lady Dalhousie."

His gaze snared that of the older lady and Joshua knew that their inclinations were as one. Lady Dalhousie had discerned and approved of his suit. Should he ask Miss Emerson for her hand in her aunt's presence? A bit late, Joshua was compelled to admit that he had no notion how such conversations were contrived. It seemed a private matter, but Miss Emerson also had need of a chaperone for the sake of her reputation.

He had never thought he might wish he had a sister, if only to better understand the niceties of proposals.

Lady Dalhousie, against expectation, came to his rescue. "I must compliment you, my lord, upon these scones and this marmalade, in particular. Both are delicious, but the marmalade is superb."

"Mrs. Baird makes it each year," he supplied. "From the oranges we order from Spain for Christmas. There are always too many to eat fresh."

"And it is perfect. Not too sweet, and the taste of the fruit is robust," Aunt Fanny said. Without a moment's hesitation, she continued. "I wonder, my lord, if I might be so bold as to ask your cook about her recipe. I would not dream of interrupting her work, but…"

Opportunity arrived and Joshua would not waste it.

In fact, he found a new admiration for Lady Dalhousie's tendency to blunt speech.

"Of course." He rang and Fairfax appeared, then escorted Lady Dalhousie toward the kitchens at his request. They would not be gone long.

"Goodness," Miss Emerson said. "My aunt must trust you beyond all to leave me alone in your presence, sir." She took a scone and smiled at him.

Joshua moved to take the seat beside Miss Emerson and she looked up at him from her scone, her surprise clear. "I would seize this chance to ask you, Miss Emerson, to do me the honor of becoming my wife."

Miss Emerson put down her scone and studied him. "I beg your pardon?"

Had he been too blunt himself?

"I propose that you might become my wife," he repeated.

She stared at him, as if his words were incomprehensible.

Perhaps she wished to hear the arguments enumerated that were in his favor.

"There are many indications in favor of the association. I believe that you approve of Addersley. Your brother has given his blessing..."

"You told Nicholas before asking me?"

"It is customary, Miss Emerson, and only rational to ascertain whether you had any previous commitments or understandings."

She inhaled sharply, though he could not reason why. "And you believe it *rational* that we should wed, even after such brief acquaintance?"

Ah, he had offended her romantic notions. He nodded, undeterred. "There is much of merit in the potential union. Your future would be assured and I would have a wife. Your lack of a dowry is of no concern to me. I would, naturally, hope for the blessing of children in short order..."

"No," she said and he stared in surprise. She set

aside her tea cup and rose to her feet, her voice gaining vigor as she continued. "No, I will not marry you, sir. I *cannot* marry you."

Joshua was perplexed. "Whyever not? It is a rational and reasonable match."

Miss Emerson's expression was resolute, though Joshua could not understand her conviction. "I do not know much of you, sir, but I am already convinced that we are utterly unsuitable to each other. No. I must decline your offer."

If she was concerned about her own contributions to the match—or lack of them—he would set her fears to rest. "But Miss Emerson, do consider the matter…"

"No!" she repeated more forcefully. "I *decline*, sir."

"But you cannot. Your aunt clearly favors the match."

"Yet I have declined," she said, her eyes flashing furiously. She straightened. "I thank you, sir, for your consideration and for flattering me with your attention, but I refuse your suit, utterly and unequivocally. If this means you will keep the puppy, I am sorry to hear as much, but you must do as you see fit."

Joshua frowned. Miss Emerson strode toward the door with purpose, the sound of her aunt's voice drawing nearer. "But why?" he asked again. "To decline is not logical, given your circumstance."

She looked back at him, more regal than he might have expected in one so young. "I will not wed for logic or good sense, or even a secure future, sir. I will wed for *love*."

What nonsense was this? "I beg your pardon?"

There was a decidedly stubborn set to her mouth. "I decline because I do not love you and you do not love me."

"Surely affection between man and wife grows with time."

"It might, in some situations," Miss Emerson ceded. "But I will never love a man who does not dance. It is simply not possible." She shook her head. "We will not suit, sir."

With that, she stepped into the foyer to greet her aunt, who was clearly triumphant in having secured Mrs. Baird's recipe. Lady Dalhousie was also sufficiently perceptive to realize that matters had not proceeded as planned. She looked between her niece, standing straight with her back to Joshua, and perhaps even discerned Joshua's own astonishment. His surprise was so overwhelming that his composure might have slipped.

Lady Dalhousie made excuses of her need to depart, due to a sudden headache, and Joshua hid his reaction to the best of his abilities. He escorted the ladies to the carriage with his thoughts churning. He stood on the steps to watch them go, knowing that Miss Emerson did not look back.

She had *declined* him.

Because he did not *dance*.

Because she would never love a man who did not dance, and she was convinced that love should govern marriage. Joshua shook his head. Perhaps a woman so lacking in the ability to logically choose was not right for him. Perhaps he should be glad that she had declined him.

But Joshua most decidedly was not glad.

His financial security, his reasonable fortune, his reputation, his house and title, even his person—he did not think himself offensive in appearance—were irrelevant to the one lady he found suitable.

Miss Emerson's decision defied belief, and yet she had made it.

That was nearly as intriguing to Joshua Hargood as the lady herself.

For he could not dismiss the possibility of changing her mind.

The prize, to be sure, was alluring indeed.

And he had been desirous of a challenge. A quest, to be sure. An errand that would consume his attention. Joshua Hargood watched his carriage vanish around the curve of the road and knew that he had found his ultimate challenge in Miss Emerson.

DAMIEN DEVRIES, the Duke of Haynesdale, could only admire the young woman he had collected from a remote region of France. She sat quietly opposite him in the coach, day after day, on their journey toward London. Mademoiselle Sylvie was quiet and agreeable. She did not complain, no matter how long they rode or how simple their occasional accommodations. Her manner was sweet and serene, not to mention that she was very pretty.

He had wondered often since retrieving the girl whether Miss Esmeralda Ballantyne had once appeared thus. It was hard to imagine the lively courtesan as so young and innocent, but even more difficult to think of her in possession of such serenity. Mlle. Sylvie was complacent and accepting of any change in her circumstance. He would have wagered that Miss Ballantyne had always been one determined to shape her own destiny, not to accept whatever was bestowed upon her and be glad of it.

The physical resemblance between the two was so great—and in more than just their coloring of jet black hair and brilliant green eyes—that Damien could not have failed to conclude that they were sisters. Mlle. Sylvie, he had quickly realized was as astute and practical as her older sister, despite having been raised in the shelter of a convent.

Upon leaving that place, he had repeated his promise of protection and vow to never touch her himself. She had been the one to suggest that she use a name other than her own, and they had decided upon Sylvie Lafleur. He had suggested that they explain her presence in his company by saying she was his ward, but she had solemnly shaken her head.

"It will be assumed to be a lie, Monsieur. Far better that you declare me to be your betrothed, though you may have no inclination to wed me."

"I do not, but not for any lack in your charms," he said, appreciating how admirably French was suited to such nuanced declarations. "If I claim you as my ward, you may be certain that most will conclude that you are my intended. It will be a tale and a rumor for your safety alone, yet one that does not demand a formal betrothal between us. I would not have you fettered with that apparent obligation, in the event that you find a suitor of merit yourself."

She nodded, appearing far wiser than her years. "I believe, Monsieur, that I have gained your protection through your interest in my sister," she said with soft assurance. "And I am pleased that she has won the esteem of a gentleman of such honor."

At the time, Damien had thought to let the girl believe what she desired, but as they approached England, he found his thoughts returning to Miss Ballantyne and her fate. He felt an urgency to reach her with all haste, to assure himself of her welfare, that he knew was not entirely without hopes of more than her thanks.

He had paid for her comforts in Fleet Prison, not caring who knew of his involvement. He had ensured that the bills were paid at her residence, so that she would have a home to which she could return. In the view of many, such actions would have bought him a mistress, perhaps even one who granted him exclusive access to her favors.

Yet Damien could not anticipate what Miss Ballantyne would conclude.

The curious thing was that despite his desire for her, despite how that one taste of her had touched a spark to his dreams, he was more concerned with her safety than any earthly satisfaction she might provide.

As well as the proving of her innocence. Her trial would be held in early May, but he would prefer to have the charges dismissed against her. That could only happen if the real culprit was found and arrested, and if that man, Jacques Desjardins, confessed to the jewel theft of which Miss Ballantyne had been accused.

This conundrum and its potential solution occupied his thoughts as they journeyed north.

Mlle. Sylvie was ill on the voyage across the Channel, which was admittedly rougher than any in Damien's recent memory. She was so unsteady and pale when they reached Dover that he was compelled to carry her to the rented carriage, which only strengthened the rumor of their joined future. Her delicacy made him fear anew for Miss Ballantyne. She had lost weight and been less robust when he had visited her, and it had been almost a fortnight since then.

Surely, she could not be cheated of knowing that her sister was safe? Or that of seeing the man who had tormented her brought to justice? It could not be thus! Damien offered the driver a greater payment for a hasty journey, though it would not be easy for Mlle. Sylvie.

The door of the carriage was closed and the driver cracked the whip, doubtless determined to earn that promised bonus. Damien glanced out the window and spotted a furtive figure hastening toward a mail coach. His heart leapt at the familiarity of the man.

He recognized that figure, even with such a fleeting glimpse, and settled back in the coach with satisfaction. They *had* been followed. He had wondered several times. And now that Jacques Desjardins was back on English soil, Damien intended to be sure that fiend never left the country alive.

He offered Mlle. Sylvie his handkerchief as the coach rocked and kept his voice low, even though they were alone in the darkened interior. "Would you be amenable to a small deceit, Mademoiselle Lafleur? I should like to set a trap for the man responsible for your sister's circumstance."

With that, the young lady's spirits were evidently revived, for she met his gaze with a resolve in her own. "Oui, monsieur. I will do whatsoever you advise to aid Esmeralda."

～

"BECAUSE HE DOES NOT *DANCE*?" Aunt Fanny sounded more like an angry hen than her usual self. Her voice rose to a pitch that made Helena wince. "Truly, you have become capricious beyond expectation. Why would you decline an eligible offer over such triviality?"

"It is not trivial," Helena argued. "And it is not the sum of my reason. We simply would not suit each other. He has little inclination to smile or laugh. He..."

"Is practical, handsome, responsible and younger than many eligible bachelors." Aunt Fanny sighed. "He is even tall, with a good chin! And doubtless he has an income of some measure, besides. Though I have yet to discover the precise amount, that house could not be kept on pennies, never mind a house in London—in Cavendish Square no less!—as well."

"He has twenty-five thousand pounds," Helena supplied, looking out the window as she braced herself for the inevitable reaction.

Aunt Fanny was so furious she nearly rocked the carriage. "Twenty-five thousand! What has seized your wits, girl? You could live in one house and he in the other for that annual sum."

"Oh!" Helena had not considered the possibility of being a wife alone in London while the viscount occupied himself with his country estate. "I thought couples lived in the same house." And truly, she had no desire for such an arrangement. She wanted a passionate marriage, one in which neither partner could consider being without the other.

The very prospect made her yearn to meet a man who would capture her heart.

Meanwhile, Aunt was fuming. "While first wed, certainly, but after you give him sons, I am certain he would indulge your whim."

Sons. That would take at least several years, if not more. Truly, Helena might not bear sons ever. Such a condition certainly did not guarantee its eventual success—and her freedom. Helena shuddered, knowing it was better she had declined.

"How many such offers do you anticipate you will receive?" Aunt Fanny continued with outrage. "You are no longer in London, Helena, with opportunity at every dance."

"Lady Haynesdale is hosting a ball."

"And just yesterday, she complained to me of the paucity of young gentlemen in the vicinity. Do you imagine they will fail to hear that you have declined the most eligible of them all?" Aunt Fanny pinched the bridge of her nose as she grimaced. "Less than a week in Nottinghamshire and you will be known far and wide as a young lady too proud to see reason."

"Am I not entitled to choose the man with whom I will spend my life?"

"No, you are not!" Aunt Fanny fairly shouted. "I will invite Nicholas to dinner that he might talk sense into you. Perhaps, if you are sufficiently contrite and charming, the viscount might be convinced to renew his addresses."

Helena folded her arms across her chest and glared out the window. Fortunately, they approached Bramble Cottage. "I do not want him to renew his addresses," she said with heat. "We will not suit each other."

"*He* believes you will suit each other!"

"He does not know me. He sees only a lady young enough to give him sons and pretty enough to grace his table. He sees a *logical* match." She spat the hateful word. "His objectives are not the sole detail of interest, Aunt!"

"But, of course, they are. Have I taught you nothing at all?"

Helena was spared more of Aunt Fanny's diatribe by the coach's halt on the drive before Bramble Cottage. A footman swept open the door, his expression hinting that their conversation had been overheard. Helena flushed but did not care what he thought. As soon as her aunt descended, she followed and hastened into the house.

She did not linger, though. She remained only long enough to collect her coat and a bonnet better suited to walking. The wind was rising and clouds gathered in the western sky, but she would not sit obediently to be berated for making the only possible choice.

"I am going for a walk," she informed her aunt, who was sufficiently astonished that she could not immediately summon a protest. By the time Lady Dalhousie had found her tongue, Helena intended to be beyond shouting distance.

She was not one to actively seek the opportunity for even such exercise as a walk, but this day would be the exception. Where would she go?

Helena halted beyond the hedge of shrubbery—her aunt had assured her that the rhododendrons would be magnificent in May—and considered her choices once she was out of view of the cottage. The road to the right led to Southpoint, but she could wait until dinner for her brother to add his voice to the criticism. Doubtless his wife would recite many dire prospects for young ladies who declined suitable offers, based upon her previous experiences as the wife of a vicar.

Helena grimaced. From Southpoint, she could proceed to Haynesdale House in one direction, and Haynesdale Hollow beyond, or toward Colsterworth in the other. She had no intention of walking so far.

The road to the left returned ultimately to Addersley and she could see the viscount's coach disappearing into the distance. This was a smaller curving road, one that ambled through the forested hills in a most inviting manner. There was little traffic upon it, which suited her well on this day. Addersley's village was beyond the manor but Helena could see some kind of structure in the forest between cottage and manor. It seemed that its roof shone, which was most unusual. She would make it her destination this day and learn something more of the countryside surrounding her prison.

Even walking was better than listening to Aunt Fanny all afternoon. Helena knew she had made the right choice, but she also knew her aunt would not be convinced of that soon. She dared not risk returning to the house for her boots, for she might be detained.

It seemed she would have to learn how to mend her slippers and soon.

Helena tied her bonnet securely and began to walk.

~

THE TRUTH of the matter was that Joshua *could* dance.

He could race horses and gamble all night long, he could drink himself witless and he could fight duel after duel. He had spent the better part of year proving that he could be every bit as much of a wastrel as his brother Gerald. While he had enjoyed some of those newfound temptations, there were intervals of that wild period in London that he could not recall—save for the disastrous end result.

He had vowed to his father that he would never succumb to such temptations again, and he would not.

He owed Charlotte's memory that much.

His word was his vow, after all.

And yet—would Miss Emerson have declined him ten years before, in London? She must have been a child then, but if she had been of age, Joshua imagined she would have found him a far more interesting suitor than she did now.

How unfair that keeping a pledge should cheat him of the one lady he desired!

Joshua paced through the empty corridors of Addersley Manor, his impatience with his situation growing step by step. Miss Emerson could not have said anything else that would so vividly fill his thoughts with the pleasures of that sojourn in London. Joshua found himself wanting to ride wildly again, wanting to feel the weight of a pistol in his hand as he paced off for a duel, wanting to savor every moment of every day as Gerald had.

Why must a man choose one path or the other?

Honor and respectability or notoriety and indulgence? There were points of merit on each side, in Joshua's view. He had no desire to be a wastrel again or live that dissipated life, but a little amusement at intervals would be welcome.

Like dancing.

He dismissed that thought.

After all, who had taught Miss Emerson that she could decide her future for herself? What she needed was a husband of honor, who would defend her against her own foolish impulses. Had she not chosen to leave London in the company of a rogue who desired only a fortune she did not possess? That showed an inclination to error and impulse that could lead her far astray. Would she make the same mistake again?

Joshua could not say and the very possibility chilled him. She could not rely upon the good fortune of meeting a solicitor's wife in the same coach, never mind one determined to act on her behalf, each time she stepped from the safer path.

But Miss Emerson was not Joshua's responsibility to defend.

Would he be compelled to watch her destroy her prospects? He did not know the men of age in the neighborhood, but there had to be some of dubious repute. If such a man could and would *dance*, she might be lost forever!

Joshua flung himself into his library, glared at the spot before the fire which might be occupied most amiably by a large dog, and seized upon a book in the hope of distracting himself.

It was regrettably, one of his father's older books, a leatherbound edition of *Robin Hood and Guy of Gisborne*. He cast it down, Miss Emerson at the fore of his thoughts.

How did a young lady arrive at a conviction that a

highwayman would be a desirable suitor? What manner of fool would wish for a thief—even one who was a nobleman in disguise and stole from the rich to give to the poor—to pursue one's affections? What if the thief won her heart? Would she happily live in the wilds of the forest with him? The notion as vexing as being declined because of his refusal to indulge in foolish fripperies.

Captain Emerson had given fair warning of the inclinations of his sister, but Joshua had not been prepared to believe her so fanciful.

He wondered if it was better she had declined him.

He could not believe it. Joshua had liked her immediately and, against every expectation, he still did. There was something about her presence that lightened his heart. She, like Gerald, could brighten a room with her arrival. She made him keenly aware of the possibilities of life—and that made him question how he chose to live. She made him want more.

Miss Emerson was the lady he wanted to wed. He knew it in his very soul.

Joshua should dismiss the incident. He should seek out another, possibly more sensible, young lady. That would be the rational choice.

And yet, his ambitions would not be so readily abandoned. He wanted to prove Miss Emerson wrong, to show her the magnitude of her error, and win her hand in his.

Joshua would never be a duke and he would never truly be a highwayman, but he was not content with his lot on this night—and he was not in a mood to lose himself in a book, however compelling the tale.

He marched through Addersley Manor in search of a trunk that was packed away but not forgotten. It was the one he had brought home from London ten years before and it had not been opened since, though it sat in the corner of his dressing room. He flung back the lid, halfway expecting to be disappointed by its contents.

One look within it and he could only smile. He lifted out a jacket, recalling visits to the tailor with Gerald. They had ordered clothes with wild abandon, in hues and fabrics he would never have chosen himself. Gerald had never been content with a conservative color or a coat that might be worn even a dozen times. Such practical considerations had been banished. And it had been amusing to indulge himself for once, to abandon his characteristic sobriety at Gerald's urging.

They had been dashing when they stepped out together, that much could not be denied.

This waistcoat, for example, in a shade of green silk that could only be called chartreuse, striped with emerald, black and with a tiny glimmer of gold. If that was not sufficient, the emerald stripes had been embroidered with ivory daisies, each one formed of ribbon and adorned with a glittering bead in its eye.

On impulse, Joshua tried it on, admiring the buttons that had the shape of a daisy in the top of each one and painted with gold. It still fit perfectly and he considered his reflection in the glass, liking that he looked a little less conservative than had become his custom.

There were enormous cravats within the trunk, boots of staggering expense that had scarce been worn, trousers and coats and breeches. The abundance was startling and now he considered the excessive cost. Joshua found himself going through them, remembering at least one incident with each garment. There were frock coats for court, shoes and hats and trousers. Joshua fingered a hole in a jacket made by a musket ball, then shook his head at a stain that might have been either claret or blood. He knew his garments had been stained by both.

He smelled the perfume of Gerald's favorite courtesan, who always had a friend, and smiled in memory of those sleepless nights. There was a dried carnation in one buttonhole, a dusty memento of a long-ago evening—undoubtedly one that had included so much dancing that the ladies' slippers were left full of holes. His handkerchiefs were monogrammed, as were his shirts, all of it packed away as tokens of another life.

Of another man.

It seemed an eon ago.

He would not think about Charlotte, or about the last time he had seen Gerald. He would not permit himself to open the floodgates of those memories. He could almost taste that fateful night, the crisp hint of winter in the air, and see the way the stars glittered overhead like diamonds. He shoved the memories aside. Once he began to review them, Joshua knew he would regret so many choices, and the weight of loss might destroy him.

No, the trick was to learn from the past, to take those lessons and chart a future with them.

Perhaps he would do that in the morning.

He might have turned away, but he spied the cloak in the bottom of the trunk. Joshua had not realized he still possessed it. He lifted it out, surprised again by the weight of so much black wool cloth. There was an enormous quantity of fabric in the generous cut of the cloak, and it was lined with heavy satin. He swung it around so that it landed on his shoulders, the flourish of donning it a gesture he recalled as well as his own name. The weighty cloak hung to his knees, a for-midable barrier to the elements, and he was glad to see that the moths had not damaged it. He drew up the hood and looked in the mirror, noting how his features vanished in the shadows.

He might have been that highwayman, the glimpse of his lavish waistcoat hinting that he was an aristocrat in disguise. Would Miss Emerson have accepted him in this garb? Joshua wondered. Would she have even recognized him? He doubted as much and for that reason alone, the cloak remained on his shoulders. He changed his boots on impulse, choosing the beautiful black ones from the trunk that were still gleaming from the bootmaker's shop. It was a waste that he had not worn them in recent years, for they were finely made. With a smile, he donned a pair of black leather gloves with long gauntlets.

His reflection could have been a different man, a man who savored life and all it offered, a man of audacity and charm, a man who might even believe in the merit of love. He might have been a man whose life merited a tale, a man to be dreaded—a man to be adored by innocent maidens. Joshua smiled at the mirror, feeling an almost-forgotten sense of power and audacity.

Indeed, he faced a reflection of his former self.

Did clothes truly make the man? In this moment, Joshua might have been convinced. He felt a plethora of possibilities, all at his fingertips, waiting to be seized.

The fact was that he had not taken a risk in a long time. It was true that he had proposed to Miss Emerson, but he had not believed there to be any possibility of failure so there was no risk in that choice.

Gerald would never have let him be so complacent.

It was time that Joshua dared a little more than had become his custom.

It was time that he lived more boldly and took advantage of opportunity more often. Perhaps that was the lesson he should take from his brother's memory and this trunk of garments. He need not be a reckless fool to savor a moment, or to celebrate the fact that he was yet alive.

Joshua had not ridden Gerald's stallion, Zephyr, of

late. The large horse was opinionated and not inclined to tolerate many riders since Gerald's departure from Addersley. The grooms, he understood, now avoided the beast and justifiably so. But all creatures benefitted from regular exercise and Zephyr was no exception.

On this day, the stallion might meet his match.

CHAPTER 5

The path through the forest was muddy after the rains and Helena wished she had worn more sturdy footwear than her slippers. It was not the first time she had erred in an impulsive rush, yet she was not inclined to turn back. No doubt, Aunt Fanny would spot her and have two reasons to chastise her. No, Helena would continue, no matter how precarious the way, and take her chances. The puppy had chewed the ribbons of these slippers, anyway.

It was cursedly difficult to climb the slight incline to her destination, but when she might have surrendered, Helena was rewarded by the sudden view through a gap in the trees. A beam of sunlight even shone down in that instant, as if it had been conjured by magic, and illuminated her destination.

It was a folly!

Helena gasped in wonder. The whimsical building had been constructed in a forest clearing, with a reflecting pond before it and shrubs on either side. The structure itself was shaped like a Japanese pagoda, though of a diminutive size. It was square, about four paces on a side, and it had been painted a glossy red. The roof was copper and fluted, the corners rising to gold-tipped points. She thought they deserved long silken tassels. On the peak of the roof, which rose from the very middle, was a golden orb. The door was bronze and the entire structure so delicate and detailed that it might have been a jewelry box. The sunlight had been glinting off the copper roof from the distance.

Helena was enchanted. Who would have guessed that any of the dour and elderly residents of this region would construct something so fanciful? Not she!

Upon closer inspection, it was clear the structure had been neglected in recent years. The cheerful red paint was peeling near the base of the walls and the exterior was marked from the patter of rain. The copper roof had turned verdigris and the golden accents were in need of polishing. The windows on either side were clouded and dark, while the bronze doors were in desperate need of cleaning.

How curious that the knob on the right door was the only element that was not mired. It must have been used more in the past.

The pond had a healthy growth of small green plants, even this early in the season, and the water was clouded. Helena thought she glimpsed a flash of orange in the depths of the water but could not be certain. The plants in the garden were overgrown and untended. Small trees and scrubby plants were growing between the pavilion and the surrounding forest, and she was certain that could not have been the original design.

The adorable pagoda had been forgotten.

Who had built it? Who had visited it? Helena tried the door but it was secured. She endeavored to peer through the window on one side, but to no avail. The window was so dirty and the interior was dark. Perhaps there were curtains inside.

Perhaps the angle was wrong. She considered the sun overhead and moved to the window on the other side of the double doors. She polished a circle of glass with her glove, resigned to washing it out herself so no one noticed how it was mired, and peered inside. Once again, it seemed that something obscured any view.

It was inevitable that being denied any thing, even a glimpse inside a locked garden pagoda, only redoubled Helena's determination to possess that very item. She circled the pavilion and discovered a window on the back side. It would be opposite the double doors of bronze. Indeed, she could almost discern something on the other side of the glass. Sadly, there was considerable mud on that side of the building and a large puddle. It appeared that the water was intended to flow from the roof to this side and thence to the pond, but the passage had been obstructed in the building's neglect. Helena was convinced she could balance on the increment of drier mud, at least long enough to take a look.

She eased alongside the pavilion, clinging to its smooth walls as best she could, gripped the lip of the window and stretched for a peek. Just as she leaned closer, a bird cried overhead and something splashed into the puddle beside her. She jumped in surprise, lost her grip and slipped.

She landed in the puddle with a splash, her foot twisted painfully beneath her hip. She immediately tried to get up but collapsed again at the fiery explosion of pain in her ankle.

She considered various words she had overhead in London, but decided they were unladylike and thus unsuitable for a potential duchess.

"Curses," she said instead, then managed to ease onto dry ground at least.

Her ankle was already beginning to swell. Her slipper was muddy, her stockings laddered, and her dress mired. She was seated on the ground, out of view of anyone who might approach the folly, unable to walk, and was keenly aware that no one knew her location. The clouds seemed to be gathering overhead with greater vigor, but she could not be much more wet than she already was.

It was a most unsatisfactory predicament.

Helena pulled herself to the path in the hope that at least she might be seen—if anyone ventured this way. It did not appear to be a strong possibility. The forest now seemed full of shadows and desolate beyond all. She had a moment of fear that she might never be found, not until she had wasted away to a pile of bones, then shook her head.

Nonsense. She had found this predicament and she would solve it.

Somehow.

There was a broken stick not ten feet away, undoubtedly debris from the forest. If she could reach it, she could use it as a cane and perhaps hobble to the edge of the forest. Chances were better of being discovered there. Helena grit her teeth and began to crawl toward the stick, dragging her injured foot. Never mind her slippers, her dress would be ruined as well, but any sacrifice was better than perishing alone.

She was halfway to the stick when she heard galloping hoofbeats. Could it be that someone sought her?

No, it could not be, and no one would look for her in this place. A galloping horse had to be on the road to Addersley Manor. At such a pace, the rider would soon be elsewhere, and she had best make the most of opportunity.

Helena took a deep breath and screamed with all her might, just as the first fat raindrops began to fall.

~

"HELP ME!"

Joshua reined in the stallion at the unexpected sound of a woman's cry, certain his ears had deceived him. Then she screamed again. He turned the horse, wondering at the lady's distress. He was near his mother's folly which no one visited any more.

Where else might the imperiled woman be? Who would walk in the forest alone? The villagers all said the folly was haunted, though he had never believed as much. He could be as skeptical as he chose, but the woman's cry made the hair rise on the back of his neck.

"Help me!" she entreated again, and he thought her voice was familiar.

Could it be Miss Emerson?

Why would she be walking alone, much less be visiting the folly?

That question nigh convinced him that it had to be Miss Emerson, for no one else of his acquaintance in the region would embark on such a venture.

The rain began to fall in heavy drops as he guided the horse along the forest path and Joshua was glad then of his heavy cloak. The weather was turning foul quickly and he drew his hood higher. He broke free of the forest to find Miss Emerson sprawled in the clearing in evident distress. Without a thought, he leapt from the saddle and strode toward her side.

"Oh!" she said, her tone so rapturous that he could make no sense of it. "There *is* a highwayman in Nottinghamshire!" And she smiled at him, an expression so dazzling that Joshua could only stare.

Indeed, his heart skipped a beat and words abandoned him. He had thought her a beauty before, but this smile was beyond brilliant and more heartfelt than any she had shown him thus far.

Joshua suddenly realized she did not know who he was. He wore his old cloak and rode Gerald's horse. She could not see his features because of the hood. Even if she saw his waistcoat or took heed of his boots, she would recognize neither.

He could pretend to be the man she wished to meet, for just a moment, only to encourage that radiant smile.

He dared not speak, lest his identity be revealed.

He bowed low to her, ensuring that the hood shadowed his face, and offered his hand to her.

She shook her head, flushing prettily. "I fell, sir," she admitted. "And my ankle will not bear my weight. Your arrival is both timely and welcome." She pushed back her bonnet, which drooped low in the rain, and regarded him with undisguised admiration.

His heart was racing, but he strove to hide her influence over him. He knelt before her, well aware of her curious scrutiny, and gestured to her delicate ankle.

She flushed crimson. "It is the left one, sir, and I would be most grateful if you could verify that it is not broken. I have no notion how to be certain but it does not bear my weight."

Joshua felt a tide of warmth as he touched her ankle, even with his gloves. It was a most perfect and slender ankle, one that made him keenly aware of how long it had been since he had savored a lady's charms. He could only imagine that her legs, now disguised by her mired skirts, were just as pleasing.

Desire simmered within him as he moved her ankle gently, and he strove to compare his actions to checking the injury of a horse. It was not in the least like checking a horse, and he would never convince any corner of his mind to believe as much for an instant.

He was holding Miss Emerson's ankle, with her permission. Once upon a time, he might have stolen a kiss from a lady in such a predicament. His brother would have convinced the lady to surrender even more.

That gave Joshua ideas that were most distracting.

He set down her foot and slid his gloved fingertips

over her ankle, hoping to show with a gesture that it was simply sprained. He felt her shiver at his touch, a most enticing reaction.

"Oh good," she said with relief. She smiled again, which did little to aid the recovery of his wits. "Goodness. My stockings are torn and my slippers are ruined, not to mention my dress," she said with a rueful sigh. "If ever I was to be taught a lesson about not changing to my boots for a walk, this would be it. I love these slippers." She touched the torn roses with a wistful fingertip, reminding him of her delight in the dog. "But now they are ruined forever and for certain." He thought she might weep over them.

He wanted to restore them, just to coax her smile.

The rain began to fall in earnest, recalling him to their circumstance, and she shivered with cold, which did even more.

Joshua offered his hand to her again, gesturing behind himself with the other, and was gifted with another smile.

"I should be most grateful if you might see me home, sir. I am in desperate need of your assistance." She tried to rise to her knees, but Joshua stepped closer and swept her into his arms. She gasped and stiffened, then melted against him with a trust that completely startled him.

When she leaned her cheek against his chest in relief, he found himself smiling with satisfaction. She was as delicate and light as he had imagined, and it was tempting indeed to carry her off to some private bower. It was clear that this lady had need of a protector and he knew he would fulfill the task admirably.

"Thank you," she whispered, a break in her voice that tore at his heart. "I was afraid that I would be here for the entire night."

He did not reply, only tightened his grip upon her.

The horse was sufficiently tired to be less skittish and he lifted her to the saddle, holding fast to the reins until he swung into the saddle behind her. He held her securely against his chest so he could draw his cloak over them both, her shivers making it clear that she was chilled. She nestled against him like a kitten, but so much more alluring that his very blood was afire.

"I do not even know your name, sir," she said and he made a non-committal sound. Her hand had fallen to the front of his waistcoat and he felt her run her hand over the silk. She bent her head and he knew she was taking note of the fine fabric—and doubtless drawing one particular conclusion.

Joshua smiled to himself as she sighed contentment.

"You dare not speak lest you reveal yourself," she guessed in a thrilled whisper. "It must be thus for all highwaymen who are in disguise." She nodded. "Then I will tell you of myself, the better that you might locate me again, if you have that desire. I am Helena Emerson, and I have recently come to live at Bramble Cottage with my aunt."

He nodded and urged the horse to a canter along the forest path. As much as he would like to prolong this interlude, the lady had need of shelter and warmth.

"I thought to learn more of the neighborhood, then fell in the mud. I was trying to look inside the folly."

He made a sound in his throat like a growl of disapproval and she nodded again.

"You are right, of course. A more sturdy choice of shoe would have been prudent, but I fear I am not always prudent. I will always wear my boots in future."

Joshua nodded vigorously, the move reminding him too much of a horse to seem romantic. Miss Emerson nestled against this chest, though, apparently content. He could feel her striving to pierce the shadows and discern his features. They left the cover of the forest and the rain slanted down upon his shoulders, driving coldly through even that heavy cloth.

"When I am recovered, will I see you again?" she asked. "I could come to the folly to meet you once more."

Oh, she was audacious! Joshua might have been inclined to scold her for being so forward, but a notorious rogue would have seized the opportunity.

He tightened his grip upon her as if in agreement.

"Oh, I am so glad!" She whispered with delight. He felt her flatten her palm against him and knew his pulse leapt at her touch. He did not know whether to be disappointed or relieved that Bramble Cottage appeared so quickly before them.

In keeping with the disguise he had not meant to undertake, Joshua halted the stallion with a flourish and leapt to the ground. Miss Emerson watched him with noted appreciation. He swept her from the saddle into his arms again and carried her through the opening in the hedge, hesitating before he set her down at the door of the cottage. They stood beneath the shelter of a small roof, the rain pouring down an arms length away.

She looked up at him with awe, and though she was drenched, Joshua knew he had never seen a more lovely lady in all his life. It was satisfying to have her regard him with such approval and he told himself that any man would savor such victory after failure.

"I hope I heal quickly," she said, her words falling in a breathless rush as if she were similarly affected by their proximity. "That I might walk in the forest again soon." She flushed as he stared down at her. "I would hope to meet you again at the pavilion, sir."

An assignation was most improper, but Joshua's intentions were honorable. If such a meeting convinced

Miss Emerson of the merit of their match, he would not decline the opportunity.

He nodded slowly again and she blessed him with another radiant smile.

"When the weather is fine again," she stipulated, then laughed. "*Whenever* it is fine, I will meet you there. I promise I will come. Will you?"

A man of dangerous repute would not be content with simple agreement. For that interval in London, even he would not have been content with that. Before Joshua could dismiss his impulse, he caught her close, lifting her higher to capture her lips beneath his own.

He felt Miss Emerson gasp. He heard her sigh. And his heart thundered when she surrendered to his kiss, parting her lips and melting against him with an abandon that hinted that there was promise in his suit.

As it was, it took all within him to halt the kiss before it went too far. It was a glorious kiss for all its short duration, one that enflamed him and left Miss Emerson flushed, her lips softened and rosy. Her eyes were full of stars as she looked up at him afterward. He placed her gently on her feet then ran his gloved thumb across her luscious mouth. She shivered, a good sign that she would be a willing partner on their wedding night, then nipped at his gloved finger playfully. Her eyes were dancing with mischief and it was all he could do to release her.

He brushed his lips across hers once more, unable to resist the temptation of another taste, then pivoted. He strode back to the horse, knowing the cloak flared around him as if he were a cavalier.

He also felt the weight of Miss Emerson's gaze upon him.

She was still standing under the shelter of the roof when he had mounted and turned the horse, so he raised a hand in salute, then gave his heels to the steed.

Had he known how long she peered after him, Joshua Hargood might have been more encouraged in his prospects.

As it was, he was pondering the complications and implications of what he had begun. It was true, Joshua was certain, that impulse was a poor master. Once it had led him to disaster, but he was not the same youth he had been then. Surely now he could avoid a repetition of such tragic events.

Was the prize not worth the risk? The prospect of winning Miss Emerson's hand in his own was a tempting one. He could already envision her in his home and by his side, her irreverent laughter and audacity enchanting him a little more every day—and night. Her company made him feel alive as he had not in years and he wanted to be the daring rogue she desired.

Joshua could not deny the thunder in his veins from Miss Emerson's sweet kiss.

No, he could only yearn for another and soon.

The question was how best to find a balance between his old ways and his nature while keeping his promise to his father.

There had to be a way to triumph in the pursuit of his goal.

Somehow, he would find it.

HELENA'S CHAMPION WAS PERFECT.

His kiss had seared her very soul.

The incident had been worthy of the most romantic of novels—and she would find him in the forest when her ankle healed.

Helena hugged the details of her rescuer to herself as Aunt Fanny fussed over her and Becky hastened to see that she had both a hot bath and a bowl of broth. The fire was made in her room, despite the lateness of the season and Aunt Fanny's frugality, and Helena was pampered in truth.

She was scarcely aware of it, her thoughts spinning as she strove to commit every detail of her gallant savior to memory. He was tall. He had a dark cloak and a powerful stride. His features had been obscured by the shadows cast by his hood, making him a delicious mystery, but he was powerful. He had swept her into his arms as if she weighed nothing at all. He was wealthy, to be sure, given that horse and his waistcoat.

And his kiss. Oh, his kiss had been a marvel, a forbidden pleasure, and surely a sample of what might come. She dared not even hint to Aunt Fanny that such an embrace had been shared.

But she wanted another such kiss.

If not more.

Who was he? Did he take refuge at the pavilion?

No, he could not do that. Where would he keep his horse if he lived there? Plus he had been riding past the forest, with a destination other than the pagoda.

Helena pondered this puzzle. He had to have a home in the vicinity. She thought of Robin Hood in his forest haven but knew that would not do for her rescuer. No, he had a house, she was certain, one of ample proportions and considerable comfort. And his nature was honorable. He had been gallant, stealing only a kiss and one she would have been happy to offer. He was a nobleman, to be sure. Perhaps his home was hidden in a hollow. Perhaps it appeared to be less than it was.

Perhaps she would visit it soon, after they met again at the folly.

She surveyed her ankle, now cleaned and securely bound, and tried to will it to heal with all speed. She had to return to the pavilion on the earliest possible sunny afternoon, the better to learn more about the most interesting man in all of Nottinghamshire—if not all of England.

How would she endure the wait?

~

HER HUSBAND'S younger sister would be the death of them, Eliza Emerson was certain. She and Nicholas had braved a rainy evening to hear of Helena's latest offense, and she did not doubt that Aunt Fanny would be fulsome in her criticism.

Helena had been at the table when they arrived, her ankle bound and her foot propped up, her manner as unrepentant as anticipated.

In fact, she seemed to be glowing with a secret held close. The girl would never cease to be trouble, Eliza was certain of it. The sooner she was married, the better.

It was only Eliza's second visit to Bramble Cottage and on that first occasion, all had been in the uproar of moving. After the better part of a week, the result was cozy and comfortable, particularly with a fire blazing on the hearth and the four of them gathered around the table in the dining room. Aunt Fanny sat at one end of the table and Nicholas at the other, Eliza facing a decidedly rebellious Helena.

There was doubtless still some disorder in the house, but the dining room had been set to rights in a most pleasing way. Eliza wagered the table linens had come from Fanny's own collection. She knew that the cottage had some furnishings, including this lovely table and six chairs, all carved of cherry, for the dining room. They were both comfortable and attractive, and of the perfect size.

It was, overall, a most welcoming room. A pair of

chiffonieres faced each other from opposite walls, offering more than sufficient storage for china and stemware. A large window overlooked the garden at the end of the room—lost in the deluge of rain on this night—and the fireplace dominated the opposite wall, at the foot of the table. Its glowing embers were most welcome, given the forbidding weather. The floors were gleaming wood with an attractive but slightly worn rug spread beneath the table. Candles flickered on the table, bathing the room in golden light.

Though Becky was no cook, the maid had managed a joint of ham with potatoes from the cold cellar and asparagus from the garden. It was simple but hearty fare. Nicholas had brought some wine in anticipation of a family dispute, and he poured it now. Eliza had worked hard on this day herself, cleaning and organizing the cupboards of Southpoint, and the meal smelled heavenly.

"Thank you, Becky," Aunt Fanny said when all the dishes were on the table. The maid, who had to be of an age with Eliza, curtsied and left the dining room.

"How lovely this room is," Eliza said, hoping to dispel some of the tension between aunt and niece.

"Bramble Cottage is most satisfactory," Aunt Fanny said. "Constance has found me a couple from Haynesdale Hollow to see to our needs, and they will arrive on the morrow. I understand that Mrs. Nixon is an excellent cook and her husband is most able. Becky speaks highly of them and she will remain, of course."

"That should suit you admirably," Eliza said.

"I thought to have just a cook and maid, but Constance is right that there will be a fair bit of work in the garden."

"I think a couple will suit you well, Aunt," Nicholas said, then lifted his glass. "Let us drink to many happy years in your new abode."

Aunt Fanny smiled at him. "And let us drink to the generosity of my beloved nephew, who has ensured my comfort in every way. Thank you, Nicholas."

Helena looked between the two of them with suspicion, obviously anticipating that they would ally together against her. They ate for a few moments in companionable silence, making a goodly dent in the quantity of ham.

Finally, Nicholas put down his fork. "Now tell us what Helena has done to so earn your ire," he invited his aunt.

Aunt Fanny's eyes flashed. "This girl declined an offer from Lord Addersley!" she said with outrage. Helena's lips set mutinously. "Surely, there could be no more suitable candidate than a man with a title, a house and a fortune, right here in the neighborhood, but this miss will not listen to sense!"

"He is respectable and responsible, to be sure," Helena said. "He is also old and *dull*."

Though Eliza might have expected such an assessment from the younger woman, Nicholas began to chuckle. She eyed him but he only shook his head, amused beyond all as the older woman continued her tirade.

"Less than a week here and she makes a most promising conquest, but she believes herself destined for better matches." Aunt Fanny fixed Helena with a stern look. "No duke will wed you, Helena. Though I wish neither to be cruel or blunt, you have no dowry and your looks will not be in your favor for much longer. You should have taken the viscount and been content. There is not an abundance of eligible gentlemen in the vicinity and you may have sacrificed your sole chance for comfort."

"I do not care," Helena said. "I will wed for love."

"You may not wed at all if you are so particular,"

Aunt Fanny said crossly. "And then you will be fortunate indeed to end your days alone here in Bramble Cottage. Nicholas may not see fit to indulge you, or he might not be able to do as much. What will you do then?"

That prospect made the younger girl pale. "I cannot wed a man so thoroughly tedious and predictable"

"Respectability is most welcome!"

"I prefer a lively companion!"

"You are a foolish chit, and I should cast you out this very night for your ingratitude and folly. Nicholas! How can you be so entertained by this vexing situation?"

"Because you would have been shocked beyond all if Helena had garnered a proposal from Joshua Hargood a decade ago. You would have forbidden her to even speak to him."

"How can this be?" Aunt Fanny demanded.

Helena looked up with avid and predictable interest.

"You must not have been in town that year," Nicholas said. "They were known as the terrors of London, he and his brother Gerald. Never had two rakehells found so much trouble. They gambled and they whored, they spent money as if it were water, they drank and they danced and I am not certain when they slept. There were duels and horse races and wicked doings at all hours of the night. The pair of them were insatiable by all accounts, and their father nearly washed his hands of them."

Helena, predictably, was listening keenly. "But he said he does not dance."

"That is not the same as being unable to dance," Eliza noted.

Aunt Fanny glared at her nephew. "What happened to change that circumstance?"

"Something dire," Nicholas said with a shrug. "I am

not certain. When I left for the continent with Haynesdale, they were in their revels. Then Gerald appeared at Badajoz, his father having bought him a commission, and that against every expectation."

"Badajoz," Eliza repeated softly, watching Nicholas for some hint that his nightmares of that battle might recur.

He smiled at her and she was reassured by the steadiness of his gaze. "I scarce had a chance to speak with him before the battle, and heard later that he was one of the few survivors. To be honest, I was consumed with Haynesdale's care in those early weeks. Evidently, Gerald continued to serve, for he was reported amongst the casualties at Waterloo." Nicholas finished his meal with a thoughtful frown. "But the change in Joshua occurred years ago."

"After that incident, whatever it was," Eliza guessed and he nodded.

"I believe Gerald continued his wastrel ways and that was at least part of why his father bought him that commission. He was always cursed lucky, and undoubtedly, all assumed he would return home, hale and perhaps even chastened."

"If he died at Waterloo, he came close to it," Aunt Fanny said.

"Heavens," Eliza said softly. "His father must have blamed himself terribly."

"I do not know," Nicholas said. "There was so much ill will between the father and Gerald, even before my departure. He must have been relieved that Joshua had abandoned that reckless life. There were whispers," he began, then shook his head. "Even now I should not repeat them. Suffice it to say that Joshua was close to his father after he abandoned his excesses."

"Reckless," Helena repeated, staring at her plate. "I cannot imagine the viscount thus."

"To Aunt's relief, no doubt," Nicholas said. "Oh, they were a pair. Joshua could fight and win with any weapon. Whenever one of them was challenged to a duel, I am certain he fought it, for his skill was beyond all else. Knife, sword, fists or pistol, he always won."

"Oh," Helena whispered. "I should like to see a duel."

Aunt Fanny shot her a reproving glance. "I forbid any such occupation or entertainment on your part."

Nicholas continued. "Gerald had a way with horses, though, in my view, he demanded too much of them. If there was a curricle race, he would be there and he would win—and he would accept the accolades from every lady in attendance. He had a fearsome charm. They both gambled, of course, and one of them was more inclined to win but as they often switched places in those days, I am uncertain who was the better at dice and cards."

"And Lord Addersley abandoned that life by choice?" Helena asked wistfully.

"Something went awry. A rakehell's life is a dangerous path, Helena, one fraught with debts and uncertainty. One must evade one's creditors—and doubtless irate husbands, too. No man successfully lives thus for long."

"I wish I had known him then," Helena said with a sigh. "It would be thrilling to be courted by a notorious rogue."

Eliza shook her head. "Though one could never be certain of his loyalties or his financial situation."

"You have entertained the attentions of such a man already," Nicholas reminded his sister. "Did you learn nothing at all from Mr. Melbourne?"

Bright color lit Helena's cheeks. "You are cruel to remind me."

"Truly, if Gerald Hargood was not dead, I would

lock you in the cellar myself," Nicholas said, earning a glare from his sister.

"Perhaps a peril has been avoided after all," Aunt Fanny said. "I had no notion the viscount had such a past."

"Can a man not repent of his sins?" Nicholas asked.

"I have always believed as much," Eliza said and their gazes met.

"You might grant the viscount a second chance, Helena," Nicholas said. "You might find more to him than you have glimpsed so far."

"I think not," his sister said, a stubborn tone to her voice.

"You might not have other suitable opportunities," Eliza warned her but the girl smiled with a confidence Eliza could not explain.

"I believe there is at least one of merit."

"Who?" Aunt Fanny demanded, but Helena only smiled mysteriously.

"Doubtless you think fondly of whoever aided your return home today," Nicholas said. "You have not told us about that encounter."

Helena lifted her chin. "I fell in the forest. A gentleman appeared in a most timely way and insisted upon my riding his horse as he escorted me home."

"Becky said the two of you rode together," Aunt Fanny said. "If so, Helena, that was most inappropriate." Eliza watched the younger woman's eyes flash.

"What was this gentleman's name?" Nicholas asked.

"He did not introduce himself." Helena spoke with confidence but Eliza was certain there was some detail she was not sharing.

"Can you describe him?" Nicholas asked, but his sister shook her head.

"I was quite overcome with pain, and he wore a hood. I could not see him clearly."

Helena exchanged a glance with Nicholas who then eyed his sister thoughtfully. When he changed the subject, complimenting his aunt on the meal, she followed his lead, much to Helena's evident relief.

This girl. Eliza would have to discover whether there were other eligible men in the vicinity and see Helena wed soon.

CHAPTER 6

"She has a scheme," Eliza said when she and Nicholas were in the carriage together. The rain was pelting against the roof of the carriage but the horse made a good pace. Nicholas had enjoyed the meal, was glad to see his aunt content with the cottage, and was anticipating an active night with his beloved.

He could not suppress his smile at Eliza's assessment, for she was right. He claimed his wife's hand and planted a kiss upon her palm. "I do not know whether to be satisfied or troubled that you have learned to read my sister so readily."

Eliza smiled briefly. "If only we could see her securely wed."

"I wish she had not declined Hargood."

"Nor I, though I have not met him."

"He would have suited her well, I think, though I can understand why she believed him too staid. He truly became the echo of his father after his reform."

"Did you know him well?"

Nicholas shook his head. "The brothers were both younger than Haynesdale and me. We would see them but we had our own schemes and adventures. I've always liked Joshua Hargood, though. Even at his most rebellious, he was honorable." He shrugged. "His brother, though, caused trouble wherever he went. He had little conscience and was utterly untrustworthy. He and Helena would have been two of a kind."

"It might be unseemly to be glad of a man's demise, but I confess myself relieved then that he is no longer present. Who can say what mischief they might have made together?"

Nicholas said nothing. He was inclined to think the mischief Helena would have found with a rogue like Gerald Hargood was entirely predictable.

He watched Eliza frown.

"Do you sense an untruth in her claim that she does not know the name of the man who aided her?"

"No, but there is some detail she is not disclosing."

"She is intrigued by him, to be sure." Eliza's gaze collided with his own. "You do not think she has com-promised herself?"

"Already? No, even she is not so impetuous as that."

"Might she have a plan to meet him again?"

"Alone? Without a chaperone?" Even as Nicholas protested, he knew his sister would do as much in a moment, if she so desired. Had he not pursued her half the length of England for that very reason? It was not unreasonable, in his view, to have hoped she might have learned a lesson from that adventure, or at least a measure of caution, but this evening's discussion im-plied otherwise. "But I cannot watch her all of the time," he said.

"Of course not! But who might he be?"

"I cannot say. I have been away from the region too long to have any accurate notion of who yet lives nearby."

"I am in the same situation. My mother will not know, for she pays no heed to gossip, even if she hears it, which is seldom."

Nicholas smiled. "That may change with Aunt Fanny nearby."

"It might, but not in time enough. Do you think you might enquire of Lord Addersley as to young men in the region?"

"By my understanding, he is also recently returned from London, but he has been back for a few months. That does give him some slight advantage over us."

"Although with his father's illness and death, he, too, may have paid no heed to rumor."

"I will try to find an opportunity to speak with him over the next few days," Nicholas said as the carriage halted at Southpoint. "I should like to know how discouraged he is by Helena's refusal."

"The better to bolster his determination?" Eliza asked and they shared a smile.

"She has a good heart," Nicholas said. "And marriage may be precisely what she needs for true happiness."

"I wish you luck in persuading her of that," his wife replied and Nicholas could not blame her for such doubts.

Truly, he would be a happy man himself when Helena was the obligation of another man.

He could only hope it turned out to be a man of whom he could approve.

HELENA MANAGED to make her way to the garden the next morning, for it was a glorious spring day and she could not abide lingering in the house. Even better, her aunt was so occupied with consideration of changes to the décor that she did not follow Helena.

Aunt would have said that she should occupy herself with her needlework, but Helena did not care for the occupation at all.

She would dream of her champion instead—and strive to solve the riddle of his identity.

She could just barely see the glimmer of the roof of the pavilion in the distance, though she wagered that once the trees were all in leaf, it would be hidden from view. How she yearned to visit there this day and seek *him* out again!

Instead, she sat on the bench and thought about him. She recalled her champion on his black horse, his cloak flaring in the wind, his face hidden in shadows, and sighed with satisfaction. She closed her eyes, recalling the strength of his arms around her, the beat of his heart beneath her hand, and her own pulse fluttered. She knew nothing about him but she would have surrendered more than a kiss to him.

His gallantry had saved her from her own impetuous choices.

Even that was romantic beyond all.

In that moment, she heard a horse approaching and looked up with curiosity and hope. Could he have come to visit her?

But no, it was only the viscount, looking fastidious and proper. She felt a little dismay, for she belatedly hoped she had not injured his feelings. His expression was as inscrutable as the day before and she did not know whether to be reassured or not.

Though it was unreasonable, she would have been glad to see him at least disappointed that she had refused him. From his manner, his proposal might have been made with indifference. There was a far cry from a love that would not be denied! The man was the very soul of composure. Did any event—either a disappointment or a triumph—stir him to a response? Helena feared not and felt a wave of sympathy for him that his experience of life should be so curtailed.

He dismounted in the yard, securing his horse's

reins to a fence post. "You have a most comfortable abode here, Miss Emerson." She was relieved that he was as polite as ever. She also was glad that he made no comment or fuss about them not having so much as a pony, nor a man to tend the outside as yet. The Nixons were to arrive this day, though the viscount could not know as much. He had almost reached her before she realized that he carried a wriggling brown bundle under one arm.

"Mischief!" she cried with delight, made to rise, then fell back onto the bench with a wince.

"Miss Emerson!" The viscount frowned with concern. "Are you injured?"

"I turned my ankle, my lord, but it will heal soon enough."

"Perhaps that is why she made a fuss this morning," he said, placing the pup on the ground before her. One end of a ribbon was tied around the pup's neck like a collar, with the other end acting as a short tether. Mischief had about ten feet of range, and the viscount gave Helena the end of the ribbon. "Perhaps she knew you had need of companionship."

Helena looked at him. Why was he doing her such a kindness? And how could this man have uttered such a fanciful comment? She thought of Nicholas' words that she might perceive more to the viscount than she had seen thus far if she troubled to look, even as she replied. "What a whimsical notion, sir."

"Is it?" He braced his hands upon his hips and looked down at the puppy, his averted attention giving Helena an opportunity study him. He was handsome, to be sure. "I have often found that dogs perceive more than people realize."

The puppy wagged and wriggled, licking Helena's outstretched hands and permitting her ears to be scratched. She pounced on a leaf that blew past and rolled to her back, offering her belly to be rubbed, and was altogether so silly that Helena could not help but laugh at her antics.

She was so occupied with the dog that she did not notice right away how the viscount was watching her. His eyes had narrowed and he almost smiled, surveying them both with unexpected avidity.

His attention was so complete that he seemed almost dangerous in that moment. He had an aura of power and competence that made Helena tingle. She realized he was tall, as tall as her champion, and as assured in the saddle. His clothing was different but she remembered Nicholas' tale of his days in London with his brother. It was easy, when his eyes darkened thus, to imagine him as a rogue.

Was he truly reformed?

Did he own a dark cloak?

Was it madness to even wonder?

"I hope that you are not dismayed with me, my lord."

He lifted a brow and she realized her question had been blunt. "Because you refused me?"

She was surprised that he should be so direct in his turn, but glad of it. "Of course."

He shook his head and crouched down, removing his glove to rub the dog's belly. Mischief was in such raptures at his attention that Helena could not fight her smile. "I would rather have an honest reply than an agreement that did not come from your heart," he said, surprising her again. His gaze was fixed upon the dog and Helena watched him, more intrigued than she might have anticipated. "We remain neighbors, though, and it would be most awkward if there was enmity between us." He frowned a little. "I chose to visit today, Miss Emerson, not just to reassure you about my promise of the dog but to ask if we might be friendly acquaintances." He looked up and she caught her breath at the heat in his eyes.

"Of course!" she said with relief and his quick smile made her heart skip a beat. It vanished far too quickly for her taste. "I thought you might be angry with me. Everyone else is."

"Because they think of a match only in terms of alliance and advantage, while you would consider your own happiness?"

"Yes." Helena blinked at him.

The viscount addressed the dog, his gaze carefully averted. His voice dropped low. "My own mother used to say that what a lady desires most is to have her own wish fulfilled. She strove to teach my brother and I both that a lady's choice was of tantamount importance, and a lady's favor was the greatest prize of all." He met her gaze again, and once more, Helena could not take a full breath. "I would never impose my view upon you or any other lady, Miss Emerson. Indeed, I must apologize for my presumption in even making my offer on such short acquaintance, and worse, for refusing to immediately accept your refusal." He stood then and bowed again.

Would he leave? Helena vehemently wanted him to linger.

"You were surprised." She was surprised to find herself excusing his choices. In truth, she was both startled and pleased by his apology. "I thank you for the honor, sir," she said and he nodded once.

Evidently, he had said all he intended to say.

"My brother mentioned knowing you in London a decade ago," Helena ventured, his quick sidelong glance making her fear she had shown too much curiosity.

"Did he?"

Evidently, he would offer little encouragement to her inquiries.

How strange that the weight of his gaze reminded her of her savior, even though she had not seen that man's eyes. She felt the same prickle of awareness, the same sense of uncommon warmth.

The same delicious sense of *possibility*.

Helena dared to plunge onward. "Nicholas said that you and your brother were rakehells of repute, and I wondered, sir, if that might give us some common ground."

"Are you a rakehell, Miss Emerson?"

To her satisfaction, the viscount was smiling at her, clearly amused. She cared only for the appearance of a most alluring dimple. The sight made her catch her breath. When he watched her intently, as he did in this moment, it was easy to believe he had wicked tendencies.

"No, but I succumbed to temptation and I wonder if you might have done the same."

"More than once, I assure you." His tone was so moderate that he might have been confessing to reading another page of a favored book before retiring. "What temptation led you astray, Miss Emerson?"

She noticed that he did not seem overly troubled by this prospect. Perhaps he lacked an appreciation for her wilder tendencies. Helena could not resist the opportunity to possibly shake his assumptions. "My favor was courted by a man I believed to be a gentleman. He was the son of a baronet and said he would inherit a goodly sum."

Lord Addersley's brows rose but he said nothing.

"He proposed that we should elope to Gretna Green."

"And you agreed." There was no question in his tone, though whether it was because he had already learned of this indiscretion or because he guessed, Helena could not say.

Helena's lips set for she didn't like to sound predictable. "I did, though it was not the adventure I anticipated. Mr. Melbourne proved to be an unsatisfactory companion even before he learned that I had no dowry or inheritance, as he had supposed. He was not gentlemanly in the least, but concerned only with his own comfort."

"I see." Once again, there was no inflection in his tone. She could not have guessed if he were outraged or indifferent. "And you regret this interlude?"

"No, that is my point entirely, sir. Matters did not proceed as I expected, yet I should never have known as much if I had declined Mr. Melbourne's invitation as was right and proper. I would have wondered all my life what it might have been like, and it would have been impossible to bear *not* knowing."

His eyes were glinting now like emeralds and Helena felt a sense of victory. "Even disappointment was better than ignorance?"

"Yes! And I met Mrs. D., which I cannot regret." At his blank look, she continued. "She was in the coach with her daughter, the wife of a solicitor in Carting Corners." He nodded that he knew the town. "So, I cannot wish to have foregone the adventure, not in the least." Once again, he seemed disinclined to speak, so she continued. "And learning of your former reputation in London, sir, I had to wonder whether you regret that interval, or whether we agree in the merit of pursuing opportunity?"

"It is unwise to overindulge in temptations," he said softly.

"Of course."

He studied her for a long moment, as if he would read every one of her secrets. Then he turned away, sobering, and she liked that he gave serious consideration to her question. "You remind me of childhood

tales, Miss Emerson, in which there is always an admonition to remain on the path when travelling through
the forest. The warnings insist that leaving the path
might offer adventure, those adventures will certainly
include peril."

"Yes," she agreed with a nod. "And that is the conundrum. Is it better to remain safe or to learn the truth?"

"I wager I know your reply, Miss Emerson, which is
the choice of every character in every recounted tale.
But I must remind you that your own adventure, as you
call it, might have ended very badly for you indeed."

Helena sighed. "So, my brother's wife has informed
me repeatedly."

"And Mrs. Emerson is right in that." He leaned
closer to make his point. "Your view is understandable,
but short-sighted, Miss Emerson, for you might gain an
experience you are unable to forget—or worse."

"I do not understand," Helen said, although she did.

"You might have been abandoned by your suitor, left
without resources, and not had the fortune to meet one
such as this Mrs. D. You might have been despoiled by
your suitor and left in shame." His eyes flashed at this
very notion and Helena could not avert her gaze. His
lips hardened to a thin line. "You might have died, Miss
Emerson, which could hardly have been an outcome to
be desired." He lifted one brow. "I may assure you that
many might have regretted that result."

Did he count himself among such company?

Curiously, Helena found herself wishing that he
might.

"It is certainly wiser to be prudent," Helena ceded
carefully. "But I should hate to lie on my deathbed,
wondering at all I had missed by such caution."

"It might be prudent for a lady so inclined to pursue
adventure to have a protector, Miss Emerson."

Helena looked up. "A protector?"

"Someone to watch over her and guarantee her safety."

Helena wrinkled her nose. "A husband, you mean."

"Or a guardian angel, though it would be simpler to ensure the attention of a husband."

Had he made a jest? Helena studied him, uncertain.

"Marriage *is* a solution found satisfactory by many." He stood then, once again indicating that he would leave. He hesitated a moment and his voice dropped low. "I wonder also, Miss Emerson, if you will ever be content with what you possess, or always be yearning for some prize you perceive on the horizon."

Helena was chastised, for there was truth in his words. "I would have made you a poor wife, Lord Addersley."

"That is one of the things we shall never know, Miss Emerson," he said so lightly that it could not have truly mattered to him. "I suppose the greater question is whether you might ever regret your choice."

"Do you regret it?"

"Of course." His smile was thin and polite, a pale shadow of the unbidden one that showed his dimple. "It would have been churlish for me to make such an offer otherwise."

Helena thought of her flight to the forest and subsequent rescue by her champion, of the incendiary kiss that stranger had given her, and flushed to her very toes. The viscount was so still that he might have been reading her guilty thoughts.

No, she could never regret any choice that had led her to her savior.

Could she convince that mysterious man to become her protector?

The viscount turned away crisply, as if he knew her interest had strayed to another man.

Helena did not wish him to be insulted and asked

the first question that rose to her lips. "But what of your own time in London, sir? Do you regret that interval?"

She thought he would not reply, but he halted and considered the toe of his boot for a long moment. When he turned back to face her, he was even more inscrutable than before. "You are right that I chose to join my brother in his revels, and there were elements of such pursuits that were pleasurable, to be sure." The viscount spoke crisply, his gaze colliding suddenly with hers again, his own so dark that her heart skipped. "But I would not be a man of much merit if I did not regret that the price of those indulgences was the life of my betrothed."

"Oh! I am sorry." Helena knew she flushed crimson, for once again she had erred in conversation with this man. His thoughts were hidden, but she suspected he felt deeply about the tragedy.

His betrothed. Had his heart been lost forever with that lady's demise? Did he feel responsible for her death? Has she been impulsive as Helena was inclined to be? Helena had a thousand questions, none of which she dared to ask in this moment.

The viscount inclined his head slightly in acknowledgement of her sympathies and changed the subject. "If I may be so bold, I had thought to ask Mrs. Jameson to call upon you. She is a dressmaker in Haynesdale Hollow and one, I understand, of considerable skill. Yesterday, Mischief ruined your slipper and since she is as yet one of my dogs, I feel obliged to replace the pair. Mrs. Jameson can ascertain the details from you and send the bill to me."

"Oh, you need not do that!" Helena was delighted by the prospect of any new garments. Aunt was frugal beyond all, but due to necessity, Helena knew.

"Perhaps not, but I will do as much all the same. I

shall return this afternoon for the dog. Good morning, Miss Emerson." He bowed again and strode to his horse, Mischief bounding after him to the limit of the lead. The puppy then sat down heavily and whimpered as he swung into the saddle. He tipped his hat one last time and rode away, even as Aunt Fanny emerged from the cottage.

Helena looked after him, wondering. Truly, he did have a similar flair to her champion. If he wore a cloak...but no, that could not be possible. The viscount could not possibly grant a woman a kiss of such ferocity that it claimed her, heart and soul. No. He would peck a lady upon her hand, politely.

Perhaps Nicholas' story of Lord Addersley's nefarious past was only a tale to increase her interest in him as a suitor.

Yes! Nicholas would readily tease her thus. That was the explanation. The brother might have been a rakehell and a rogue, but never the viscount himself.

"Was that Lord Addersley? He has called again in such short order?" Aunt Fanny's hopes were more than clear.

"He brought the puppy for a visit, Aunt Fanny. He does not renew his addresses." Even as she said the words, Helena became aware of a slight disappointment in that.

Her aunt beamed. "Does he not?"

"Indeed, you will be pleased to know, Aunt, that he chastised me for being overly impulsive and reckless."

"Did he?" Aunt Fanny surveyed her then shook her head. "I suppose you cannot help such inclinations, child, not with your mother as she was."

Helena straightened for she was never told much about her mother. "I know so little of her," she began, but Aunt turned with purpose.

"I see no cause to give you more ideas than you already have," Aunt said grimly then smiled after the departing viscount. "Lord Addersley called, and already. What promise there is in that." With a delighted smile, Aunt spun and returned to the cottage, leaving Helena alone with the puppy again.

Did the viscount intend to court her yet? Helena was certain he did not, but her aunt's reaction revealed that not everyone would agree.

For her part, Helena was more interested in knowing when she might see her mysterious savior again.

~

THEY WERE to be amiable acquaintances.

Joshua was pleased with his progress, incremental as it might be.

Matters might yet be resolved well.

And the lady had erred in the past by trusting a suitor who was unworthy of her confidence. Joshua felt outrage stir that this Mr. Melbourne should have been less than honorable with Miss Emerson, tempting her to leave her family on a flight to Scotland, then failing to ensure her welfare once he learned the truth of her financial circumstance. The man was no more than a base fiend!

Yet Miss Emerson had no regrets, for now she knew.

Joshua had to think about this. It was such an unexpected view. He would have thought she might be disappointed in the true nature of the man she had hoped to wed. He might have expected her to protest against her lover having to concern himself with financial realities instead of the inclination of his heart, thus giving more credit to the man than might be due. He might have expected her to be contrite that she had erred thus.

But Miss Emerson was none of those.

And Joshua could not condemn her, not after her question about his own experiences. He did not regret that year in London. He and Gerald had enjoyed a marvelous time. He had lived more boldly and extravagantly than at any other time in his life. He had taken risks. He had gambled—and often won. He had no desire to return to that life, but he was glad he had experienced it.

How curious to share Miss Emerson's uncommon view.

He did believe she had need of a protector. The world could be unkind to daring females. But if she had a defender at her side, they two might venture far beyond the experiences of most people. They might savor an audacious life together, each pulling the other back from excess.

He could nigh hear his father turning in his grave in disapproval of such a notion, but what harm was there in giving Miss Emerson a measure of the excitement she craved? What if she encountered a highwayman whose moral code could be trusted?

The potential rewards were not small from his side of the matter. Partaking of highly satisfactory kisses and potentially winning her agreement to his suit were not advantages to be overlooked. He would like nothing better than to safely provide the adventure she sought.

Donning a cloak and riding out in disguise might see his future secured.

But then a prolonged deception could not lead to a good result. Joshua knew it would be dishonest to trick her. When his ruse was inevitably revealed, she might despise him.

Instead, he would be a riddle that she might solve. By day, he would call upon her, and show himself as an attentive companion, one whose honor was beyond question, one whose conversation and company were satisfactory. In the evenings, he would appear to her, perhaps take her for a ride, almost certainly accept a kiss. But his intentions were honorable and he would ensure that scandal never touched her name. He would guarantee the propriety of their secret meetings.

And once her ankle healed, when she came to the forest to meet the cloaked stranger as arranged, Joshua would reveal himself. The ruse would be dismissed, as was right and good, and the lady would see his true merit. There would be honesty between them.

Joshua simply had to be triumphant in winning her approval before that encounter.

He had brought the puppy.

He would replace her slippers.

In fact, he looked forward to being a little wicked, just for Miss Emerson.

The plan was perfection itself.

WHEN NICHOLAS ARRIVED at Bramble Cottage that afternoon, Helena saw her opportunity. He had given a ride to Mr. and Mrs. Nixon from Haynesdale village at the dowager's request, and the men unloaded their two trunks quickly. Mr. Nixon carried the trunks to the chamber by the kitchen that the couple were to have as their own, while Aunt Fanny showed Mrs. Nixon the kitchen and house. Helena was quick to help Nicholas with the provisions brought to them from Southpoint, and he granted her a smile when they were alone in the kitchen.

"You, helping me," he said, his eyes sparkling as he teased her. "Whatever is it that you want, Helena?"

"Simply to be of assistance," she said and he laughed out loud.

"More than that, to be sure. How much will this assistance cost me?"

She swatted his arm, for he always guessed her intentions. "No more than a tale."

"One of the Duke of Haynesdale, I wager. You aim high in that, Helena."

Helena was startled to realize that she had almost forgotten about the duke. "No, I do not." She frowned. "Will you tell me about Mother?"

Nicholas sobered and leaned against the table, folding his arms across his chest. His manner turned wary, which hinted there was some detail Helena might not wish to know.

That only, of course, increased her desire to learn it.

"What about her?" he asked softly.

"What was she like? What did she look like? How did she meet Father? How did she die?"

He frowned at the floor for a moment, Aunt Fanny's tones carrying to their ears. "She was very much like you, Helena," he said finally, his brows drawing together in recollection. "She was lovely, truly lovely, and she liked nothing better than to laugh and dance. I don't think Father could have found a more merry companion." He met her gaze. "She made him smile again, and for that, I would forgive her almost anything."

"Was there so much to forgive?"

Nicholas' brows rose. "She was heedless. If she wished to do a thing, she would do it, and no one could persuade her otherwise. She spent money like water and nigh beggared Father with her spending. She did not gamble, but she adored dresses and shoes, bonnets and gloves and other fripperies. I do not think I ever saw the same dress upon her twice." Helena winced for she dearly loved dresses and other fripperies herself. "Worse, she convinced Father to buy finer horses and new carriages, to rent more luxurious accommodations each time they went to London. She loved the parties and the dancing, and I would wager, the attentions of so many gentlemen."

"But surely she loved Father."

"I believe she did. I hope she did. He adored her." Nicholas straightened. "Her nature was why he died, after all."

"What do you mean?"

"He had a new curricle and a new pair of horses. Very young and sprightly, they were, not as well trained as I might have preferred. The tale is that she insisted that she would take the reins, and though she seldom did as much, he let her. It was late at night. They had been at a masquerade and I am certain that both of them had enjoyed the claret."

Helena felt her hand rise to her lips, as she guessed the result of this choice. She knew her parents had died in a carriage accident, but not like this. Not so recklessly as this.

Not so needlessly as this.

"They collided with a mail coach. There was some suggestion that she tried to race ahead of it through the intersection, rather than waiting for it to pass."

"It was bad?"

"Terrible," Nicholas said grimly. "At least they died immediately." He frowned. "The horses had to be destroyed as well."

"Goodness," Helena whispered, understanding why no one had told her this tale.

"I doubt Father would have regretted it, even if he could have done as much. She was his joy and his destruction, but he would never have taken away a single one of her smiles."

"Oh, Nicholas. I had no idea."

He surveyed her. "Who would tell you such a story, Helena, when you are her very echo?"

But Helena had turned away. It would be one thing to suffer herself as a result of one of her choices, but to cause injury to another—to a loved one—was an outcome she could not even bear to consider. Her throat was tight when Nicholas laid a hand on her shoulder.

"I think you are more clever than your mother was, Helena," he said quietly. "But there comes a time when a clever person relies upon good sense rather than good fortune."

"That sounds like something Viscount Addersley might say."

Her brother smiled. "Perhaps it does." He kissed her forehead. "Just think before you choose. I could do without another pursuit of you and some worthless fop with a scheme."

Helena smiled at him. "I don't think I ever thanked you properly for your timely arrival."

"Greater thanks to Mrs. D., and to your conviction that I would come."

"You always have taken care of me, Nicholas, even when I did not deserve it."

He winked at her. "And the best reward would be for you to choose a good husband to assume that responsibility."

And not ensure that man's early demise with her folly. Helena heard the unspoken words.

"Do you think I was wrong to decline Viscount Addersley?"

"I think a woman knows her own heart, and is the one to recognize her best match."

"But you like him."

"I find him somber, but he is reliable and re-spectable." Nicholas nodded at her. "I would have been surprised if you had accepted a man so different in nature from you, but the match might have proven to be a good one." He shrugged. "We shall never know." He changed the subject then, perhaps sensing that he had given Helena much to consider. "Could you take these pots of jam and put them on the shelf? Eliza favors this basket and will want it back."

She could die foolish.

She could die foolishly.

Or Helena could begin to use her wits.

It was not an overly difficult choice, when she considered it thus.

CHAPTER 7

It had been years since Joshua had visited Haynesdale Hollow and he was glad to see the recent improvements. The road had been widened and several cottages that he knew were occupied by Haynesdale's tenants had new roofs. The duke was serious about tending his responsibilities and Joshua would take a lesson from that. He was in the midst of reviewing all the obligations now beneath his hand. It was good to know that he could ask Haynesdale for advice in any such matters, upon that gentleman's return.

He thought again of the mysterious notes, frowning.

He was tethering his horse outside the inn when a young boy darted toward him, then halted, palm up. "A penny to spare, my lord?" the boy asked.

When Joshua glanced toward the boy, he could not keep himself from staring. A ghost might have been conjured before him. The boy's hair was dark and his eyes were clear green. He was slender and lanky, his clothing worn but clean, a wariness in his gaze. He might have been nine or ten years of age. None of that was particularly worthy of note—it was the boy's striking resemblance to Gerald many years before that silenced Joshua.

"Have ye, sir?" the boy asked, pushing his hand closer and Joshua realized he had been gaping. He reached into his pocket and found a halfpenny, then cast it toward the boy. "Thank you, sir!" the boy said with delight, his smile making Joshua blink with surprise.

He could *be* Gerald, standing before him.

"Don't be bothering the gentleman, Francis," a woman chided.

The boy flushed then showed off his prize. "He gave me a half-penny, mum."

"How kindly that was of him," she said and curtsied before Joshua, keeping her eyes downcast. "I thank you, sir, for your generosity to my son." She was blond, her hair so curly that it had worked free of her braids in wisps that surrounded her face. There were freckles scattered across her nose and cheeks, and he imagined she had once been a pretty maid. She was still pretty, but now she looked to be tired and a little strained. That was no surprise given the size of the basket of laundry she carried.

He imagined that once she might have been as pretty as Charlotte. Certainly, her coloring was the same.

To his relief, the boy assumed the burden of the woman's basket and she smiled at him fondly, then looked fully at Joshua.

It was her turn to stare in surprise. "Sir!" she whispered, her eyes lighting with a joy Joshua could not explain. "You are back!"

Joshua was indeed back, but he could not fathom how she recognized him. He retreated a step, even as he studied her anew. No, he did not know her. "Have we met, madame?"

The innkeeper emerged in that moment, wiping his hands upon his apron as he looked between the two of them. Darney was stout and balding, a man with a merry laugh who had no tolerance for any trouble in his inn.

"Met?" The woman gave a surprisingly bitter laugh, as if angered by Joshua's response. "I should say as much, sir, after all those nights. *Met!*" Her gaze was decidedly less friendly than it had been and her son looked between them with curiosity.

The innkeeper cleared his throat. "I believe you are mistaken, Mrs. Lewis."

Joshua frowned. "Indeed, madame."

"But…" she began with heat, as if to argue the point.

"This," said the innkeeper grandly. "Is Lord Addersley, seventh viscount of Addersley."

"Oh!" the woman said and crimson flooded her cheeks. She dropped her gaze again and retreated, flushing furiously, as she stammered apologies. When she and her son had backed a dozen steps away, they turned as one and hastened away, only the boy sparing a glance over his shoulder at Joshua.

It seemed likely to Joshua that he had been mistaken for his brother, and given the boy's resemblance to Gerald, he could guess how this Mrs. Lewis had known him. Their liaison must have occurred before his father bought Gerald's commission, given the age of the boy.

"I do apologize, my lord, for this incident," Darney said, urging Joshua toward the common room. "I wish I had noticed your arrival sooner and I might have prevented it. How may we be of service on this day?"

"I would ask you to see my horse tended."

"As you wish, my lord. It is always our pleasure to serve you." The innkeeper bowed, as fulsome as ever, but Joshua looked after the woman, who had now vanished from view. "Again, I apologize, sir."

"You cannot take responsibility for the entire village, Mr. Darney," Joshua said. "What do you know of this lady?"

The innkeeper frowned. "Mrs. Lewis is kinder than others in her family. The boy can work hard. You need not trouble yourself about either of them, sir."

Joshua understood that the subject was closed. "I thank you. Would you direct me to Mrs. Jameson's establishment?"

Darney's eyes lit, as no doubt he speculated upon Joshua's need to find a ladies' dressmaker. He pointed Joshua in the opposite direction from Mrs. Lewis' departure. Joshua patted Specter's rump and took his leave of the innkeeper.

He was considering the implications of his suspicions. He would have to check with Mr. Newson as to whether the child was known and if any arrangements had been made for him. Joshua had no doubt that his father would not have confided such a tale in him, or that his father would have insisted upon such a gesture if he had known of the boy's existence.

The question was whether Gerald had confessed his deed to their father.

Or indeed whether he had even known of the boy's conception. Could the boy's resemblance to Gerald be coincidence? Joshua thought not.

Mother and son had been cleanly garbed but not richly so, which made Joshua conclude there might be no arrangement.

That was just wrong.

He was before Mrs. Jameson's shop before he wondered how many other such children there might be, sired by Gerald and as yet unacknowledged.

He and Mr. Newson might have to contrive a plan.

To Helena's dismay, Aunt Fanny insisted upon waiting with her in the garden for the viscount's return. Helena did not doubt that her aunt meant to interfere and she was embarrassed at even the prospect.

Mrs. Nixon, busily arranging her domain, looked up with interest at the pair of them as she brought out a pail of water to be emptied. She was older even than Becky, a woman so slender as to be sinewy, but serious of manner and sufficiently diligent to please even Aunt Fanny. Within hours of her arrival, she had sorted the rest of the house, and had embarked upon a mission to scrub the kitchen spotless.

Her husband was her veritable opposite, a plump man somewhat shorter than his wife, inclined to silence as his wife was garrulous. Truly, Mrs. Nixon never seemed to fall silent, and Helena already recognized that her aunt would be relying upon the new housekeeper for tidings of all and sundry. The husband moved more slowly than his wife but with no less persistence: he had already trimmed the shrubbery at the front of the house and tamed it into respectable order.

"Begging your pardon, but has the lady declined a suitor?" the housekeeper asked now, eyes bright, and Helena braced herself for another chiding.

Aunt Fanny turned importantly to her new servant. "No less than the viscount himself."

"Lord Addersley?' Nixon's eyes rounded as Aunt Fanny nodded. "Well, I never." Helena was prepared for the worst, but Nixon nodded wisely.

"For the foolish reason that he does not dance," Aunt Fanny added, her tone acid.

"Well, there is folly in such a reason, to be sure, but there is sense in it as well," Nixon ceded, dumping out her water. She filled with clean water. "There are *stories*, after all, mum." Her tone was ominous, as sure an invitation to Aunt's curiosity as to Helena's own.

"Stories?" Helena echoed. She could not imagine that there were any dark tales about the viscount, save perhaps that once he had remained awake until as late as ten in the evening, reviewing his accounts. Doubtless that could only occur when he was chasing down an errant shilling, or waiting for the hot brick for his bed to be sufficiently warm.

"I remember when he lost his betrothed," Nixon said, securely capturing Helena's attention.

"He had a betrothed?" Aunt asked.

Helena strove to hide her interest. She would like little more than to learn the full tale of the viscount's lost beloved.

"Oh, aye, yes, some ten years ago, it was. They say he was broken-hearted over her death. Did he not abandon his wild ways immediately and become a sober son to his father once more?" Nixon shook her head sadly. "It is better, in my view, to refuse a suit from a man whose heart has been claimed by another than to be his second choice of wife."

"I should not like a man to compromise by wedding me," Helena said with heat.

"And there is wisdom in that," Mrs. Nixon said. "They say he has never smiled since that sorry night of her death."

"I have seen him smile," Helena offered, only to earn a skeptical glance from the other woman.

"Have you now, miss? Perhaps his lordship recovers from the loss by increments. I wager he has yet to laugh again, though he was never inclined to merriment by my understanding."

Helena dropped her gaze, thinking of that dimple.

"But what happened to his betrothed?" Aunt Fanny asked. "I would not indulge in gossip about one's neighbors, but it would be better that we have some inkling of past events, the better to not inadvertently cause offense to his lordship."

Mrs. Nixon nodded wisely in agreement with that. "I have no taste for rumor-mongering myself, mum, but this is the truth as told to me by the daughter of the former housekeeper of Addersley Manor, who had it from the butler of Addersley House in London herself."

Helena was intrigued beyond all.

"I should so appreciate your confidence," Aunt Fanny said.

"The marriage was arranged by the old viscount, it was said, and Miss Havilland was considered the perfect candidate by all. She was a lovely young lady, so merry and a delight to all she met. A beauty, too, with her golden curls. So light on her feet she was that she did not seem to be of this earth but an angel set down amongst us." Mrs. Nixon shook her head. "Truly, I have never seen a young lady so pretty, and her father an earl besides."

Helena felt a dark pang of something rather like envy, but strove to dismiss it as unsuitable. Miss Havilland, after all, was dead.

"But she must have died so young," Aunt Fanny said and Helena was glad for once to be in her aunt's company. She could simply listen without seeming inquisitive.

"Not even eighteen years of age, mum."

"Was she not of a robust constitution?"

"Oh, she was, mum, as healthy as ever a lady might be."

Aunt Fanny and Helena exchanged glances of confusion. Before either could ask, Mrs. Nixon leaned closer, clearly bursting to confess the truth.

"She was *shot*, mum."

"Shot?!" Helena and Aunt Fanny echoed as one.

"But how could that be?" Aunt Fanny demanded.

"By whom?" Helena asked at the same time.

Mrs. Nixon shook her head. "There was a duel between his lordship and another man, a challenge issued over honor or some such. The young lady feared for her betrothed and she crept out of her father's house to follow them. 'Tis said she flung herself at his lordship as the shots were fired, wanting only to ensure his safety, but was killed herself instead."

"Goodness!" Helena whispered, thinking this tale might have come from a book.

It could also explain the viscount leaving the life of a rakehell behind, his heart broken by the loss of his beloved—when she had been trying to save him.

And she had been witless enough to remind him of it!

This, she realized, would also explain the viscount's admonition about impulsive choices. If his betrothed had been prudent, that lady might yet be alive.

And he would be happily wed.

She began to understand why he might not be inclined to frivolity.

"A sad, sad day, to be sure," Mrs. Nixon intoned, showing a grisly satisfaction in the tale. "Her father rent his hair, they said, for though he had four sons, she was his only daughter and his delight. The old viscount took it hard, for he was fond of the girl, too, but his lordship, well, he has not looked at a lady since." She dropped her voice to a whisper. "They say he labored in secret alongside the old viscount on business for the war, but I cannot say as that is true. Certainly, though they were in London, neither he nor his father have been seen much in society these past ten years, by all accounts."

Business for the war? What manner of business? Helena wanted very much to know. For an impossibly dull man, Lord Addersley was suddenly proving to be worthy of fascination.

Perhaps he was just a man with *secrets*.

"What a tale!" Aunt Fanny whispered. "So tragic."

"'Tis indeed, mum, but I had best return to my labor."

"Thank you, Nixon." Aunt Fanny's hand fluttered at her chest. "What an ordeal the poor man has survived, but Mrs. Nixon is right." She patted Helena's hand. "You would not be happy as any man's second choice, my dear. It is best you did decline him."

Helena, though, felt her heart softening toward the viscount. If he had lost his beloved, it made sense that he did not wish to love again.

Truly, it showed an admirable conviction to have abandoned society and foregone matrimony for an entire decade out of respect for the lady he had lost. Of course, he would not wish to dance without her. Of course, he would become a recluse of sorts, given such disappointment.

Was his heart lost forever? Had she escaped a match that would have been dutiful at best? Helena could not regret that, but she was no longer as convinced that marrying the viscount would have been an error.

She heard hoofbeats and knew Lord Addersley returned to collect the dog, but Aunt Fanny was no longer interested in the viscount and his doings.

"Mr. Nixon!" Aunt said, standing up with indignation. "I beg you not to cut those rhododendrons before they bloom!"

"But they obscure the view, mum."

"And they can remain thus until they have flowered." Aunt Fanny hastened away to see that her will was done, even as the viscount rode into view.

He seemed to be distracted by some concern, for he did not look immediately at Helena. He dismounted and strode toward her with such purpose that he might have been impatient. He tipped his hat and inclined his head, speaking crisply. "Miss Emerson."

Mischief gave a little yip of glee and raced toward him, falling over her feet in her haste. His smile flashed as he crouched down to pat the dog and Helena wished he had smiled for her.

Then he looked up, gaze simmering, and did smile for her. The expression seemed forced, as if something troubled him, and she marveled that she could discern more of her thoughts than he must wish her to see. "You are uncommonly quiet, Miss Emerson. Has Mischief committed some deed to lose your favor?"

~

SHE HAD LEARNED something of him in his absence.

Joshua could fairly smell the change in Miss Emerson. Someone had told her something that made her look upon him with greater favor.

Though that was welcome, he wished he knew what it was.

And yet, he did not have time to linger and ease the tale from her.

The situation of Mrs. Lewis meant that Joshua intended to speak with Mr. Newson before that man left his offices in Addersley village. He was caught between his objectives, between his responsibilities as viscount and his desire for this particular lady's favor.

Miss Emerson cleared her throat as if hesitant to speak, which in itself was curious. She was also markedly somber, a situation he already knew to be rare. "Mischief has been a delight."

"Good."

"Though I have learned a most troubling tale, one

that prompts me to give consideration to your own advice."

"Indeed?"

She impaled him with a glance, her eyes so blue that he was certain he might drown within them. "I did not realize that my mother and I were so similar. She died when I was two, in an accident with my father." She took a breath, as if for fortitude. "It was her error, sir, that caused their untimely demises. Had she not been so reckless in her choice, in her wish to drive the curricle even though she knew little of such a task, I might yet be in possession of my parents."

"I see," Joshua said softly, watching as her tears rose.

Her throat worked. "I had not considered the price of curiosity before our conversation, sir, and I must thank you for your warning." She lifted her chin, looking both fragile and resolute. "I mean to improve my choices in future."

"Surely you cannot mean to forgo experiences?"

"No, but I shall endeavor to be more prudent in my choices." She smiled at him. "Perhaps you are right that I should find a protector."

Joshua inclined his head. "I am delighted to have made a useful suggestion, Miss Emerson."

She glanced down at the dog, uncharacteristically hesitant to speak. "Are you quite certain, my lord, that there are no highwaymen in the vicinity?"

Joshua frowned at the unexpected query. "Quite sure."

"But I thought I saw one last night, a man riding a dark horse and wearing a dark cloak." She eyed him, as if she knew. "He was quite dashing and rode in the direction of the forest."

Ah! Had she guessed the truth?

Did she wish for him to reveal himself?

Joshua could not guess, which intrigued him all the

more. Few people surprised him, but Miss Emerson already made a habit of it. He spoke firmly. "A highwayman, Miss Emerson, could hardly be considered a suitable admirer for a lady."

"You are right, of course, sir, but can you not see the allure of a mysterious stranger?"

"I see little appeal in danger, to be sure."

"Mystery and passion are the very essence of romance, Lord Addersley."

"Mystery, danger *and* romance." He kept his tone light but shook his head, all the more convinced that she had need of a protector. "Truly, Miss Emerson, you demand a great deal of any man bold enough to court your favor."

"Not so much as that. It is all well and good for a man to be responsible and serious, but it is encouraging to see some hint of his ardor. In fact, I think it would be most compelling for a man of great control to show that he is overwhelmed, just for a moment." She lifted her gaze to his, her manner expectant.

What a beguiling creature she was. "In rage?"

"No, not in anger. In—" she took a breath, evidently rapturous, then exhaled, eyes shining. "In—desire." This last word rode on a whisper and might have been the most enticing sound Joshua had ever heard. Miss Emerson smiled a little at him, her eyes shining, and he was uncertain he could summon a coherent word to his lips at all.

He cleared his throat, knowing he sounded stern. "You would not be pleased if such a man seized a kiss— or more—against your will."

"No, I would not," she agreed readily. "But when a man is always composed, it is difficult to believe that his heart beats at all."

"If his heart failed to beat, he would lie dead at your feet."

Miss Emerson laughed. "Do you read poetry, my lord?"

"No. I did when compelled to do as much as a boy, but I find little relevance in it now."

The lady did not appear to be surprised. "Because poetry is often about yearning and love, even about being overwhelmed by desire. I have always wondered what it would be like to have someone write poetry to me."

Joshua would never manage that feat. "How might a man otherwise show such an aspiration, in a respectful manner?"

He watched Miss Emerson consider this, and again had the sense that she revealed only a fraction of her thoughts on the matter. "His gaze might linger," she said finally, lifting her chin to meet his gaze. "His eyes might *darken*."

"Indeed?" Joshua smiled, knowing his skepticism was so clear that he had no need to declare it.

She bristled. "Your eyes become darker at intervals, sir."

"They do?"

"They do," she said with conviction. "I believe it is when you feel strongly about the topic at hand." Once again, she bestowed a smile upon him. "It is a most thrilling sight."

Thrilling. There was some detail about him, albeit one he could not control, that Miss Emerson found thrilling.

Even when he was not disguised himself as a rogue.

This was a most satisfactory revelation.

Their gazes locked for what might have been an eternity. "Indeed," Joshua said finally, the word no more than a murmur. Miss Emerson caught her breath and flushed in a most delightful manner, and he averted his gaze as everything tightened within him.

He was feeling rather reckless himself, though it was utterly unsuitable for him to act upon such urges.

"He might be impulsive in his choices or generous in his gifts," Miss Emerson continued, her ability to discern his thoughts not as troubling as it should have been.

Joshua could conclude that their minds were as one.

But she had refused him.

"I see," he murmured. He did not dare to look at her but kept his gaze fixed on Mischief. The pup lolled at his feet, rolling to her back as he rubbed her belly. When the silence stretched too long between them, he felt compelled to say *something*.

"I thank you for the clarification, Miss Emerson," he said. "I believe Mrs. Jameson may call on the morrow."

"Thank you!" She waited, as if expecting his own guarantee of a visit, but Joshua was uncertain when Mr. Newson would be available to confer with him this afternoon. He would rather surprise Miss Emerson with an unexpected appearance, than make a promise he might have to break.

Miss Emerson rose to her feet, balancing her weight on her uninjured foot as she curtsied gracefully. "Thank you again for bringing Mischief, and for the slippers, sir."

Joshua nodded and touched his hat, utterly at a loss for words. He scooped up the dog and returned to his horse. He had never imagined that one's eyes might darken, much less that such an incident would provoke such enthusiasm in a lady.

He wondered how he might contrive to make it occur with some predictability.

He knew, as he turned the horse, that he would ride out this night in the direction of Bramble Cottage and that prospect filled him with anticipation.

~

THE NIGHT WAS CLEAR, the slimmest crescent of a silver moon high overhead. Helena sat at her window, and stared into the shadows of the night. She was thinking about Lord Addersley, recalling the gentle strength of his hands as he patted Mischief and of his kindness in bringing the puppy to visit her. It seemed there was more to him than people like Becky insisted. Helena would have wagered a pair of slippers—perhaps the ones he insisted upon buying for her—that his veins did not run with ice water.

She shivered a little at the notion of passion simmering beneath his composure and wished she might know for sure.

And what of her champion? She closed her eyes in recollection of his sultry kiss, all the more exciting because it was a forbidden and stolen pleasure.

Aunt had scolded her for her distraction at dinner, and sent her early to bed to ensure that her ankle healed more quickly. Helena had no interest in any of her books, not with the remembered caress of her champion to feed her imagination.

Did she know him without his disguise? She could not say for certain. Though they were of a size, his manner and that of the viscount were so different. He possessed an audacity and a verve that Lord Addersley in his polite restraint did not possess. He had to be another man, someone she had not yet met—officially.

Did she dare to hope he might seek her out again?

Might she manage to see his face if he did?

Or should she take Nicholas' warning to heart and turn aside her champion?

No, she could not do that. She could be more prudent though. She could speak to him at the gate. She could refuse to ride out with him, at least until he revealed himself.

She supposed she would not have been who she was if the sensible choices had not sounded so very dull.

The hour grew late and Bramble Cottage fell quiet. Helena must have dozed for she was suddenly awakened by the sound of hoofbeats. She straightened in curiosity with predictable speed, lighting the lantern and opening the window wide. She could not see the road from her window, nor even the forest where the folly was located.

The hoofbeats grew louder. She fully expected the horse and rider to pass on by, continuing toward Southpoint, but the sound of the horse faded from earshot too soon. Had the rider left the road? Helena scarce dared to hope. Her lips parted in surprise when she saw the silhouette of a large horse walking across the fields behind Bramble Cottage. A man strode before the horse, leading it with confidence away from the road.

Horse and rider were no more than a shadow against the darkness, but Helena's heart rose to her throat in recognition of the rider's long cloak.

He came to her again!

Any doubt was banished when he halted and glanced. He seemed to look directly at her window and even as her heart stopped, he raised a hand.

He beckoned.

Helena realized that she must be silhouetted in the window against the light of the lamp.

Her champion had come for her!

She spun from the window seat and seized an old pair of slippers. Her boots would not go over the wrapping on her ankle, she was certain. She had not yet undressed for the night, so seized her spencer and looked out the window again. He was moving closer, leading the horse toward the hedge that surrounded the cottage.

There was no time to find her bonnet or rebraid her hair. She had no notion how long he would linger—or what he would do if Nixon raised a hue and cry.

But Helena could not miss the opportunity to see him again.

She crept down the stairs, her heart in her throat. Her ankle had recovered enough that she could hobble along, though not with any speed. She already knew which stairs were inclined to creak and managed to either avoid them or tread on the other end.

Nixon was holding forth in the kitchens, telling her husband about the benefits and flaws of the household and comparing Aunt to former employers. Her spouse was whistling to himself somewhere in the kitchen, clearly disinterested in his wife's diatribe. Helena paused at the bottom of the stairs and dared to peek around the corner. She was certain the pounding of her pulse would be overheard.

Mr. Nixon was sitting by the fire, and looked to be whittling something. His concentration appeared to be complete. His wife was out of view, though she could clearly be heard.

Helena took a breath and slipped across the small gap between the base of the stairs, certain she would be caught.

When she was not, she opened the door the barest increment and slipped into the night. Only when the door was secured behind her did she dare to breathe.

Then she smiled.

There was only the silhouette of her champion and the nicker of his horse at the opening of the hedge.

"You came!" she whispered and flung herself toward

him. His hood was drawn up again, but he stepped forward to meet her before she had taken two steps. He caught her close and lifted her from the ground. He moved his head so that he had to be looking at her injured ankle.

In the darkness.

Helena smiled up at him, loving the firm grip of his hands upon her waist. She followed his gaze downward and sought to reassure him. "It improves steadily, but I am impatient with my progress all the same. I was certain I could not endure the wait until we meet again in the forest."

He seemed to glare sternly down at her.

"Oh, I will do as I am bidden," she assured him.

He chuckled then, a dark and seductive sound, and shook his head as if doubtful.

"You are right. I am not inclined to be sensible, but I strive to make a change."

His attention seemed to sharpen.

She sighed. "I mean to be more cautious in future, lest I lead others astray with my recklessness. I could not bear to cause injury to another in my quest to savor all."

He lifted her closer and kissed her then, an approval of her words that did not last nearly long enough to satisfy. It did, however leave Helena breathless—and striving to see his features in the shadows of his hood. "I am so glad you came," she confessed in a whisper. "I feared I would not see you again soon."

He lifted her toward the saddle with purpose.

"A ride?" she asked and he nodded. "I should love a ride in the moonlight more than anything else," she confessed, not hiding her enthusiasm. "But I should be prudent and decline your invitation, I know I should. I am sorry."

He shook his head and placed her in the saddle,

guiding her hands to the pommel. His own hands were gloved, but when she hoped he might swing up behind her, he stepped back. He placed one hand over his heart, then bowed to her, blowing her a kiss when he straightened.

"You give me your promise that all will be well?" she guessed, her heart warming.

He nodded with an authority she could not doubt, then waited, one hand up, for her decision.

Helena took a fortifying breath, wishing she could see his eyes, wishing she knew his identity. She looked up at the moon and the stars, certain she had never shared so wondrous a moment with anyone, and did not wish for it to end.

She might discover who he was.

She fixed him with a look. "I will go, but only for a short ride, and only because you have promised to defend my welfare."

He bowed again, then turned to lead the horse away from the cottage.

Although she was disappointed that he did not ride with her, Helena appreciated his choice. She felt safe in his company, even without knowing his name, her mysterious stranger who kissed so ardently but did not speak.

Did she think he would recognize her voice?

Did she know him?

She studied him, struck again by the similarity of his dimensions and posture to the viscount. But he could not be Viscount Addersley, could he?

He led the horse away from Bramble Cottage, away from the road, away from all the locations Helena already knew. There were only fields and hills in this direction, at least as far as she could see from her window, and she wondered at his destination.

Helena didn't care. She trusted him completely. She

smiled to herself, thinking that she was leaving the path to wander forbidden territory in the company of an alluring stranger—and doing as much willingly.

Helena would not turn back for any price. Her heart told her to believe in her champion and she did.

CHAPTER 8

$\mathcal{M}$iss Emerson was radiant.

If she had known that she had completely conquered Joshua's heart, he wagered she would have been more glorious yet.

She was like Gerald in that she preferred to be triumphant, but there was a joy in her response that was utterly unlike Gerald. Perhaps she would be content with her situation, if she had the one she desired most. Gerald, in contrast, had been insatiable in his desires.

Perhaps he had done the lady a disservice in assuming she must be the same.

When she smiled at him as she did on this night, her eyes shining with pleasure and her cheeks flushed, he thought her the most glorious lady in all the world. If his invitation was responsible for her satisfaction, he could not see how he would resist offering another and another.

It was a night made for wooing, still and cool but not cold. Thousands of stars glittered overhead and the silvery crescent of the moon rode high. As he led Zephyr away from Bramble Cottage and into the hills, the sounds of the forest became more noticeable to Joshua. He could not longer detect the scent of the fire from the chimney at Lady Dalhousie's abode, and the distant road was devoid of traffic. The sound of the horse's footfalls were muted by the grasses underfoot. The forest and its shadows pressed closer on either side, the rustlings of wild creatures more readily detected. He spotted a fox trotting about its business with purpose and pointed it out to Miss Emerson.

She caught her breath and Joshua was certain the fox heard her. It glanced their way then redoubled its pace, vanishing into the shadows of a copse of trees. The silhouette of an owl passed overhead, gliding silently through the night as it hunted, and when the stallion shook his head, the jingle of his trap seemed overly loud.

"We might be the sole occupants of the world," Miss Emerson whispered with an awe Joshua shared. He could have walked all night, content in the knowledge that the venture made her happy. He liked that she had shown some caution and strove to change her impulsiveness. He would see her safe, no matter what.

"What is that?" she demanded suddenly and he glanced over his shoulder to find her pointing to a small rise ahead.

It was the ruin of the original Haynesdale keep, and all that was left of the old motte-and-bailey medieval structure. Thinking it made as good a destination as any, he led the horse toward it with purpose.

"A ruin!" she whispered with delight. "Are they standing stones placed by the ancients?"

Joshua smiled as he shook his head.

"An abbey, then, or a church, left in shambles after the dissolution of the monasteries," she guessed and he was impressed that she had been granted so much of an education. He knew that some families did not see their daughters tutored in more than the domestic arts.

"You are surprised," she said proudly. "I had a tutor

when I was younger, though I did not excel at my studies. I did learn a little French, but I liked history very much. Can you imagine what it was like to live at the Tudor court? I should love to visit Hampton Palace one day above all things. Aunt promised to take me to the Tower to see the crown jewels but she never did." She sighed. "I doubt I shall ever see them now, much less Anne Boleyn's grave."

If ever he had the opportunity, Joshua would ensure she had that excursion.

He was glad of the silence necessitated by his ruse, or he might have promised her more than was appropriate.

He had no sooner thought as much than he caught a whiff of woodsmoke. He stopped and Zephyr halted behind him, taking the opportunity to nibble at the shoulder of his cloak. Joshua remained utterly still and listened.

Yes. There was movement within the ruins and he could just barely discern a ribbon of smoke rising from it. Someone had taken refuge there. He recalled that there was still a structure of a sort, though the roof was only partial, it would provide some shelter from the elements. The keep had been built on a mound and would originally have had a wooden palisade around the central tower. The wood was gone, of course, but the deep ditch dug outside those walls was still a furrow in the ground. It was impossible to see much at this hour and this distance, but the hair prickled on the back of his neck in warning.

He knew there were numerous soldiers returned from the war, decommissioned and unable to find paid positions. He had hired as many as possible at Addersley Manor, but there was a limit to his own resources. The less fortunate of such men turned to banditry and lived rough.

This was no place for Miss Emerson.

He pivoted smartly and led the horse back in the direction they had come.

"I thought we would explore the ruins," Miss Emerson protested just as Joshua heard a sound from that very location. He swung into the saddle behind her with purpose, thinking only of her safety, catching her around the waist as he gave Zephyr his heels. The stallion was more than happy to break into a canter and then a gallop, tossing his head as he raced back toward Bramble Cottage.

"Oh!" Miss Emerson had been seated side-saddle, but she turned toward him now, as she had that previous time. Her hand landed upon his waistcoat, the feel of her exploring caress sufficiently to make Joshua's heart leap. When she leaned her cheek against him, her trust complete, he once again felt that dizzying tide of desire. He could smell her scent, that of her skin mingled with a touch of lavender, a feminine combination that prompted him to spread his hand across her back and draw her closer.

Another lady might have been shocked or dismayed, but Miss Emerson laughed lightly. She wound an arm around his waist, pressing herself against Joshua in a way that made him forget everything but the lady who was virtually in his arms. "Oh, sir, I fail utterly in denying temptation," she whispered, but Joshua did not care.

He could be wicked for her, and she might be as impulsive as she liked in his company.

Bramble Cottage appeared all too soon and Zephyr apparently knew their destination. He halted of his own volition in the shadow of the surrounding hedges, exhaled mightily and shook his head, then reached to nibble at the budding flowers.

Joshua did not chastise the creature in this moment.

There was only Miss Emerson and his relief that she was safely home again. He touched her chin with a fingertip, lifting her face, and bent to capture her lips beneath his own.

The lady, perhaps predictably, responded with an enthusiasm that could not be denied.

~

HE HAD TAKEN her to his refuge.

Helena readily guessed the truth, and loved that his impulse had been to share his secret with her. It made perfect sense that he had changed his mind in the last moment, but she had divined the truth.

She had to learn more about the ruins, whatever they were.

For the moment, though, there was only his wondrous kiss. This time, his caress was more confident and demanding, as if he was encouraged by her response. Helena had no inclination to be reserved. She had never felt such pleasure or such surety of a man's honor. This time, he cupped her nape in one broad palm, the leather of his glove smooth against her skin. This time, his kiss was deeper, as if he would sear her very soul with his touch.

Or make it impossible for her to even notice another man, now that they had met.

Helena leaned against him, surrendering fully, trying to show his victory with her response. He made a little growl that she found satisfying beyond all, then tore his lips from hers. She felt him looking down at her and wished she could pierce the shadows of his hood. She reached for the edge of the fabric, but he moved away, leaping from the saddle.

"Helena!" Aunt called from the house and Helena winced. "Where are you, girl?" She looked up at her own window and spotted her aunt in that chamber, where she had left the lamp burning, and grimaced.

Her champion locked his hands around her waist and lifted her down, retreating a step to kiss her hand. Such a salute would not suffice, not now.

Helena flung herself against him, moving with speed that he could not be noble and turn her aside. She reached up and slipped her fingers into his hair, pulling his head down that she might kiss him again. Again, he made a low sound of capitulation, as if he could not resist the temptation she offered, then his arms were around her and his mouth closed over hers once more.

Helena closed her eyes, wishing Aunt a thousand miles away, as her lover lifted her from the ground to hold her captive against his chest. She wanted his kiss to last forever. She wanted him to lift her back into the saddle and ride away with her. She wanted to learn more of all that could pass between man and wife, and she wanted to do it with him. Impulse, she was certain, could not steer her false when her heart clamored to be with this man.

But he set her on her feet again, a small sound revealing his reluctance to do as much, then escorted her to the opening in the hedge as if she was a queen. He bowed low, just as Aunt shouted again, and kissed her hand.

Then he lifted his head, as if he would study her, though she could not see his face. He turned her hand over and she felt the warmth of his lips against her palm as he planted a kiss there. He closed her fingers over the imprint, as if he would advise her to hold fast to that invisible token, and Helena knew she could love this man with all her heart and soul.

Lord Addersley said she had need of a protector, but Helena was certain she had found one.

He kissed his own fingertips and might have backed away, but Helena closed the distance between them hastily. She needed to know. He caught her one hand in his when she reached for him. Her one hand was held captive against that fine waistcoat, but she reached boldly into the shadows of the hood with the other.

He inhaled sharply and retreated, but she had felt the cleft in his chin.

It could not be. She knew only one man with a cleft in his chin, one of a height and breadth with this one, one who rode with assurance but otherwise did not share this man's élan.

How could her champion be Lord Addersley?

His manner was so different. His very nature had to be different. Lord Addersley could not have an increment of romance within him. Doubtless he had fallen asleep with the company of a serious book by this hour.

"Helena!" Aunt shouted again, the sound stirring her companion to action. He pointed to the opening and Helena slipped through it reluctantly, yearning to accompany him instead—wherever he might ride. The horse did not move, and she knew he waited for her to be safely within the house. She crossed the yard, then lingered in the shadows of the kitchen doorway. She heard the horse stamp as he mounted, then he rode past the opening, revealing himself one last time.

He raised a hand in farewell and Helena blew him a kiss. He feigned catching it and crushing it against his heart, a whimsical gesture that proved once and for all that he could not be Lord Addersley.

Only when she opened the door did he turn the horse. Helena would not have been the girl she was if she had not remained in the doorway, listening to the sound of his horse's retreat.

She sighed at the romance of it all, then Aunt Fanny appeared in her dressing gown, her expression furious.

"Where have you been, child? Why would you be in the yard at this hour of the night?" Aunt peered at her closely. "There is a glimmer in your eye that hints at mischief."

"I cannot imagine how that might be, Aunt. I simply went out to look at the stars." Helena slipped past her aunt, knowing she was incapable of disguising her satisfaction. Her aunt made a sound of disbelief and followed her up the stairs, as if to be certain that Helena retired to her chamber.

She stood at the window, looking into the night. How could she reconcile her need to be with her mysterious stranger and her awareness that she had to be more prudent in her choices? Her heart told her to trust him, but she had trusted Mr. Melbourne, too. Helena sat down on her bed and frowned at the floor.

There was only one possible solution. She must do all in her power to unveil the identity of her mysterious stranger, and that before their rendezvous at the folly.

~

LATE THAT NIGHT, Joshua dreamed.

He stirred restlessly, but his eyes did not open. The nightmare that had become so infrequent as to be forgotten was upon him again. Try as he might, he could not compel himself to awaken—even though he knew the horror he would relive.

He was on the field at Wimbledon again, the weight of the revolver in his hand. The moon was but a sliver of light above, clouds flitting across it so that even its meagre light vanished at intervals. Gerald was fairly vibrating in anticipation, but Joshua felt the usual cold stillness within him.

There was a task before him, one at which he would

succeed. There was no room for emotion, much less excitement, when brandishing a weapon.

They had argued all evening about Joshua's intentions. Gerald was certain that his opponent should be killed outright. Joshua had no intention of committing such an act. As was so often the case, Joshua took Gerald's place, assuming his part for the challenge he had issued. Not for the first time, Joshua felt he had assumed a habit that he did not like.

Gerald should pay the price of his own deeds.

But Gerald did not practice and he was not a good shot as a result. Gerald preferred to drink and dance and gamble, to issue challenges for duels that he would never be compelled to fight.

Because he had Joshua.

"This will be the last time," Joshua said quietly as the other men arrived. They were no more than silhouettes in the darkness, distinctive by the shape of their hats and the flare of their great coats. Their boots made no sound on the grass, and they might have been specters come to claim another for their company.

"Of course," Gerald agreed easily, but there was no conviction in his words.

They had exchanged clothes, as had become their custom, Joshua wearing one of Gerald's more flamboyant silk waistcoats, richly embroidered in green and gold. He wore his brother's favored frockcoat of emerald green wool with the velvet collar, and the great silver and malachite pin in his cravat that was as distinctive as a signature. The brim of his hat shielded his face from view, but Gerald stood behind him in his own more conservative garments. Yet again, Joshua was struck at how the change in garments altered their stances. He stood with legs braced against the ground, one hand on his hip, as he never did. Gerald seemed to become smaller in stature and quieter in Joshua's clothes.

There was no question of their deception being discovered in the shadows.

The combatants shook hands in silence. Gerald loaded the revolvers and handed the other one to his opponent's second. The weapons were checked, their readiness verified by all parties, then Joshua stood back-to-back with Gerald's rival.

His pulse did not even accelerate in these duels he had no desire to fight. They were calculations, no more and no less. He had noticed the other man's grim manner and guessed he would aim to kill. How good a marksman was he? The rumors were not favorable, but any man could be fortunate with a single shot. Joshua intended to graze his opponent's shoulder. It would be a warning, resulting in an injury that would cause some discomfort but not maim, much less kill. Gerald's honor would be defended and no one would be seriously hurt. It was the best compromise he knew.

They counted together, pacing off the distance, the night seeming overly silent around them.

As Joshua pivoted and raised the revolver, he had a sudden and unwelcome portent of doom. The shadows seemed overly thick, the moon claimed by those clouds in the wrong moment, and he hesitated. The clouds cleared, revealing his opponent in the distance. The other revolver was fired, the sound cracking against the night. Joshua fired then was assaulted from one side. The weight of some person collided with him, sending him off-balance. He recognized a woman's perfume, but could make no sense of it before she screamed, almost deafening him.

"No!" she cried and he recognized Charlotte's voice, even as her weight took him to the ground. He felt the blood of his betrothed spread warmly over him, he heard her gasp in pain – and he could make no sense of her presence there.

"Charlotte!" Gerald shouted but Joshua's blood had already gone cold.

For the lady sprawled atop him was dead.

She might have been his betrothed, but it was his brother she had been intent upon saving.

Joshua awakened suddenly, sitting bolt upright in the bed. His breath was coming quickly, his heart racing, his skin damp with perspiration. He felt the full sting of betrayal again, the cold conviction that Gerald had betrayed him, that his brother's connection with his own fiancé was more than intimate. He knew, too, that Charlotte had chosen Gerald over him, for he had heard the anguish in her voice.

He gripped the linens, took a breath, and rose to stare out the window at the first glimmer of dawn's light. Once again, he felt a that painful sense of betrayal.

Neither Gerald nor Charlotte had given any sign of their apparent affection before that night. Neither had confessed the truth to him, which meant they were both willing for Joshua to wed Charlotte as arranged. He knew without doubt that their relations would continue after his own nuptial vows were exchanged with the lady. Gerald never surrendered a pleasure for the sake of propriety. He could not imagine that Charlotte would be able to resist the invitations of the man she truly loved.

Would the infants presented as his sons truly have been Gerald's sons? The notion was sickening. Joshua paced his room, heartsick once again. He had lost a betrothed and a brother in that night, as well as any inclination to trust another.

He had not been able to mourn Charlotte, not knowing of her deception. He had never loved her, though he had been fond of her. If he had loved her, he would have been destroyed by her deceit.

He remembered now his resolve on that morning that he would never risk loving a woman.

He stared out at this morning, the sky turning pink above the forest that sheltered his mother's garden folly. His heart clenched at even the thought of Miss Emerson and her enticing kisses. Her enthusiasm was seductive—and dangerous. Who knew how many kisses she had returned with such ardor? Who knew how many men would capture her attention in future?

Who might have guessed that she could persuade him to abandon his promise to his father in so short a time? Miss Emerson was perilous to his convictions, and worse, the price of his surrender to temptation might be the lady herself.

All could have gone awry the night before and readily so. He should not have taken her for a ride in the moonlight. He should not have taken such a risk.

No, the lady was right in her refusal of him: they would not suit. If he ignored what had to be a fleeting and thus unreliable desire and considered the matter with his usual logic, he could see that any joy Helena might bring him would be short-lived.

He could be a good husband to her, but he would not make her happy—thus she would not be a good wife to him. Captain Emerson had been right and he knew his sister far better than Joshua ever would.

He was fortunate that she had refused him, although on this particular morning, Joshua Hargood did not feel lucky in the least.

First thing that next morning, Joshua rode toward the ruins of the medieval keep with a small party of men. If someone had taken up occupation there, he should see them routed in the duke's absence. He was accompanied by half a dozen men from Addersley Manor and they rode in silence down the road and past Bramble Cottage.

He did not so much as glance toward that structure.

They found no one in the ruins, though there were indications that someone had sheltered there in the cellar. There had been a fire kindled near the door recently, given the ashes left behind. Joshua found some refuse, perhaps the remains of a meal, tossed in a corner of the cellar. It had not decomposed or been eaten by wild creatures, hinting that it had not been there long. There were boot prints in the dirt, and he guessed that it had been one man alone.

One of the men with him spied boot prints dried in the mud. It had not rained for several days, but the prints in the dirt hinted that the visitor had been here after the mud had dried. He sent his men into the woods surrounding the ruin but they found little more.

There was no one to rout. It was not possible for him to keep a watch upon the place from the distance of Addersley Manor and the ruins were not his to monitor.

He could only hope that the man, whoever he was, did not become more bold and trouble those at Bramble Cottage. It was the closest residence, a fact that Joshua heartily disliked. Perhaps Miss Emerson would remain inside at night, showing some uncharacteristic temperance.

He shook his head at the very notion. At least she could not venture far with her injured ankle.

Joshua summoned his men and turned toward home, resolving to tell the duke of this as soon as that man returned.

In the meantime, it was his obligation to warn the

residents of Bramble Cottage. He would keep his visit brief—even though his anticipation rose with every step closer.

~

BECKY, it seemed, was to be Helena's constant companion in future.

She argued against this edict from her aunt, citing her injured ankle as evidence that she could not find much trouble. Aunt Fanny only snorted, making it clear that no one believed Helena's tale of looking at the stars.

Her aunt left the two of them in the garden, Helena's embroidery at the ready. Becky dutifully did some mending for Helena's aunt, her stitches so small and neat that Helena saw no point in even attempting to echo them.

The sound of a party of horses was a welcome distraction.

The appearance of Lord Addersley sent a surprising surge of pleasure through Helena. She told herself that she was simply glad of a diversion but it was more than that. When his gaze slid over her with an appreciation he quickly disguised, she tingled to her very toes, feeling that she had glimpsed a secret he would have preferred to hide.

Greetings were exchanged, though he did not take a seat. "I wished to ensure that you have not been troubled here at Bramble Cottage of late," he said, his manner particularly formal.

"Troubled by whom?" Helena asked.

He frowned into the distance, clearly distracted. "There have been reports of men in the ruins, so in the duke's absence, I felt obliged to see if there was truth in the rumor."

"The ruins?"

"The ruins of old Haynesdale castle," Becky provided. "They have been there since the time of King Arthur."

Helena looked to the viscount for affirmation of this, but he was watching Becky with some amusement. "I think not so long as that, Becky," he said. "The motte-and-bailey was likely a twelfth century structure. When it finally burned several hundred years later, the lords of Haynesdale moved their abode to its current location."

"Motte-and-bailey?" Helena asked.

The viscount drew a circle in the dirt, with another inside it and a dot in the middle. "That is the design of a medieval fortification. First there are earthworks around the perimeter, a hill and a moat or both, then there would have been a wooden palisade encircling the residence itself. Originally, it would have all been of wood, but this one evidently was partly constructed of stone at some point. The foundation walls and a cellar remain reasonably intact."

"It was the dungeon," Becky said with enthusiasm. "Where villains were left to die. They say as the ghosts of those who did end their days there haunt the hills around the ruins." She nodded with authority at this confession.

The viscount almost smiled, his eyes glimmering in that way Helena could only admire. "There have been more than ghosts in residence, unless the specters have developed earthly appetites. We found remnants of a fire and a small collection of discarded foodstuffs."

Helena feared then for her champion. "Did you rout whoever was there?"

He shrugged, much to her relief. "We saw no one, just signs of occupation." He frowned again. "I would suggest, Miss Emerson, that no one from your household venture out at night until this situation is resolved, which may not occur before the duke's return." He fixed her with a steady look. "Men driven to desperation may be unpredictable, even dangerous."

"But who are they?" Becky demanded.

The viscount was somber. "There are many men who served valiantly during the war who now find themselves decommissioned and without pay. They may or may not have homes to which they can return after such a long absence, or there may be reasons they choose not to do as much. Not every wife welcomes the return of an injured man, or even one beset by nightmares."

"How terrible for them!" Helena said. She thought of her champion, denied a spot at his own hearth, turned out into the night, after years of loyal service to the crown, and her heart tore in two.

"It is unjust, in my view, but I can only do so much." Lord Addersley was rueful. "I have employed as many returning soldiers as possible, as has the duke."

"I will ask Nicholas if he might have a post for one or two in his stables," Helena said with vigor.

The viscount nodded approval. "That is a fine sentiment, Miss Emerson, whether your brother has that capacity or not."

"What can you tell me of the ruins?" she asked. "There must be some tale of its history."

The viscount considered her query for a moment, then took a seat. He appeared to only perch on the chair, as if pressing matters awaited his attention, and she appreciated that he took the time to answer her question. She had to gather information wherever she could if she was to aid her champion.

"There is a tale, of course, and one of which you may well approve, Miss Emerson," he said. "For it is a sage of romance, even with a measure of danger."

"Oh!" she said with delight.

He smiled, very quickly, and she wished he had not sobered so soon. "I am no storyteller, but the gist of the tale is this. There was a Lord Haynesdale whose first son was born when he was in his winter years. There was treachery in his household, for he had become frail and many men of ambition surrounded him. His wife feared for her son, so she marked his skin with his father's signet ring, heating it in the fire so that its emblem would be burned into his flesh."

"Oh!" Helena gasped.

"In that way, there would always be indisputable proof of the boy's identity."

"How barbaric."

"But effective, Miss Emerson. For the infant was sent away with a trusty servant to defend him, and that guardian fled to France with the lord's heir. When that person died some years later, the young boy knew his legacy but could do little to recover it himself. He had the good fortune to be adopted by a knight in search of a squire, a younger son who had joined the Templars and departed upon crusade. And so it was that the boy traveled to Palestine in the care of the knight and trained as a knight himself. By the time the knight returned to France, the young boy had become a man, and when he was granted his spurs, he decided to seek out his own legacy. He returned to Haynesdale with a companion, only to find that all had gone awry in his father's holding in his absence."

"I think you do not do yourself justice, sir," Helena said when he paused for breath. "You tell a fine tale. I am enraptured."

The viscount's eyes gleamed. "I believe it is the tale itself that holds you enthralled, Miss Emerson, but I will take such compliments as they come."

Becky giggled, but Helena was aware only of the

viscount's gaze fixed upon her. "It is true," she confessed, feeling a little discomfited by his attention. "I do love a romantic tale."

"Then you will be heartened to know the rest. The knight's companion was robbed by a pair of urchins in the forest near the keep of Haynesdale and the knight gave chase. He discovered when he caught one of them that she was a maiden, a pretty young woman with flashing eyes and a sharp tongue. He knew, with the conviction that some men possess, that this was the lady who would claim his heart."

"Oh!" Helena and Becky sighed together.

"The lady, however, was unconvinced. She had little regard for knights, given her experience of those who had laid claim to Haynesdale—who were, by all accounts, a disreputable and untrustworthy lot. The maiden confided in the knight, telling him that those who held Haynesdale were not the rightful lord or his son, but usurpers, and further, that their demands upon the villagers had been so excessive that those common people had taken to the forests. They waited only for the return of the rightful heir to rise up and fight for justice."

"This is much like the tale of Robin Hood," Helena said with approval.

"The heir concocted a scheme with the defiant maiden. He suggested that they should pretend to be wed, and further, disguise themselves as an aristocratic couple on a journey. In this way, they might gain access to the keep and learn the weakness of those who had seized control. He did not tell her that he was the rightful heir himself, for he had kept the secret all his life and could not confess it readily."

"But she saw the mark on his flesh and knew who he had to be," Helena guessed.

The viscount granted her an intent look. "She did,

indeed, and so his secret was revealed, even as her alliance to him became complete."

"Did she see it when he took a bath?" Becky asked. "Or when he slept?"

The viscount chuckled. "I wager she might have seen it as a result of their guise of being man and wife." His gaze slid to meet Helena's and she felt herself flush, even though she could not look away.

She was thinking of those passages of amorous advice and wishing she might read them again. She halfway thought the viscount knew as much and was amused by her curiosity.

Though he was not surprised by it. Helena was certain he expected her to be audacious and perhaps even awaited her to be so.

"And the rest, sir?" Becky prompted in the tone of one who knew the tale already.

Helena could guess. "And they fought the usurpers along with the villagers, won back the holding, and he reclaimed his legacy in triumph," she said with satisfaction.

"I believe they even lived happily ever after," the viscount added, giving a little bow.

"Is it true, though?" Helena had to ask.

"As far as I know. It is the tale that is frequently told of the ruins, and I understand the duke does trace his lineage at least as far back as Bartholomew and Anna."

Becky nodded with enthusiasm. "The first time I heard the tale, your brother sang it, sir. It was in the common room at the inn in Haynesdale village, and he scarce stopped for breath." She shook her head. "There must have been a hundred verses!"

"There is a version in rhyming verse," the viscount said. "And my brother knew it all." He shook his head in recollection. "Our tutor was most annoyed that Gerald could sing the entire lay of *Bartholomew's Return*, but could not recite a list of the monarchs of England." He smiled, a little sadly to Helena's thinking, and made to rise to his feet. "We used to play in the ruins as boys, though I had nigh forgotten as much. He loved that place beyond all."

Becky sighed and shook her head. "God bless his soul, sir," she murmured and the viscount nodded in acknowledgement of that.

"Perhaps it is your brother who occupies the ruins," Helena suggested before she could keep the words from springing to her lips.

Indeed, it made perfect sense that her champion might be the notorious and charming Gerald. There might be space in that ruin for his horse to have shelter and he might have taken refuge in a familiar ruin. That would also explain the similarities and the differences between Lord Addersley and Helena's champion.

Did brothers not often share a height and build? Might they both have a cleft in their chins? Yet one was dashing and one was sedate, their respective natures distinguishing them from each other despite their physical similarities.

But the viscount shook his head and his tone was severe. "That cannot be, Miss Emerson. My brother died in the battle of Waterloo."

"But are you certain?" Helena asked. "There might have been an error."

"Miss!" Becky said, sounding as horrified as Aunt might have done.

The viscount only studied her, his gaze colder than she had ever seen it. "Impossible, Miss Emerson," he said curtly. "Your affection for tales leads you astray in this matter." He touched the brim of his hat and bowed so precisely that she knew he was annoyed with her. "Good day."

"Oh miss," Becky whispered. "You have offended

him in truth. Why would you ask him such a thing? To suggest that a dead man yet lives is impertinent beyond all."

But Helena could only wonder. Her notion made good sense, to her thinking. She knew, though, that no one wished to give it consideration.

Why not? Were people glad that Master Gerald had died?

There was a tale and one she intended to uncover, though she could not do as much with Becky by her side. Her ankle had to mend and quickly! Surely then she would be able to evade Becky and meet her champion at the folly as planned.

And she would know the truth of his name.

That happy situation could not be contrived too soon for Helena.

CHAPTER 9

Gerald alive.

Impossible!

And yet…and yet. As much as Joshua was inclined to discard the possibility, he had to consider it. There *was* the official document delivering the news of Gerald's demise, which should be utterly trustworthy. Joshua had to wonder about battlefields, though, about the difficulty of accurate identification. He could not dismiss the fact that Gerald had not returned home in any form. His brother's remains, such as they were, must be interred near Waterloo. Joshua did not even know if there was a stone to mark the place.

In fact, he did not even know how much of Gerald had been available to be identified.

What if there had been an error?

It was a notion that had never occurred to him, and would never have without Miss Emerson. Surely it was a reminder of Miss Emerson's ability to challenge his expectations and assumptions—which could not be a good thing.

If only this notion were so readily dismissed. As Joshua rode for Addersley Manor, he pondered the possibility of Gerald's survival. There was no evidence that his brother lived. Indeed, there were no bills, which had always been the surest sign of his brother's existence.

But Joshua could not entirely forget Mrs. Lewis' response to the sight of him. There had been something of her declaration that did not sound as if she had been awaiting her lover's return for a decade. The more he reviewed the encounter, the more Joshua had to wonder if Mrs. Lewis had seen Gerald since their son's conception.

Gerald might have survived and found a patron.

More likely, it would be a patroness.

How might Mrs. Lewis figure into such a situation, if indeed there was one?

There was only one way to know for certain. Joshua would have to visit the lady in question.

First, Mr. Newson. Perhaps he might have welcome tidings to deliver to Mrs. Lewis as a result and a respectable reason to call upon her.

He checked his watch and touched his heels to the horse.

BACK IN LONDON, Miss Esmeralda Ballantyne found herself abruptly returned to her own home. Though she was weakened and much thinner, her spirit was unquenched. Oh, she knew who was responsible for her situation, for the paying of her bills, for the contentment of her servants and the security of her house, even her own release.

And she knew enough of men to guess what the Duke of Haynesdale wanted from her in return. Even the prospect of being the mistress of one man, of becoming even more beholden to him than she already was, chafed at her.

In such circumstance, she might as well be that man's property, one of his chattels, or his indentured slave. The one thing Esmeralda prized above all others was her freedom, and liberty to make her own choices.

But that might have been lost, through no fault of her own.

A curse upon Jacques Desjardins!

If ever Esmeralda had resented that the rules of society and even the law of the land gave more to men than to women, that had been nothing compared to her current fury at the injustice of it all.

She could not deny that the Duke of Haynesdale had a claim upon her—yet she could not entirely explain his willingness to incur her obligation. There had been that old feud between them, and his comments in recent times about her chosen profession showed that his views were unchanged. Why would he even wish for a courtesan as a mistress? His interference in her life would undoubtedly come at a price Esmeralda did not wish to pay.

What could she do about the matter? She paced and she pondered. She would sleep and she would eat, regaining her strength with every passing day. If she called upon him, doubtless he would not see her. She had to wait for him to appear at her door, which did not suit her well.

And so it was that she opened her mail and discovered a note requesting that she add yet more to her book in process, *The Ladies' Essential Guide to the Art of Seduction.*

More.

There was a great deal more advice that she could give.

Without undue consideration, Esmeralda dipped her quill into the ink and wrote a passage to invoke change in her gender.

. . .

*U*PON THE MATTER *of feminine capitulation...*

It is the expectation of many men, and indeed of society at large, that women should be biddable and docile, always taking the counsel of men with regards to their behavior. I would suggest to you, gentle reader, that there is a delight to be found in challenging such expectations, particularly in matters of intimacy.

In the bedroom, in privacy with one's lover, a lady can reveal her own urges as nowhere else in the world. Be bold in your caresses, and forthright in your demands. Instead of lying back and accepting whatsoever your partner deigns to offer, tell him what you wish of him. Make the first address. Touch him as you wish—or touch yourself as he watches. I have written of boldness before, but the combined power of audacity and surprise cannot be underestimated, nor can its ability to change the foundation of a relationship be overlooked...

~

M*R.* N*EWSON WAS* adamant when finally they met that afternoon, but Joshua had expected a protest from the older man. He was determined to see the question of Mrs. Lewis resolved to his satisfaction. Duty, honor and integrity were his guidelines in this matter.

"I do not believe it appropriate that we discuss this matter, my lord." The older man flicked a baleful glance at Joshua.

"But I would ensure all is set to rights," Joshua insisted.

"All was arranged to your father's satisfaction."

"I fear it may not be to mine."

"I gave my word, sir..."

"And I must defend my name, Mr. Newson," Joshua

said crisply, interrupting his manager. "There is a child in Haynesdale Hollow who could be my brother Gerald at six years of age. His name is Francis Lewis and his mother greeted me like a returned lover." Joshua fixed the older man with a quelling look. "I must know the tale and the resolution my father chose."

Mr. Newson polished his pince-nez. "You cannot act upon every coincidence, sir."

"I doubt it is a coincidence. I suspect Gerald was the boy's father and the mother, quite reasonably, mistook me for Gerald."

"It is not your concern, sir."

"It *is* my concern," Joshua insisted. "If the boy is of my blood, he should be provided for."

"Your father did not share your view."

"My father is dead, Mr. Newson. I insist upon knowing what provisions, if any, were made for Gerald's progeny."

The older man was shocked. "You speak as if there was an entire village of such children! There were none!"

"There is one for certain."

"There were women, to be sure, but they were light-skirts and doxies, every one of them."

"Mrs. Lewis does not appear to be either. She looks to be a respectable woman, albeit one burdened with the obligation of raising a son alone."

"I would not be so readily deceived, sir."

Joshua cleared his throat and straightened. "Tell me, Mr. Newson, or I will find another manager. I must know all that occurs within the sphere of my responsibilities."

"But this was years ago…"

It was in that moment Joshua guessed the truth.

"Was Mrs. Lewis the reason my father bought Gerald a commission?"

Mr. Newson pinched the bridge of his nose. "I swore to keep silent forever," he said heavily. "But I vow to you, sir, your father and I did not know there was a child."

"There is."

Mr. Newson sighed, and took a moment to consider his options. Joshua watched him, knowing his expression was impassive—and not welcoming.

Finally, the older man turned and retrieved a ledger from a bookcase, opening it on the table before Joshua. "Your brother had a habit of seducing young ladies, most of whom, as mentioned, were in the trade of winning the affections of young gentlemen like himself. In London, he spent considerable sums on such women, so much that your father ordered him back to Nottinghamshire."

"I remember the women," Joshua said. "I remember the debts."

But Joshua did not recall Gerald being banished from London to the country.

"I doubt you knew the full extent of it, sir. Your father wished to protect you from your brother's…inclinations." Mr. Newson opened the ledger to a page and offered it to Joshua. There was a list of debts, some paid directly to women, some to dressmakers, furriers, shoemakers and jewelers. The sum at the base of the page was staggering, a culmination of extravagance made by both brothers. One date seized Joshua's attention, the date when all had gone awry, and he anticipated that the spending would at least slow after it.

He had abandoned that life, after all.

But Mr. Newson turned the page to reveal that the expenditures continued and at a much higher rate. Gerald had redoubled his own indulgences when alone in his revels, spending more than he and Joshua had spent together.

"That was for his final year in London," Mr. Newson said. "He nearly beggared the estate, sir."

Joshua sat down, astonished. "I knew he overspent his allowance."

"That tally does not include his gambling debts," Mr. Newson said, his tone heavy with disapproval. "We didn't even learn of all of them until he had left for the Continent." Mr. Newson dropped a heavy finger to the ledger. "You will notice, however, that the spending slows in September of that year."

"And dwindles to very little at all. What expenses remain are from tradesmen in Haynesdale Hollow, not London." Joshua looked up, awaiting an explanation.

"That was when he finally heeded your father, sir and returned to Nottinghamshire as bidden."

"But Father and I were yet in London."

"Aye, and Addersley Manor was closed. It was expected that Master Gerald would open part of the house, but he never did. Your father believed the diminished spending marked Master Gerald's involvement with a young lady in the region, perhaps one of some means." He raised his brows. "I thought perhaps he charmed an affluent widow. You see that they are for provisions rather than clothing, lavish meals instead of horses and carriages."

"I see." Gerald, evidently, had frequented Mr. Darney's inn.

"Your brother came to your father, requesting funds and a settlement for his nuptials."

"He meant to wed her."

Mr. Newson nodded. "He spoke of it, but his lordship would not hear of what he called an unsuitable match. I never knew the lady's name." Mr. Newson coughed delicately. "I also believe his lordship believed the fancy to be a fleeting one, as was characteristic of Master Gerald's liaisons. They argued heatedly—you were in London at the time, sir, when your father came back to meet with Master Gerald—and his lordship chose to buy a commission for Master Gerald. Master Gerald left Addersley Manor immediately to join his company, by his lordship's design, and never crossed its threshold again."

"It was arranged so quickly as that?"

Mr. Newson coughed again. "It is possible that the argument was precipitated by your father's presentation of this plan, and your brother's insistence that he meant to wed was a response. I was not in attendance and cannot be certain." He sighed. "Your father was riled beyond all, to be sure. The tale was not shared with his usual coherence and attention to detail."

Had Gerald even said farewell to Mrs. Lewis? Joshua wondered whether his brother had had the opportunity. Had he truly loved her?

Had Gerald known about the child?

You are returned!' she had said, with such joy. It seemed to Joshua that Mrs. Lewis held his brother in affection, even if no one else did.

Had she seen his brother since that day of his departure?

Joshua revealed the note he had received, the second one, and offered it to Mr. Newson. The older man's gaze flew over it, then he looked up.

"You think this is about the child?"

"I think someone believes Mrs. Lewis has been poorly served."

"But she is married. Her name makes that clear."

"I wonder," Joshua said, knowing that his own cook called herself Mrs. Baird but was unwed. He met the older man's gaze. "But I intend to find out. I will not see Gerald's child raised in poverty."

Mr. Newson took a deep breath and frowned. "I understand your impulse, sir, but be warned that people of that class may seek to win an advantage undeserved. Consider the note!"

Joshua found himself bristling on Mrs. Lewis' account. "If she had intended to demand funds from Addersley, would she not have done as much by now?"

"She might have done, sir," Mr. Newson ceded heavily. "Perhaps she awaited your return or that of your father."

Joshua thought she had been waiting for Gerald. "I do not think she wrote this note or the earlier one, but I will uncover the truth."

"You cannot be granting coin to any woman with a son who resembles your brother, my lord."

"Or the line might extend all the way to London," Joshua said flatly. "I appreciate your concern, Newson, but I must repair this situation. The lady lives nearby, Newson, and the resemblance between her son and Gerald is powerful. I will do what is right in my brother's name and memory."

And he might, in the course of doing as much, be able to put Miss Emerson's notion to rest.

The older man caught his breath, grimaced, then nodded reluctant agreement. "We should set a threshold upon it, sir, that your good nature not be exploited."

"We will do what is right, Newson, and that is that."

JOSHUA FELT restless when he returned home. Finding evidence of the occupation at the ruins but not the individuals responsible gave him the sense of a task left unfinished. He could see no way to ensure Miss Emerson's safety, if she did venture from Bramble Cottage, and yet he had no responsibility to defend her.

If she had accepted his suit, he might have insisted

that she and her aunt—or she and Becky—come to Addersley Manor until all was resolved.

The fact was that he did not trust her to be sensible.

The very disruption of his usual serenity should have been proof that they were better apart, but Joshua could not dismiss his attraction to her. It was folly. Her presence led him astray and compelled him to forget his habits, but he could not regret a moment in her company.

Even knowing all of this, he felt cheated by his own decision to not pause at Bramble Cottage this day, thereby denying himself even a moment of her company. He felt disgruntled, all for the lack of a certain lady's smile.

He stared across the garden, hands shoved in his pockets, and considered that he felt alive for the first time in a decade. Helena made him smile. Her companionship gave him joy. In her presence, he felt the promise of the future and the wonder of every small delight. And in his heart, he could not truly believe that such an association could be ill-fated or wrong.

How unlike him to be conflicted!

Joshua shook his head, guessing that it was Miss Emerson's habit to disrupt the equilibrium of clear-thinking men.

He found himself unable to keep from imagining her in residence at Addersley Manor. The house felt appallingly empty to him in his solitude and devoid of charm.

He marched through it, seeking some element that would give him pleasure or at least offer a distraction. Instead, he recalled Miss Emerson's favorable comments about this detail or that, and the sight of her in each room.

How had Miss Helena Emerson so securely captured his heart?

It was true. Joshua loved her.

He had loved her from that first glimpse.

It was an astonishing realization. He knew he admired her, of course, and that he found her alluring. But it was more than that. He was enchanted by her lively spirit, her penchant for laughter, even her audacity. She might vex him with her insistence upon following impulse, but in another way, he admired her boldness.

Joshua liked how he felt in her presence.

There was the peril of her. If they were reckless together, dire consequences could result. He could not countenance as much.

He must forget her.

He did not wish to do as much, but it was the only sensible choice.

How curious that for the first time in his life, he had no desire to be sensible!

Joshua was scowling at the interminably long table in the dining room when he realized that something was missing. There should be another pair of sterling candlesticks on the table. He searched the rest of the room but found no sign of them.

He recalled then that the small ormolu clock had also been missing.

In no mood to tolerate thefts in his household, Joshua rang for Fairfax.

Fairfax was clearly shocked that the candlesticks were gone. He was similarly bewildered that the ormolu clock was missing and could not fathom how he had overlooked its loss. "I am shocked, my lord. There has never been any such trouble in this house, and none of the servants are newly arrived."

"Perhaps someone has a new need for funds," Joshua suggested.

Fairfax cleared his throat and looked more prim

than usual. "Perhaps it was someone from outside the house, sir."

"But who could have entered the house without detection?"

Fairfax dropped his gaze. "You did have guests, sir, and guests most interested in the décor of your home."

Lady Dalhousie and Miss Emerson? Joshua's astonishment was so complete that it must have shown, for the butler shook his head.

"Older ladies, I regret to inform you, sir, can be... acquisitive when their tastes exceed their means, particularly if they were accustomed to luxuries in the past." He cleared his throat again. "And if I may be so bold as to speak plainly, sir?"

Joshua considered his butler. "Please do, Fairfax. You know that I rely upon your insights."

The older man beamed. "I would say, sir, that my estimation of the young lady was much diminished by her decision to refuse you."

Joshua was touched by his butler's loyalty. "Apparently, she cannot bear the prospect of wedding a man who does not dance, Fairfax."

The butler frowned. "But you had a dancing master to tutor you and Master Gerald, sir. I recall that you both excelled at dancing."

"My father demanded my promise to abandon such frivolities and I mean to keep my vow."

"I can well imagine his disapproval of the excesses possible in London, sir, but dancing?"

"He expressly included it as a deed to be avoided."

The butler frowned. He made to turn away, then turned back again, his indecision and consternation such that Joshua had to ask.

"Is there something you would say, Fairfax?"

"Only that I cannot credit it, sir. I believe your assertion, of course, for you made it, but your father, also, danced himself with notable grace and enthusiasm. Why, he and your mother hosted any number of gatherings with dancing, sometimes as many as one a month." He smiled in recollection. "Your mother loved to dance."

"I do not recall him dancing," Joshua was compelled to note, for it was true.

The butler grimaced. "I fear, sir, that there was only one partner he desired. I never knew him to dance after your mother's demise."

Joshua nodded. "But he danced, you say?"

"Oh yes, sir. If I may be so bold to make a suggestion, perhaps it was your dancing companions in London of which he disapproved."

It could be true. Joshua and Gerald had danced with courtesans, actresses, whores and widows of dubious repute.

They had danced in gaming dens, at gatherings where Cyprians were in attendance, at the theatre and at other venues of dubious repute.

They had danced in various squares, at all hours of the night, and in the dew of drunken mornings. Such dancing had often been accompanied by indulgence in other pleasures, like that of brandy, and invariably led to other excesses.

But dancing at Haynesdale House, under the watchful gazes of dozens of his respectable neighbors, escorting ladies of impeccable reputations, in a sedate and orderly manner, might not fall under his father's injunction.

It was certainly a matter to consider.

Joshua nodded. "Thank you, Fairfax. That is a notion to consider. In the meantime, since we have no good notion of when these items vanished, I see little point in alerting the household to our suspicions."

"Doubtless, they have been sold already, sir," Fairfax agreed.

Joshua consulted his watch. "It is too late to ride to Haynesdale Hollow and consult with the silversmith there, but I will do as much in the morning."

"Excellent, my lord. In the meantime, I would compile a list of every item we know to have vanished. If you might provide assistance, sir. There are some items I have not seen for years, though it is possible your father had them sent to London without my knowledge."

"We will work together, Fairfax," Joshua resolved, opening the console to begin the task.

EVEN THOUGH MRS. JAMESON had called and there was the promise of new satin slippers in Helena's future, the day passed slowly.

It was, to Helena's thinking, a portent of her future at Bramble Cottage—interminable days one after the other, stretching long into her future, only the rare prospect of new slippers to provide a measure of interest.

Aunt had been sorting linens with a vengeance, inspired by Nixon's energetic cleaning of the house to put every detail in order. Mr. Nixon worked steadily for all his casual manner, and made remarkable progress on the overgrown hedges and garden. The surroundings of Bramble Cottage looked markedly more civilized. Becky had finished the mending, happily sitting with the restless Helena most of the day.

Helena had missed her champion. She had missed Mischief. She had missed the viscount, and she recalled the tale he had shared. She was impatient to do more than sit and heal, but had no choice in the matter.

She supposed there was a lesson in that, a reminder that following impulse could lead her astray. There was Mr. Melbourne, a lesson in the price of misplaced trust, and now her ankle, a lesson in the folly of solitary excursions. Try as she might, she could not consider her night ride with her champion to be a lesson in any kind of folly.

It had been lovely and romantic. He was so gallant. Her trust was not misplaced there, even though she was not certain of his name. But what a tale that would be! The viscount's brother, alive and well, returned to Addersley to take her, Miss Helena Emerson, as his bride.

There was a future to dream about.

Yet Helena passed a sleepless night. She was torn between the hope that her champion would come to her again, and the fear that he would not. What would she would do if he did appear? Did she dare to break the injunction against leaving the house alone to meet him? The viscount would not have hesitated to avoid temptation, but Helena knew she did not possess his resolve. How had he abandoned all pleasures, even at his father's dictate, and done so at once? She could not even deny the temptation of one small digression.

In the end, she did not have to choose for her champion did not come.

She overslept the next morning, much to the chagrin of Aunt Fanny. Aunt was always hoping someone would call but no one came to Bramble Cottage. There was no risk in being late to dress.

Helena heard the viscount's horse near noon and her hopes of company rose, but he rode past their gate. By the time Helena reached the hedge, he was no more than a silhouette in the distance—though she knew it was him. She told herself that he was late for an appointment, and that he would undoubtedly halt on his return.

~

"But you sold them to me, my lord," the silversmith said, his manner puzzled. He and Joshua stood in the man's shop in Haynesdale Hollow, the silversmith wearing his apron and spectacles.

"I most certainly did not," Joshua replied. "When was this?"

"A few days ago." The tall and angular smith pulled out a ledger and adjusted his spectacles. There was a precision about his manner that Joshua liked. "Monday April 21," he read. "A fine pair of sterling candlesticks from Lord Addersley, hallmarked Fraser & Sons London." He turned the ledger so Joshua could read it.

"And yet I have never stepped into your establishment before."

The silversmith frowned and turned the pages of the ledger. "I must disagree, my lord. You tried to sell me a clock not a fortnight ago. I did not buy it, for the sole potential customer for such a token would be the duke, and I know His Grace prefers to acquire his timepieces in London." He shook his head. "I made no note of it, alas, but it was during that stint of rain we had of several days running."

Joshua remembered the rain, and the missing clock. "And you are certain it was me?" He watched the other man, wondering whether he frequently traded in stolen items and was covering for the thief.

The silversmith removed his glasses and scrutinized Joshua. "To be sure, my lord, now that you stand before me, I can see that it was not you. The man who presented himself as you shared your coloring and had your height, he might even have worn that coat or one similar, but it was not you. I recall now that he was inclined to keep his face turned away and he did not remove his hat." The silversmith frowned as he considered Joshua's hat. "It was less fine than yours, to be sure."

The conclusion was evident. Someone in his household or near to it was stealing from Addersley Manor and impersonating Joshua to sell the items. Who could it be? He would ask Fairfax to line up all the staff and judge which of the men was of similar height to himself.

It could be a maid and a man working together, though, in which case the man might not be employed at Addersley. Somehow he would find the villain and put an end to this.

He bought his own candlesticks back, the silversmith offering him the same price he himself had paid to the villain. Joshua thanked him, thinking that more than fair. "Where else might he have tried to sell the clock?"

The silversmith shrugged. "Nowhere in Haynesdale Hollow, my lord. I reckon he would have to go as far as Colsterworth. There is a goldsmith there who sells watches and clocks as well."

Did the thief have a horse or access to one? Joshua could not say. For the moment, he would return home and strive to identify the villain.

Someone must have seen something. A stranger could not enter his home without being observed.

He thought of the notes and wondered if the two might be linked.

LORD ADDERSLEY DID NOT HALT upon his return that day.

Helena abandoned her tea at the sound of hoofbeats to hasten to the door. But the viscount rode past, seemingly without even a glance in her direction. He certainly did not slow his horse.

Helena was disappointed, for he always brought tidings to them.

She sat up watching for her champion until well after midnight, but he did not appear either. She heard no horse. She saw no shadow in the distance.

It seemed her curiosity was to be punished—as the curiosity of every heroine in every fairy tale was inclined to be. She winced, remembering the viscount's comparison. Had she not touched her champion's face and discovered the cleft in his chin?

She had strayed from the path to wander in the forest, curious to know its hidden charms. She had looked inside the locked cupboard forbidden to her. She had lit a candle to look upon the face of her mysterious lover.

And in so doing, she had lost his regard. Helena knew that as well as she knew her own name. Curiosity was always punished in such tales.

Helena had to find a way to set matters to rights, but if her champion no longer came to her, she could not see how it might be done.

She had a will, though, so there had to be a way.

She thought about that cleft in his chin, and in the middle of the night, she began to wonder. Lord Addersley said it was impossible for her champion to be his lost brother. His conviction of his brother's death had been unshakable. Undoubtedly, he had more evidence than he wished to share, evidence that proved to him that his brother was dead.

Her own brother, of course, might have taken an opposing view to tease her, but Lord Addersley had always told Helena the complete truth, even when it was unwelcome. If he said his brother was dead, she should believe him.

But if her champion was not the viscount's brother, who might he be? It was true that he might be a former soldier, reduced to poverty by the loss of his commission, but Helena doubted such a man would share any traits, even size, with the viscount.

How many men had she ever encountered with a cleft in their chins? Of similar height and breadth? With such elegant manners? At such ease on a horse? Possessed of fine clothing and boots?

Helena frowned at the ceiling. In this region, there was only one man who fit that description. Though she fought against the conclusion, she could not evade it.

What if her champion *was* the viscount?

What if the viscount had a secret identity, like the highwayman or Robin Hood?

She sat up abruptly in bed, her thoughts spinning.

He would have to have a good reason for undertaking such a disguise, of course, one that required a secrecy that was outside his nature. It was not difficult to imagine him perpetuating a disguise with good cause, or even being evasive about the truth. He was honest, to be sure, and trustworthy, but he was also honorable.

What was the cause?

She could not ask him outright, of course, for if the viscount kept a secret, there must be good cause. He was not a frivolous man or one inclined to jests. Had someone not implied that he had worked as a spy during the war? Did his quest have anything to do with the men who had occupied the ruins?

Helena dared not even hope that his ruse was for her sake. No, she had simply witnessed the truth by accident, by being in the wrong place at the wrong time, and his gallantry had demanded that he see her safe.

There was so much more to the viscount than met the eye!

And Helena wanted to know every detail.

Would he keep their rendezvous at the folly, when

her ankle was healed and the weather was finer? Helena wished for that outcome with all her might as the rain fell, pounding upon the roof and ensuring her captivity at the cottage was complete.

When she finally slept, she dreamed of the thawing of a taciturn viscount with a dimple—and in her dream, the viscount kissed with all the beguiling assurance of a highwayman.

~

NICHOLAS SENT the carriage to Bramble Cottage on Sunday morning, and the family all went to church together in Haynesdale Hollow. Helena spent the service surveying all the young men present, but failed to find one who might be her champion.

The viscount, she could not fail to note, was not there. She supposed there was a church at Addersley village and he was obliged to attend services there, but found herself disappointed in his absence all the same.

The dowager came to Aunt Fanny when they were leaving the church, her delight obvious to all. The reason soon became clear. "I have had a letter from Damien," she confided in Aunt Fanny, her words sufficiently loud to carry to others. "He will arrive in time for the ball, though I had no such expectation."

"How wonderful," Aunt said, granting Helena a significant glance.

Helena sighed, finding herself with little interest of the duke's doings.

"You may have your dance after all, Helena," Nicholas teased but Lady Haynesdale laughed.

"Oh, Damien does not dance. You must know as much Captain Haynesdale. He did not even dance before his leg was injured and now—" she made a sweeping gesture with one hand. She then leaned closer to Aunt Fanny. "The most interesting detail is that he is bringing his ward, a Mademoiselle Sylvie LaFleur."

"I was not aware that Haynesdale had a ward," Nicholas said.

"Nor I!" agreed Lady Constance with a laugh. "But his adventures are legion. Doubtless he will have a tale of it to share when he arrives. He is expecting another guest as well, an elderly lady called Mrs. Oliver."

Mrs. Oliver? Was that not the name of the author of that scandalous advice Helena had found in Eliza's possession? Helena cast a quick sidelong glance at Eliza, whose eyes had widened in alarm. Even Nicholas developed a sudden fascination with the ground before his boots.

Helena was not mistaken then. It was the same Mrs. Oliver. Who was she and why was she coming to Haynesdale at all? She listened avidly, hoping to learn as much as possible of these promising tidings, but the subject was changed all too swiftly.

The dowager said her farewells and hastened away, even as Aunt Fanny watched her go. "A *ward*," Aunt said under her breath. "The duke unexpectedly has a ward, who is French." She shook her head primly. "I wager she is young and lovely and of no blood relation at all."

Nicholas laughed. "And you think he plans to wed her?"

"I think the situation utterly obvious, Nicholas," Aunt said primly. Nicholas handed them all into the carriage.

"Then I will take your wager, Aunt, for I know Damien has no intent to marry at all. I am certain that if ever he did take a wife, it would be a lady close to his own age. He has little patience with young ladies."

Helena assumed this was a warning targeted for her ears, but she was less interested in the duke's inclinations than before. Indeed, she could only recall how very elderly he was, and reliant upon his cane. He made no effort to be charming, in her recollection, or even to be polite. The viscount was a much more agreeable companion and much more attractive, as well.

"A pretty young chit might change his thinking," Aunt insisted. "It has happened before."

"Not Damien."

"It is his duty to wed and father at least one son."

"And never has there been a man so disinterested in the expectations of others." Nicholas shook his head. "When do you think he would wed this young lady?"

"I will not speculate upon the circumstances of others," Aunt huffed, although Helena knew she routinely did as much. A wager with Nicholas, though, would reveal her interest in the affairs of others, and in a way that she might deem vulgar as well.

Helena's brother, however, knew the perfect bait.

"A new hat for you if I am wrong," he said and Aunt's eyes lit with predictable interest.

"*Any* hat?"

"Any hat the dressmaker in Haynesdale Hollow can contrive for you."

Aunt, Helena knew, believed herself in need of a hat, and if one could be had at no expense to herself, all the better.

"And if I am wrong?" that lady asked. "What will you demand for your side?"

"I will be content with the satisfaction of having been right," Nicholas said with a smile.

"I will take your wager," Aunt said as the carriage began to roll. "I will take your wager and teach you a lesson, Nicholas Emerson, about the folly of believing a man cannot change his view. Love," she informed him loftily, "can soften the most resilient heart."

"It will have a quest in claiming Damien's," Eliza said under her breath.

Nicholas laughed and shook Aunt's hand. For her part, Helena looked out the window, marveling that her interest in the duke should have diminished so very much in so little time. It was a puzzle and almost certainly the influence of a docile country life. Soon, she thought with a sigh, she might even find enjoyment in her needlework.

CHAPTER 10

Joshua found himself missing the society of Miss Helena Emerson. He had been occupied with church services the day before, and a spring tea hosted by the ladies of Addersley village. There had been speculation about the progression of the strawberries in the gardens of Addersley Manor, as well as queries as to whether he might resume his mother's old habit of hosting a strawberry picnic and tea in the gardens.

He had a clear sense of the right answer in the view of his tenants. He made the excuse that he could only manage such a social event with the assistance of a wife and was subsequently introduced to a variety of young ladies considered to be eligible in the vicinity.

For once, he had welcomed the prospect of dining alone.

By Monday, however, he was keenly aware of his solitude, particularly in the absence of one delightful lady. A visit to the stables confirmed that Hoskins believed the puppies of an age to go to their new homes. He immediately resolved upon a visit to Bramble Cottage on his way to collect the documents from Newson for Mrs. Lewis.

As he dressed for his ride, his gaze fell upon the waistcoat he had worn the day he had come upon Miss Emerson with her injured ankle. Had she guessed the identity of her admirer? Joshua thought she might have done, the feel of her fingertips upon his chin all too easy to recall. On impulse, he chose the waistcoat, over-coming Reed's insistence that it was too elaborate for a call to his manager.

Perhaps Miss Emerson had need of a little as-sistance in deriving the truth.

He had a devil of a time getting away from the sta-bles, for Hoskins was filled with advice for the pup's future. The ostler recounted the best feeding times, the best nourishment for the dog, the condition of its bed, and the commencement of its training.

"She might be your own child, off to live elsewhere," Joshua teased when the other man paused for breath and Hoskins grinned.

"They are a fine lot of puppies, my lord. I would not see any of them come to harm."

"Perhaps I should suggest to Miss Emerson and Lady Dalhousie that you might call on the morrow to ensure that all is as it should be for Mischief. Miss Emerson has never had a dog, to my understanding, and might be glad of your advice." Lady Dalhousie seemed to know a great deal about dogs, and Joshua had no doubt that all would be settled admirably, but he wished to reassure his ostler.

"I should like to do as much, sir. It would be no trouble."

"And it would set your fears to rest."

"Only if all is as it should be, sir."

Joshua nodded. "And if it is not, you can offer sug-gestions to see that it is so. I shall make some of my own today."

Hoskins nodded with relief and scratched the puppy's ears. "Thank you, sir."

"Come along, Mischief. Your new lady awaits you."

The day was overcast, with a promise of rain in the afternoon. As he rode past the copse of trees that surrounded the folly, Joshua could only recall Miss Emerson's demand that he meet her there on the first fine afternoon. His visit this day would give him the opportunity to ascertain the state of her ankle, and better to guess her intentions.

Of course, he knew her intentions. She would go alone to the folly in the hope of a rendezvous. He considered whether he should let her be disappointed or not as he rode toward Bramble Cottage. When he rode through the opening in the rhododendron hedge—now rather wider than it had been—he found Miss Emerson in the yard. She wore a dark blue dress with white edging, one that he knew would favor her eyes.

He was pleased when she looked up and smiled in welcome at him, then turned her steps toward him. He was not surprised when the dog yipped with joy at the sight of her, for he shared that feeling of elation. He dismounted and set down the puppy, which had grown in just a week, and Mischief darted toward Miss Emerson.

She made a great fuss over the puppy. Mischief rolled to her back to have her belly rubbed, then ran around Miss Emerson and barked. Joshua's horse snorted and stood his ground, well accustomed to dogs and not in the least bit interested in them.

"Hoskins has declared it to be time for Mischief to leave her mother," he said.

"Will she miss her mother and siblings terribly?"

"She may, or she may be too enchanted with you and her new life for that."

"Aunt has insisted that she have a bed in the kitchen

to begin, for she will have to learn what can be done and where. Aunt says she must learn her manners and that it may take several months."

"It may indeed. Although in my experience, a tired puppy is more inclined to behave."

Miss Emerson laughed. "Then I will be glad it does not rain as yet, for we will play for a while."

"Is your ankle sufficiently healed for such activity?"

"It is!" Miss Emerson smiled as she approached him. The dress did indeed favor her coloring, making her eyes look more blue and her skin more creamy. He watched her gaze linger upon his waistcoat and knew he did not imagine that her gaze had warmed when she looked up at him again. "I thank you for bringing her, my lord. You must have considerably more important affairs to attend."

"As it is, I must ride to Haynesdale village to see my manager today."

"Why is he so far from Addersley Manor?"

"It is not so far as that, and the affairs of the manor have been too simple in recent years to fully occupy the time of a manager. Mr. Newson is a solicitor with other business affairs to manage in addition to mine." He was positively garrulous in this lady's presence. Did she realize her effect upon him?

"I see." She smiled down at the dog again, who was nudging at her slippers. "Not another pair, Mischief," she chided. "You might lose your taste for ribbon roses." She seized a stick from the gardener's trimming and cast it for the dog, who bounded after it.

"Hoskins expressed a desire to ensure that Mischief was well settled here. Would you mind if he called on the morrow, and perhaps made a few suggestions?"

"I should not mind at all. Indeed, I would welcome his advice. Aunt has many views, but your ostler must know so much about ensuring the wellbeing of dogs."

"He does indeed." They both looked down at the puppy, happily rolling in the grass with the stick. "You might acquaint her with the house and grounds today, so that she becomes familiar with it all."

"I will." Miss Emerson eyed him, her manner expectant. Joshua could only think of one thing she must desire of him—his departure.

"I will be on my way," he said, checking his pocket watch as if he did not already know the time. "Mr. Newson will be waiting upon me."

Miss Emerson, to his surprise, walked back to his horse alongside him. "I hope that your affairs are readily concluded," she said. "Have you heard that the duke is expected this week?"

"No, I had not."

That was good, as Joshua could consult with him about the men occupying the ruins. It was less good because Miss Emerson was rumored to have a *tendre* for the duke. The last thing Joshua needed at this early date was competition for his suit.

He reminded himself that he had already been declined.

"His mother was quite pleased when she shared the tidings after church yesterday."

Joshua considered Miss Emerson, who looked to be indifferent to this news, which made no sense at all. "I expect she would be," he said with care, then reached for the saddle.

She seemed suddenly agitated. "To be sure, sir, it was very kind of you to bring Mischief and I thank you for that favor."

"We are friendly acquaintances, Miss Emerson," he said, thinking it a timely reminder.

"Yes!" she said, her eyes lighting. "And so I would like to take this opportunity to ask your advice."

If she asked him how to win the duke's attention,

Joshua did not know what he would say. "Of course," he said, resting his hand upon his horse's saddle.

"I know that you have business and would not delay you from important affairs, but I did wonder, sir, just how you did it." She turned an earnest gaze upon him.

"Did it?"

"You said that your father insisted that you abandon your life as a rakehell and by all accounts, you simply did it. You surrendered the pleasures of dancing and gambling and attending parties. I can only imagine that there was excitement in the fighting of duels and satisfaction in shopping without consideration to expense, in horses and carriages and—" she took a breath "—the company of ladies. Did you truly change it all immediately and completely?"

"I did. Not without some yearning to assume my old ways, but the work my father invited me to share with him was more than sufficiently rewarding. I suspect also that it suited me better than a life of revels."

"Truly?"

"There is satisfaction in believing one's efforts to be of merit."

"Oh, I can believe as much. Perhaps that is the key."

"Is there a matter troubling you, Miss Emerson?"

She clasped her hands together and appealed to him. "I endeavor to change my ways, to be less susceptible to temptation and to think before I surrender to impulse." She sighed. "But it is so very hard. I am curious, particularly it seems to forbidden adventures, and even knowing that much could go awry, I still am willing to undertake the risk to know."

"I see." Joshua looked into the distance, keenly aware that she was watching him, her manner expectant and hopeful. In truth, he would have done anything for her, but knew that such a pledge was not what she sought in this moment. "Perhaps you have need of a distraction,

Miss Emerson. I had the task I shared with my father, which was most intriguing and challenging."

She dropped her voice to a delighted whisper. "Were you truly a spy? That is what they say."

Joshua could not halt his smile. He liked that she listened to gossip about him, for it showed a measure of interest. He leaned toward her and whispered in reply. "Not a spy, but one who sought tidings in the messages sent by spies."

"Oh. That would like solving a giant riddle."

"Oftentimes it was."

"But what manner of tidings might you find?"

"A man in a town might send word that a great deal of wine had been delivered to a local address. Another might confide that all the fodder for horses in that town had been quietly acquired. We might assemble a number of such individual indications and thus derive a location where the enemy intended to meet in consultation or even move their forces."

"How very clever!" she said with delight. "But please do not tell me more. I would not jeopardize your confidence."

"The war is over, Miss Emerson."

"But there are always continuing hostilities in one corner of the world or another," she said. "A man of your skills might be needed again and if so, I wager it might be a secret." She frowned and looked away. "I cannot think of a distraction that might occupy me, at least not a suitable one."

Joshua dared to say it. "You might wed. A wife can have many obligations."

She laughed. "But I have foolishly refused the only suitor I had. You see how impulse steers me false?"

Joshua looked at her, unable to believe the encouragement he found in her expression. Had she changed her mind?

Had she guessed that he had been the one to come to her aid?

She smiled a little and reached out a fingertip to his waistcoat, not quite touching it. "What a fine garment, sir, with such delightful needlework."

"I thank you. It is a relic of those days in London, and one I have not worn with sufficient frequency."

"I think it suits you most well," she said, granting him an admiring glance that made him catch his breath. She raised her gaze to his. "Perhaps there are some elements of those days that are worthy of retaining."

"You are correct, of course. There is little to be gained in keeping good garments and boots locked away, for the sake of the memories they provoke."

She sobered then. "I am sorry about the loss of your betrothed."

"As am I, Miss Emerson, and I thank you for your sympathy. It has been many years, though."

"But surely love does not fade so readily as that."

She was watching him closely and Joshua abruptly understood her concern. "Ours was an arranged marriage, Miss Emerson," he said gently. "One settled between our fathers and presented as an ideal solution. It was my duty to wed Miss Havilland and hers to wed me. We would have done as much if she had lived. You must not, however, conclude that my heart was broken forever."

"Oh."

Joshua found himself making an impulsive confession. "In fact, Miss Emerson, Miss Havilland mistook me for my brother. The duel was Gerald's to fight, but he was a poor shot so I took his place as was our habit. She strove to save Gerald, not me. He had claimed her heart and I believe she possessed his."

"You did not know?"

"Not until her demise."

She blinked and looked away, then back at him again, outrage lighting her eyes. "But you would have married her. She would have been your wife, even though she loved your brother."

"Yes."

Her breast heaved with outrage on his behalf. "But that, that is *wicked*, sir. I did not know Miss Havilland, but I dare to suggest, sir, that she did not deserve a husband of your ilk."

Joshua could only blink in his amazement.

Miss Emerson was flushed with indignation and held his gaze boldly, utterly convinced of her view.

And his merit.

Well.

Joshua cleared his throat, halfway thinking that to take encouragement from this sign might jeopardize his prospects of success again. Curiously, he felt the need to take that chance.

Perhaps the lady already influenced his views.

"I wonder, Miss Emerson, if Mrs. Jameson gave you any notion of when your new slippers might be finished? I would expect that you might wish to wear them to Lady Haynesdale's ball on Friday."

"She said anytime after the morrow."

"I find myself summoned by the dowager duchess to confer with her on Wednesday afternoon on some matter," he said.

"Oh. We heard the duke was expected this week."

"Perhaps then I might also have the opportunity to consult with him." Joshua returned to the subject at hand. "I could offer you conveyance to Haynesdale Hollow, Miss Emerson, if that suited your convenience, that you might collect your new slippers. It would be no trouble at all."

Miss Emerson's smile was dazzling in its brilliance and the sight made Joshua's heart leap with satisfaction.

"I should like that very much." She curtsied to him, her eyes brimming with delight. "I thank you for your kindness, sir."

"It will be no trouble at all, Miss Emerson." He bowed to her, accepting her offered hand and kissing its back. Her hand was bare, her skin warm, and he felt her shiver when his lips brushed against the back of her hand. Her fingers tightened ever so slightly on his and he dared to be encouraged anew. He did not realize that his voice dropped low, or even that his eyes had darkened with satisfaction when he glanced upward to meet her gaze. "Indeed, it will be my pleasure to be of service to you." He did hear the lady catch her breath and see her flush.

"Perhaps you might have time to stop for tea on your return home today," she said, her voice breathless, and Joshua was powerless to decline.

HELENA'S CHAMPION was Lord Addersley.

But a week ago, she might have been disappointed to learn that a man she believed to be dull had rescued her with such flair, but now, she saw the error of her conclusions. The viscount had secrets upon secrets, a veritable hidden life. Truly, it would take a lifetime to learn all about him—and when his gaze grew so dark, his manner so intent, Helena could not wait to begin.

Better yet, he had not loved his betrothed. No wonder he had recited the merit of an arranged marriage between virtual strangers—that had been his own circumstance. She could only hope that his words today indicated a significant change in his thinking.

He certainly attributed the change to her, which was more than encouraging.

She spent the day recalling the heady pleasure of his

kisses and imagining a future as his viscountess. Curiously, she was less interested in what might be changed about Addersley Manor than what she might experience on her wedding night—as well as the days and nights beyond that.

Never would she decline an opportunity with such haste again!

The rain had begun by the time he returned that afternoon, a gentle drizzle that made the cottage seem cozy and welcoming. Truly, Helena had never spent such a contented interval in that abode as the hour he sat with them in the parlor. Mischief, exhausted from her antics outside, snored on the hearth and Aunt was fulsome upon the conditions and discipline necessary for the proper care of dogs.

Lord Addersley sat politely and sipped his tea as he gave every appearance of listening, his gaze sliding occasionally to Helena, who was similarly attentive. Their gazes clung more than once, and she delighted in noticing a glimmer of humor in his eyes when Aunt made some outrageous claim. She watched his lips tighten slightly in disagreement and saw him straighten with interest at other comments. The man offered a thousand miniscule clues to his perspective, to one who knew how to look.

Helena delighted in her newfound awareness of him.

She wanted to know all about him.

For some reason, perhaps because the viscount asked Aunt's permission for the excursion to Haynesdale Hollow planned for Wednesday, Aunt saw fit to tell him the tale of her brother and wife's demise. She bemoaned the willfulness of Helena's mother and her brother's second wife, that lady's impulsive inclinations and the curricle accident that had claimed their lives too soon. Helena was embarrassed to have this story shared and kept her gaze fixed upon her tea cup, though she knew full well that the viscount was studying her.

Doubtless Aunt meant to remind him that he and Helena were poorly suited.

He made his excuses and rose to leave immediately after the conclusion of that tale.

Helena walked to the door with him, Mischief awakening to follow her, and wondered what he was thinking.

"So, you are said to resemble your mother," he said when they reached the door.

Helena dared to look up. "In all her shortcomings, it seems."

The viscount was dismissive. "I suspect her merits outweighed any such shortcomings, particularly in your father's view."

Helena met his gaze to find him smiling just a little. "Do you?"

"If your merry nature is as hers, I wager she brought joy to his life. My own father missed my mother so severely, I could wish that he might have encountered another lady who prompted his smile."

"But her folly cost them their lives."

"And perhaps they were complicit in events of that evening." He shrugged. "Perhaps it was not folly or whimsy behind her choice. They attended a celebration, your aunt said, so your father might not have been fit to take the reins himself." He nodded. "A curricle, though, is not the simplest of conveyances to govern, and who can say what might have startled the horses at night in town."

Helena smiled at him, liking the suggestion that her mother might not have been completely at fault. "I thank you, sir. I have always been told that she was feckless and that her nature cost my father his life."

The viscount donned his hat. "Your aunt has her view, of course, but she was not there, Miss Emerson, thus her interpretation may not be true." He met her gaze. "If I may be so bold as to speak plainly, if you resemble her so much, I doubt your father had any regrets in taking her to wife."

Tears pricked at Helena's eyes and her heart swelled. Emboldened by his kindness, she dared to make a most audacious suggestion when he turned to the door. "I believe, sir, that you said you *do* not dance, not that you *cannot* dance."

She thought heard him chuckle when his face was averted but by the time he turned to her, his expression was inscrutable. She had to look into his eyes to see the faintest twinkle, and she felt immediately that they shared a secret.

Ice in his veins. What a preposterous notion! Only someone so foolish as to decline to look at the man could believe as much.

"I wondered when you might raise that topic, Miss Emerson," he said, his tone indulgent. He watched her closely, such heat in his eyes that she felt warm and keenly aware of him. She recalled those kisses, yearned for another, and felt herself flush.

"Perhaps you could only be so absolute in making those changes dictated by your father because you had a welcome distraction in the labor you shared with him."

The viscount, instead of dismissing her suggestion, gave it consideration. "Perhaps." His gaze lingered upon her as he waited for her to continue.

"And in the absence of that distraction, perhaps you might indulge in one of those activities, perhaps the most innocuous of all of them."

He frowned a little, but Helena knew he meant to tease her. "There are those who would insist that dancing is an introduction to pleasure and thus might readily lead one to surrender to more."

Undaunted, she raised her chin to challenge him. "Was your father one of such people?"

"I have no recollection of him doing as much, to be sure." The viscount smiled, and that dimple sent a surge of triumph to Helena's toes. "He always insisted that he derived no pleasure from it, but I have been reminded that my mother loved to dance."

"You suspect, then, that he might have said one thing but done another?"

"I suspect that any pleasure he found in dancing was lost when she could no longer be his partner." He frowned slightly. "There may have been other considerations as well."

Helena hastened to speak, certain she had saddened him with a reminder of his father, so recently passed. "I have to find such a sign of affection to be admirable."

"As do I, Miss Emerson. I think a marriage more likely to be a happy one when there is affection between husband and wife."

"I thought you did not believe in wedding for love."

His gaze slipped away while he considered this. "It is true that I have held that view, though in recent days, I have come to consider the merit of the opposing perspective. Perhaps it is better for a couple to already have a measure of affection for each other before exchanging their vows, rather than simply hoping for the best in committing to a virtual stranger."

"I would think the likelihood of a happy match might be increased."

He chuckled and this time she had the satisfaction of seeing his amusement. Her heart nearly stopped when the dimple reappeared and his eyes glimmered. "I come to share your view, Miss Emerson." He reached for his hat. "I bid you good day."

"One last query, if you please, sir." Helena smiled, her fingertips brushing his sleeve. Her aunt called from the parlor but it was easy to ignore the summons when the viscount looked at her with such avidity. "I wonder, then, if you might indulge in just one dance at Lady Haynesdale's ball. To indulge in one small amusement might make it easier to adhere to the rest of your father's injunctions. It also would do Lady Haynesdale honor as a hostess if you were to make such an exception." She argued the matter too much and she knew it, but Helena desperately wanted to convince him.

"But none to a partner who so tempted me to dance?" he asked, his voice low.

Helena could not imagine how she had thought this man dull. He was alluring beyond all when he spoke to her thus. "Perhaps a little to the lady in question."

He smiled and bent over her hand. "Perhaps more than a little, Miss Emerson." Once again, he kissed her hand and she felt the slight brush of his mouth upon her skin, a most scandalous and wondrous sensation. He bent further to pat Mischief, then pivoted to leave, sparing a glance at the grey skies before he strode to his horse. Helena waited and watched, not truly surprised when he lifted his hand in farewell, his pose precisely that of her champion.

Would he renew his addresses? She could only hope.

Truly, if hoping could change future prospects, any reticence on the viscount's part had no chance against the vigor of Helena's desire.

Wednesday might have been an eternity away.

WHEN HE ARRIVED in Haynesdale Hollow, Joshua asked Mr. Darney to show him the way to Mrs. Lewis' home. When they stood before the plain wooden door, down an alley from the main thoroughfare of Haynesdale Hollow, he spoke. "I would prevail upon you further, Mr. Darney, and request that you remain as my witness for this interview. I will see you compensated for your trouble, of course."

"Your custom at the inn and the occasional favorable word amongst your fellow gentry is all the compensation I require, sir."

"Thank you, Mr. Darney." Joshua raised a fist to knock.

The door was opened promptly as if the occupant was already aware of their arrival. A burly man stood there in his shirtsleeves, his expression forbidding. "Aye?"

"I seek Mrs. Lewis. Is she receiving visitors?"

"Receiving visitors," the man said, sneering as he mimicked Joshua's accent.

"Give us no trouble now, William," Darney said. "This will be to your sister's benefit."

"Benefit," the man, evidently named William, muttered, then turned to shout. "Alice! There's a *gentleman* here to speak with you."

Joshua ignored his tone. The woman he had seen the week before appeared from a shadowed doorway, wiping her hands. Her gaze darted between the men with some concern. "What is it?" she asked as if she feared dreadful tidings.

"I have come about your son," Joshua said. "Francis, who I met the other day. He is the son of my brother, Gerald, is he not?"

She lifted her chin. "He is."

"Not as he ever cared about the boy," William muttered. He retreated but did not leave the room, which was almost barren. He folded his arms across his chest and listened, his expression suspicious.

"Then he has Hargood blood," Joshua said, removing the document from his jacket.

"Hargood blood," William sneered. "Francis is your brother's get and no fancy talk will change that fact."

"I can see that he is my brother's son," Joshua replied. "And I have come to address that fact."

"You cannot take him from me!" Mrs. Lewis protested.

"I have no such intention."

"You all hated Gerald. Your father sent him away. Gerald said he would come back. He said he would marry me."

"Perhaps that was his intention, but my brother will not return home again. I apologize if you were not informed that he died at Waterloo."

"He never did," she said darkly but Joshua could not begin to undermine her skepticism.

"As Francis is my nephew," he continued, "I would see him educated, as befits a member of my family. I see several options."

"You cannot take him from me," Mrs. Lewis repeated.

"I would not do as much. I could, however, offer you a post at Addersley Manor, Mrs. Lewis. I cannot guarantee your acceptance among the staff, though it is possible that your fondness for my brother will find you some alliances. It is equally possible that some of my household will disapprove of you bearing a child out of wedlock, even Gerald's child."

"She cannot leave Haynesdale Hollow," her brother protested.

Mrs. Lewis lifted her chin. "I will only live at Addersley Manor as its mistress."

Joshua blinked in his surprise. He was not about to wed this woman over Gerald's affair. "That is out of the question, Mrs. Lewis. If you are disinclined to accept a post, that is your choice. I have arranged for an annuity that will pay you regular dividends." He presented the document but William snatched it from his hand.

"She cannot read," he said roughly, then opened it to read the details. "It is not sufficient!"

"It is more than I am obligated to provide," Joshua said, recalling Mr. Newson's warning all too well.

"You will have your nephew live like a pauper?"

"He will eat and have shelter, if those funds are managed well, and I am prepared to pay for his apprenticeship, should he choose to learn a trade."

"A trade?" Mrs. Lewis said. "He will be a viscount's son!"

"Best teach him how to dance," William said with a guffaw.

Joshua exchanged a glance with Darney. "I thank you for your presence and your patience in this matter," he said and Darney nodded.

"I have heard the boy say that he would like to become a blacksmith," the innkeeper said.

"He will be one of the gentry!" Mrs. Lewis insisted, and it was clear to Joshua that the unlikely prospect had seized her thoughts to the exclusion of all others.

He could only continue as if he conversed with sensible people. "If he makes such a choice and the tradesman in question is prepared to take him on, then you have only to send word to me or to Mr. Newson in the village to arrange the details."

"You should give Alice the money now."

"And you will take it from me," Darney said. "I can collect it from you in my public room."

"Alice owes me!" William insisted. "Who else has seen to her welfare and shelter? Not her fine man, that is for certain. The gentry care only for their own comforts, and not for the results of their deeds."

Darney clicked his tongue. "I would not be so quick

to complain, William, when you have a newfound annuity in your hands."

"It is not enough," that man repeated stubbornly.

Mrs. Lewis cupped a hand over her belly. "What of the next one?" she asked. "He will arrive by September."

"You cannot expect me to provide for all your bastards, Mrs. Lewis."

"This one is your brother's get, too," she said, her eyes a little wild. "I will see provision for the second, as well."

"That cannot be so, Mrs. Lewis," Joshua said. "My brother is dead."

"I will tell everyone that the child is yours!" she threatened, shaking a fist at him. "I will be a viscountess and my children will be raised as gentry, as is right and proper."

"I regret, Mrs. Lewis, that other obligations do not allow me to linger. I wish you a good day." Joshua tipped his hat and turned to leave.

"Ice in his veins," William muttered. "'Tis what they say of him and 'tis all true."

"On the contrary, William," Darney said from the threshold. "The gentleman has set a matter to rights by his own volition, with no obligation to do as much. You should thank his lordship."

"Thank him? For a miserable annuity instead of Alice's due!"

Joshua strode out of the house, having no interest in continuing such a futile discussion. The woman was mad, thinking he would wed her, or that she could extort the care and feeding of a stranger's child from him. He tugged at his gloves, more than a little annoyed by the exchange.

"I shall ensure that everyone remembered you have been gone from Nottingham for the better part of a decade, sir, and only returned two months ago. Whoever the father of that child, it cannot be you."

"I thank you, Darney, for your consideration. I recall that your wife is a good cook. Perhaps I might enjoy an early supper at the inn before riding home."

The innkeeper beamed. "It would be my pleasure, sir, to be sure."

The pair proceeded back to the main thoroughfare, Joshua noting that his boots would have to be cleaned again.

"Sir!" someone called from behind him but he did not turn. "Lord Addersley?"

Joshua glanced back to find the boy Francis hastening after him, his eyes alight. "Is it true, sir? Did you say I could be apprenticed to learn a trade?"

"I did indeed, Francis. If you find a tradesman willing to have you as his apprentice, you have only to speak to Mr. Newson. If all parties are agreeable, we shall see it arranged."

"Oh, sir! I should like more than anything to be a blacksmith."

"Then you must present yourself as a willing candidate to that man, and perhaps work for him for a while to earn his agreement. Mr. Darney can assist you in your address to Mr. Newson, if necessary."

"Thank you, sir!" the boy bowed low before him. "I will watch your horse whenever you come to town, sir. You have only to call me."

"Thank you, Francis."

The boy bowed again, then darted down the street, doubtless headed for the smithy without delay. No matter how awkward the exchange, Joshua knew he had done the right thing, and he believed that Francis would make the most of his newfound opportunity.

The boy also could not be blamed for the nature of his relations, but with this small advantage, he might well escape their influence, which could only be an improvement.

"He is a good lad," Darney said quietly. "Your suggestion is both generous and sensible, sir."

"The boy's conception is not his fault. He should have the opportunity to make something of himself."

"Ah, since he is not to be a viscount," Darney rolled his eyes as he laughed. "Ah well, he will not be the first to have compromised his mother's aspirations." He chuckled and Joshua smiled a little, glad to have the task behind him. "There is beef stew today, sir, and a plum tart. I must say, my Louisa makes a plum tart beyond all others."

"That sounds most excellent, Darney. I look forward to the meal." He would pause to speak to Mr. Newson before returning home.

Then he had the promise of a rendezvous with Miss Emerson at the folly to consume his thoughts. He had no doubt that she would venture there, and the morrow promised to be fine. He looked forward to having all confusion between them cleared, and could only hope to end the encounter with a kiss.

That possibility put a spring in Joshua's step as little else could have done.

*H*is cloak was gone.

Joshua could not believe it, but the garment had vanished as surely as if it had never been. He became vexed as he sought it. Reed had no notion of what had happened to it, and had not taken it for mending or cleaning. It was not within his wardrobe or even in the trunk of garments from London.

The thief who had invaded his home repeatedly had changed tactics, in a most incomprehensible way.

Who would steal a cloak?

It was a very good cloak, but hardly worth taking the risk of such an intrusion.

Because of the hunt, Joshua was late leaving for the folly. He had no doubt that Miss Emerson would be there, awaiting him. She would never have resisted the temptation of such an assignation, especially now that she had guessed the truth of his ruse. He would ride there, apologize to her for the deception, and ensure that all was clear between them.

He hoped for a kiss or another sign of encouragement.

He had not yet decided whether to ask for her hand again before or after Lady Haynesdale's ball. If the night was fine, Miss Emerson might find favor in a moonlight proposal.

He wore his usual coat and hat, tugging on his gloves as he strode toward the stables. Specter was saddled and waiting. Joshua halfway thought the stallion was disappointed that he had ridden Zephyr on his night ventures, for on this day, the horse was even more responsive than was his custom. He barely needed any encouragement to canter from the yard, then was urged to a gallop with ease.

The stallion was not the only one impatient to reach the folly.

~

TUESDAY DAWNED SUNNY AND CLEAR, a day filled with promise to Helena's view. She would go to the folly, as planned, and meet her champion—the viscount. Her ankle was sufficiently recovered, but she wore her sturdy boots, just to be sure. She would be *sensible*. She took Mischief with her, thinking the run would be good for the pup.

Mischief raced ahead of her across the meadow. Once on the path through the forest, Helena called the dog closer, not wanting to lose her. The pavilion's roof gleamed in the sunlight and, even better, a man leaned against it, arms folded across his chest.

Waiting.

Helena stopped on the path, fighting her sense that something was amiss. The man wore the familiar cloak and his hood was raised. She did not like that she could not see his face. Where was his horse? Why did she feel imperiled?

"Good morning," she said, as if naught was amiss between them. She did not move forward, though.

He inclined his head but did not speak, moving

away from the wall with a fluid grace that seemed almost predatory. "Have you come to surrender to me?" he asked gruffly and Helena was astonished that he should be so forthright.

"I hoped to speak with you, to be sure," she said, her wariness growing.

He laughed and it was a harsh sound. "We can talk later." He stepped toward her quickly. "I would ask for a kiss first." He reached for her arm in a sudden gesture. Helena retreated a step, and Mischief growled.

The dog placed herself between them. Her ears were back and the hair rose on the back of her neck. She bristled as she growled at the man.

But Mischief liked Lord Addersley.

Who stood before Helena? She thought of the men at the ruins, and her own suspicion that Lord Addersley's brother might yet be alive.

"I will share no kiss with a man who hides his face," she said, speaking as if she were more confident than she was.

"You will share with me what you have offered freely to others," he snarled and lunged toward her. Mischief jumped and snapped at him, prompting him to swear and recoil. He kicked at the dog and Helena cried out, but Mischief evaded his boot. The dog leapt after him, snarling and he retreated so quickly that his hood fell back.

He was not Lord Addersley, though there was a strong resemblance between them. He had a cleft in his chin and the same coloring. He was of a height and breadth with the viscount, but seemed much rougher and less fastidiously groomed. More, he seemed to be worn or even ravaged by some ordeal. He was lean, if not gaunt, and the wild fury in his eyes made Helena shiver. She knew instinctively that he was unpredictable and untrustworthy.

And she was alone, save for Mischief.

"Call off your dog!" he shouted and pulled a knife from his belt. "Or I will kill it!" He might have been a madman, given the wildness in his eyes, and she did not doubt he would fulfill his threat.

"Come, Mischief, come!" she cried and the dog came to her, still growling. Helena did not delay but pivoted to run from the pavilion and the glade, calling the dog. Mischief raced beside her, needing little encouragement to leave the man behind.

There were no pursuing footsteps. Relief flooded through Helena and she looked back from the shelter of the forest. She could not see the man at all. The pavilion appeared to be abandoned, the glade as peaceful as before, but still, she did not trust him. Her heart was racing and Mischief was fast by her side. The dog's ears were up and her posture alert.

They hastened together along the path.

How could he have known that she had offered kisses to Lord Addersley? He must have been watching them, on one night or the other. Helena shivered.

But how had he obtained Lord Addersley's cloak?

At the edge of the forest, Helena turned toward Addersley Manor instead of Bramble Cottage, determined to share what she had learned with the viscount.

To her relief, a large horse was galloping toward her, the viscount himself in the saddle.

Her champion arrived!

~

To Joshua's surprise, Miss Emerson was running down the road toward him, Mischief at her heels. Her bonnet had slipped askew and she ran with complete disregard for her skirts. It was clear she was in some distress, though he could not imagine the cause. He reined in the horse and swung from the saddle in time to catch her in his embrace.

"He was there!" she said against his chest, but Joshua could make no sense of her claim.

"Who? I expected you to be at the folly."

"I was, but he was there before me." She spoke in spurts, panting as she caught her breath. "Waiting, with his hood drawn up. But something was wrong, I knew it immediately." She lifted her face, her gaze burning. "He vowed he would hurt Mischief when she growled at him. He had a knife!"

Joshua took her shoulders in his hands and held her gaze. "Who?"

"I cannot be certain but I think he must be your brother. He favors you." She stretched a gloved fingertip to the cleft in his chin as Joshua's heart sank. "But looks less reliable." She shivered. "Indeed, there is a desperation about him that is most frightening."

Gerald. Alive!

It defied belief, but who else could the man be?

Joshua looked toward the grove of trees, but of course, there was no sign of her attacker. That man, whether he was Gerald or not, would be hidden by the foliage if he lingered by the folly.

"Are you disappointed that he lives?" Miss Emerson asked softly.

Joshua was startled by the question. "I am not certain that he does, as yet, but if he does, of course I am not disappointed. He is my brother, and I have mourned his loss."

She smiled, pleased with his reply.

Joshua shook his head. "But I cannot understand his choice. To hide in the forest makes no sense. Why not write to me or to my father? Why not come to Addersley Manor? For that reason alone, I doubt that he is

Gerald. My brother must know that he would be welcomed at his own home."

Miss Emerson wrinkled her nose. "Does he?" she asked to Joshua's surprise. "Your father sent him away, remember." She leaned closer. "Perhaps he *did* write to your father but was rebuffed."

Joshua stared at her in shock. He could not countenance that. His father had been so devastated by the loss of Gerald. He would have welcomed the return of his son on any terms.

He was struck then by a sudden thought. Had Mrs. Lewis welcomed Gerald?

That might explain the child she expected. If Gerald had returned to Nottingham before Christmas…all suddenly made a treacherous sense.

Joshua felt that details changed with undue haste. He was aware that Miss Emerson awaited his decision. "What did this man say to you?"

Her lips tightened. "That he would have from me what I gave willingly to others. He must have seen us… together." Her words gave Joshua a chill and she shivered again. "He must have been *watching*." Her view of that was clear, and it was a perspective Joshua shared.

"Did you see where he went?"

She shook her head. "I ran, and when I looked back, he had vanished."

"Did he have a horse?"

Miss Emerson considered this for a moment before she shook her head again. "I do not think so. I did not see or hear one."

Joshua looked again toward the folly, hidden behind the trees. The man, whether it was Gerald or not, could not have gone far on foot. He could not pursue him and leave Miss Emerson undefended, especially given that she had been threatened. Praise be that he had ridden Specter on this day.

"Can you ride, Miss Emerson?"

"Of course. Nicholas taught me years ago, but I did wear breeches for the lessons." She rolled her eyes. "Much to Aunt's disapproval." She smiled at him. "I can ride with assurance, sir."

"Excellent." Joshua fitted his hands around her waist and lifted her to the saddle. "You must return to the safety of Bramble Cottage," he instructed, relieved when she nodded understanding. Specter exhaled mightily but held his ground. Mischief had the sense to refrain from barking as she circled the horse, striving to reach her mistress. "And you will not leave the cottage alone until this is resolved."

"I will not," she promised to his relief.

She must have been frightened.

And that was all the encouragement Joshua needed to slap Specter's rump, encouraging the horse to run, and step back. If there was one thing he had learned, it was that ladies could not be safe when men fought each other.

He would have said anything to ensure Miss Emerson's departure, but was relieved it had not been necessary. Perhaps her reputation for having little sense was undeserved.

He straightened his cravat and began to march along the path toward the folly. In moments, he would know whether Gerald lived or not. In his heart, he hoped it was Gerald.

No matter what his brother had done since last they had met.

HELENA LOOKED BACK at the viscount, noting how he strode with purpose toward the forest and the folly. He looked so bold and confident, precisely as she had imagined him that first day, charging into peril with no regard for his own safety. He would do what was right and vanquish the villain single-handedly, showing a valor that few other men possessed…

Her heart stopped cold. If the desperate villain with the knife was Gerald, the risk to the viscount might be greater than he realized.

And if Gerald dispatched his older brother, *he* would become viscount.

Had this been his plan? Had he set a trap for Lord Addersley? Had she unwittingly aided his plan? Helena could not bear the prospect. She turned the horse and urged him to a canter in pursuit of Lord Addersley. She had to warn him!

She cursed her skirts even as they made good progress, for her perch was more precarious than she might prefer. In breeches, she could have galloped the horse and reached the viscount more quickly. He had already vanished into the forest on the shadowed path, and she leaned over the horse's neck as she touched her heel to his side. She hung on as the horse approached a gallop, then Lord Addersley came into view.

He spun to face her, but his expression was not relieved.

No, it was thunderous. Never had his emotions been so clearly displayed, but Helena could not admire the change.

"Miss Emerson!" he said, his tone moderate but the words bitten off with precision. He raised a hand and the horse slowed in obedience, even as he marched toward her. His eyes were flashing with fury and his lips drawn to a thin line as he seized the reins. "I sent you home," he reminded her.

"I had to warn you, sir…"

"You were obliged to do no such thing, Miss Emerson. You gave me your promise that you would return to Bramble Cottage and remain there in safety, and you did as much not five minutes ago."

"I did, but…"

"There is no negotiation in this matter, Miss Emerson. Turn the horse. Now."

Helena turned the horse as instructed. "I simply wanted to ensure that you understood the danger," she began again.

"Either I confront a desperate villain alone, or I meet my brother again," the viscount said crisply. "I am well aware of the nuances of peril in either situation, while you, Miss Emerson, persist in showing a decided lack of good sense."

"He might kill you!"

"The possibility, while less than desirable, is not out of the question."

He knew. He knew the danger before himself, and he proceeded anyway. Helena stared at him, in awe of his bravery. He was just as she had imagined him that first day, a man who could not be halted from doing what he believed to be right. Her admiration of him was nigh overwhelming.

"I do not think you should be alone," she dared to say, wanting to witness his triumph.

"And there our perspectives diverge," he replied and his voice hardened yet more. "Again. Truly, Miss Emerson, I can only be relieved that you showed the foresight to refuse me, for you were right." Helena gasped but he continued. "We are not remotely suited to each other. I could never pledge myself to a woman so utterly determined to proceed foolishly in every situation."

"Oh!" Helena was astonished by his severity and by his censure.

His expression was relentless, though, his gaze dark and angry. He lifted one hand and pointed toward

Bramble Cottage, an imperative she had been persuaded to follow. "Go home, Miss Emerson. Immediately."

Helena lifted her chin. "If you are left dead at the folly, I shall find another way to fetch my slippers."

"I am most relieved to hear as much," he said, averting his face before she could be certain whether she had heard a thread of amusement in his tone.

He granted her another solemn look, one that hinted at a disdain for her that nigh broke Helena's heart in two. She whistled to the dog as she turned away, then urged the horse to a canter. She never looked back, though she felt the weight of the viscount's gaze upon her.

He probably did not trust her to do as she had said she would.

He probably did not believe she would keep her promise.

She would prove him wrong, though Helena was not in the least bit certain that he would even know.

The viscount no longer admired her. He no longer believed they were suited—and he changed his thinking in the precise moment that Helena realized the magnitude of her error in refusing him.

She was a fool, to be sure, though she did not know the cure for that malady.

❧

JOSHUA WOULD HAVE SAID anything to see Miss Emerson out of danger.

He would have insulted her even more brutally, if need be, to ensure that she had no chance of being injured in whatever battle he entered. He watched until she was out of view, not entirely trusting her to follow his bidding.

It had been a tragedy to lose Miss Havilland. To see Miss Emerson injured as a result of his deeds, or worse, was a possibility that sickened Joshua. He would never recover from his guilt over such an error—and that was independent of who the lady in question chose to wed.

He might have been a forlorn suitor in a romantic tale, one with no hope of gaining the admiration of the lady in question but destined to serve her willingly for all his days and nights.

Perhaps he was the fool.

When the sound of Specter's hoofbeats had faded, he pivoted and continued into the forest. Sufficient time had passed that the villain could be safely away, even on foot, but Joshua saw him as soon as the clearing came into view. He stood, leaning against the folly, the insouciance in his stance so very familiar. He wore Joshua's cloak, cast over one shoulder and the hood back. Joshua studied him as he approached, his footsteps as unwavering as the other man's gaze. Gerald. It was Gerald. His hair was longer; his features were more haggard; there was a bitterness in his smile and a hardness in his eyes that Joshua did not recall. He was more wiry than he had been and dirtier than once he would have preferred. His garments were worn and his boots were dull.

Joshua stopped when half a dozen steps remained between them. "It is you," he said, hearing his own relief.

"And you are not surprised," Gerald replied. "How did you guess?"

"I did not."

"Ah, did she do the guessing?"

"She saw the resemblance between us, yes." Joshua shook his head. Something was amiss. He could feel the animosity coming from his younger brother but could not explain it. "We had a letter that you were killed at Waterloo."

Gerald lifted his hands and stepped closer. "And yet, here I am."

"Why did you not write? Father and I would have been glad of such happy tidings."

Gerald's eyes narrowed. "Are you so certain of that?"

"Of course!" Even as he said the words, Joshua wondered.

"Are you truly so trusting, Joshua? Did you believe everything he told you?" Gerald began to stroll around Joshua, menace in every step. "Do you not think I tired of hearing how you were the favored one, how you were the better to assume the title, how relieved Father was that I had not been born first?"

"The praise I heard was all for you, your skill at dancing, your charm and easy manner."

Gerald laughed. "Perhaps he secretly despised both of us."

"I do not think so."

"Perhaps he blamed Mother for only bearing two sons, both so very unsuitable."

"Gerald! You cannot speak thus of the dead…"

"And how did he speak of me?" Gerald asked abruptly. His eyes were bright, his very manner unpredictable, and Joshua realized the peril of his situation. He had trusted that his brother would not do him injury, but in this moment, he was not so certain.

"He did not," Joshua had to admit.

"Never?"

"Never. He told me only that he had bought your commission and that you were gone." Joshua held his brother's gaze. "I never knew why you were dispatched, and still I do not. We never had the opportunity to say farewell, and I regretted that."

Gerald scoffed at that. "After what happened with

Charlotte? I cannot believe even you to be so bloodless as that, Joshua."

"She died by her own error," Joshua said carefully.

"She died because she loved me. She died because I courted her and I won her heart, because I wanted her for myself. No one would arrange such a match for me, the younger son, and I wanted what you were given so readily."

"You should have told me that you loved Miss Havilland."

"But I did not. She was yours, so I took her and made her mine. It was that simple."

"Gerald!"

His brother pointed toward Bramble Cottage. "Just as that one is yours, so I will take her and make her mine."

"Miss Emerson has declined my proposal."

"But you want her, and she wants you. I'm not going to let there be a happy ending for you, Joshua."

"You will not threaten Miss Emerson in my presence."

"Threaten her? I will take her, Joshua. I will have her beneath me, and I will claim her maidenhead, whether she is willing or nay, and I—"

Gerald never finished his threat, for Joshua decked him. Surprise was on his side, and Gerald fell backward, blood spurting from his nose. He looked from the blood on his hand to Joshua, his astonishment clear.

"I advised you to refrain from threatening Miss Emerson," Joshua said. He might have turned his back on the brother he once had known, but he saw the flash of anger in this man's eyes and retreated a step instead. Gerald flung himself at Joshua, and Joshua saw the flash of the knife.

A little too late he understood why Mrs. Lewis had been so convinced that she would be a viscountess, and

Francis would inherit the title: Gerald meant to kill Joshua.

They grappled together, fighting as they had as boys, but the stakes were higher and the struggle was fierce. This time, Joshua fought for his life.

He had always won when they fought, and he hoped his good fortune held.

~

THE VISCOUNT DID NOT COME.

Helena sat outside with Mischief, waiting for his appearance, her agitation rising with every passing hour. It was evening when Hoskins came for the horse, though he spoke only briefly to Nixon and brought no tidings from Addersley Manor.

Helena could not contain her anxiety. She paced so that Aunt sent her to bed for the sake of silence. She was restless in her room, so concerned that Mischief watched her avidly. She knew she would never sleep without knowing whatever had happened in the forest, but there was no way to discover the truth.

Did the viscount truly believe they were so ill suited? Helena had believed him in the moment, but as the hours passed, she wondered if he had simply wanted to ensure that she left him alone. Had he been protecting her, as he had done before? Or had he truly been dismissing her forever?

She hated the uncertainty of that as much as her ignorance of his fate.

The hair prickled on the back of her neck after midnight and she knew something would happen. She heard the hoofbeats and her heart lunged to her throat. Her candle was still lit—despite many admonitions to extinguish it—and she went to the window, fearful of what she might see.

A lone rider appeared, his silhouette as familiar as the horse and his cloak. He lifted a hand, beckoning to her, but something was amiss. Helena stared at him, unable to name what detail ensured that she was filled with dread, but she would not answer his summons.

She doused the candle with a deliberate gesture, plunging the room into darkness. He stared toward the cottage for long moments, then gave the horse his heels and raced toward the ruins of the old keep.

He was not the viscount. Helena was certain of it.

What had happened at the folly?

More importantly, what had happened to the viscount?

~

JOSHUA ACHED.

His eye was blackened and his ribs were bruised. Gerald had the worse end of the pummeling, and had fled after his knife had been seized by Joshua and cast into the pond. Joshua had retrieved it after his brother's flight and knew he should not have been surprised that it was a weapon from his father's collection in the library.

He walked home, feeling every rising bruise, and sent Hoskins to retrieve Specter from Bramble Cottage. He did not specifically forbid the sharing of any tidings, but simply did not think of sending word of his survival until the ostler was gone.

The knife made him realize that Gerald might be the thief taking items from Addersley Manor. His brother would be aweare which items were of value and also the ones whose disappearance was less likely to be noticed. His thefts could be executed quickly and effectively.

And Gerald knew ways into the house. He had always been able to lift the latch on the library doors from the outside, a trick that Joshua had never mastered. A consultation with the horrified Fairfax had ensured that all would be secured that night.

Joshua retired early, partaking only of a hearty broth and a hot bath. He would hope that the duke might have arrived on the morrow so he could consult with that man about Gerald.

He had bidden Hoskins to ensure with a quiet word that the man employed at Bramble Cottage secured that house. He did not retire until Reed brought him word of Hoskins' safe return.

Knowing that Miss Emerson was safe – for the moment – was all he needed to be able to sleep.

HELENA HEARD the pony cart arrive at Bramble Cottage early the next morning, and hurried to finish dressing and hasten downstairs. She could only guess that it was a delivery from town, and hoped there might be news of the viscount.

She found Aunt at breakfast, the door to the kitchen more ajar than was typical and Aunt herself in the seat closest to the door. It was not her customary place, and she waved Helena to silence as soon as she entered the room. Helena slipped into a place at the table and poured herself a cup of tea, glad that the voices carried readily from the kitchen.

Nixon was speaking to someone, a woman who Helena did not know. Evidently she and Nixon were familiar acquaintances.

"Butcher and his wife," Aunt mouthed and Helena nodded.

She had to guess that the wife had accompanied her

husband on his deliveries because of the tidings that might be shared. She was soon proven right.

"A blackened eye, I tell you, and bruises all over himself, as what I hear," confided the butcher's wife. "They say his valet had to carry him to bed and that he may never be the same again. Such a fight it must have been!"

Surely she could not mean Lord Addersley? Helena's heart rose to her throat at these tidings.

"But the viscount yet lives?" Nixon asked.

"He does." The butcher's wife might have been disappointed.

"One must wonder at the state of his opponent," Nixon said.

"Indeed! They say he confronted the thief who has been stealing from Addersley Manor."

"Oh, a desperate villain!"

Had Gerald been stealing from the house? Helena wished she could ask the viscount for more detail. And who had appeared in the fields the night before? The horse and cloak, she was certain, had been the same. According to this tale, the viscount had been too injured to ride out. How would Gerald have gotten the horse?

He might be a thief through and through.

"And one yet at large," the butcher's wife said. "You should see your doors locked at night."

"We will. The ostler from Addersley Manor brought us a warning, but with less detail."

"These are sorry times. Roger says there will be a duel yet, on the green of Addersley village."

"A duel!" Mrs. Nixon breathed in horror.

"People forget what a dissolute life the viscount lived in London a decade ago, but I remember well enough. The old viscount was most unhappy with his sons, though more disappointed in his heir. He expected better of the boy than gambling, dueling and whoring."

"Indeed. Any father would."

"And even in this matter, I say the viscount should have shown greater care for his responsibilities. Why would he confront a villain alone, let alone so far from the house and any assistance? There is the rash choice of a foolhardy man and matters might have ended even more poorly. With the old viscount dead and buried, and his lordship's younger brother dead at Waterloo, there is no one to assume the title."

"He should have married by now," Nixon said. "There should be children already."

"Indeed. He neglects his duties." The butcher's wife's voice dropped low. "I heard he offered for your mistress's niece but she declined him."

Helena's cheeks burned.

"That she did," Nixon acknowledged. "I learned of it upon my arrival. Though I might have found fault with that choice mere days ago, these tidings convince me that the girl was fortunate in her decision."

"I should say as much, for only now do we hear the tale of the viscount's mistress."

Mistress! Helena gripped the handle of her tea cup, certain it could not be true.

"Mistress!" Nixon echoed in horror.

"*Mistress?*" Aunt mouthed in outrage, glared at Helena as if the fault were hers, then leaned closer to the open door.

"Mistress. There can be no mistake." The butcher's wife continued in a scandalized whisper, one that was still easy to hear from the other room. "Her name is Mrs. Lewis," she said with the satisfaction of one with a juicy tale to share. "She lives in Haynesdale Hollow with her brother and son."

"Son?" Nixon asked.

"Son," the butcher's wife affirmed. "A boy of nine summers who is the very image of the viscount at that age, by all accounts—and worse, the viscount purchased an annuity for Mrs. Lewis just this past week. I had it from she who cleans Mr. Newson's house on Mondays, so it is true. Was there ever a more sure sign of guilt?"

Helena could not even look at Aunt, so great was her dismay.

"An annuity does indicate an…interest in that lady's fortunes."

"More than that," the butcher's wife said. "He pledged to pay for an apprenticeship for the boy, and this against the advice of Mr. Newson. He is open-handed, to be sure."

"To take responsibility for both mother and boy does indicate he had a part in the boy's conception."

The butcher's wife laughed. "A part? Goodness, Mildred, Mrs. Lewis is with child again. The alliance continues to this very day. Evidently the second child's conception has tempted him to acknowledge the truth."

Aunt turned to Helena in dismay. Helena straightened with fury. How dare the viscount propose to her when he already had a mistress and a son—and perhaps another son to arrive soon? How dare he so deceive her?

How dare he be so much like Mr. Melbourne, a man concerned only with his own advantage—and one who had managed to fool her all the same.

"I hear that Mrs. Lewis is telling all that she will be a viscountess soon, and that her son has no need of an apprenticeship for he will be viscount himself."

"No!"

"Yes!"

He would marry his mistress? Helena was appalled.

It was true that those who eavesdropped seldom heard anything to their advantage.

She rose from the table and left the room, Mischief at her heels, unable to believe she had so misjudged Lord Addersley.

It was an unfortunate moment to realize how securely that man had captured her admiration.

Perhaps his declaration of her unsuitability the day before had been the truth of his estimation.

Perhaps he would not even keep their appointment on this day.

Perhaps it was for the best if Helena forgot Viscount Addersley completely. She threw the ball for Mischief, unable to summon any interest in the duke's pending return even so.

Why did men have to be so very vexing?

CHAPTER 12

*J*oshua had no notion what to expect from Miss Emerson, though he doubted he would receive much of a welcome. He owed her an apology for his dismissal of the day before, though he hoped she would understand that he had needed to ensure her safety at any cost. He hoped she did not find his blackened eye offensive. It remained slightly swollen and had turned a glorious shade of purple.

He dressed with care in a navy coat and buff trousers, his best black boots and a perfectly tied cravat. He had a notion of how to regain the lady's favor so had Molly harnessed to the gig, then spent the entire drive to Bramble Cottage trying to compose his apology.

To his relief, she was in the garden outside the cottage and alone except for Mischief. She was not dressed for a journey to town, which was a disappointing sign. It was the way she lifted her head to glance toward him, her outrage so clear in her posture that Joshua feared he might not be able to regain her approval.

"Miss Emerson," he said as he alighted from the gig. He secured Molly's reins and gave her a pat. Mischief came running to him, her tail wagging so hard that she almost stumbled.

Miss Emerson held her ground and eyed him, her expression unwelcoming.

If anything, she was even more beautiful when her eyes flashed with fury. Her lips were set and she held herself tall, like a warrior intending to strike him dead. Her gaze lingered upon his blackened eye for a moment, but she did not speak of it.

He bowed, feeling a measure of stiffness that he could not entirely hide.

"You are injured," she said, her words clipped.

"I fear I am, but not severely. We fought but he escaped."

She stared at him, her features seemingly carved in stone. "Thank you for delivering such tidings. Good day, sir." She began to turn away.

"I do owe you an apology, Miss Emerson, for my comments of yesterday afternoon."

She glanced over her shoulder at him, her expression icy. "Surely the fact that you could never pledge yourself to a woman so utterly determined to proceed foolishly in every situation has not changed."

"I spoke harshly, I admit, but it was imperative that you return home and with speed. I had to ensure your safety, Miss Emerson, and you were disinclined to take my counsel."

"I think there is more to the matter than that, sir."

"Indeed?" Joshua was puzzled.

"And her name is Mrs. Lewis." She fairly spat the last two words.

She was angrier than he had ever seen her, and Joshua could make little sense of her reaction.

"What do you know of Mrs. Lewis?"

"That you have bought an annuity for her and her son, that her son resembles you greatly and that she is expecting another." Her eyes flashed. "That you should have a mistress and hide this detail from me, even when you made an offer for my hand, is outrageous beyond every expectation. That you concealed the fact of a son is even more appalling..."

"She is Gerald's mistress," Joshua said softly. "I encountered her for the first time last week, and recognized that her son had to be Gerald's son, as well."

Miss Emerson fell silent, an encouraging sign.

Indeed, her very anger was encouraging, for he had thought her indifferent to him and any details of his life.

He offered his hand. "Will you walk around the garden with me while I explain?"

She hesitated the barest moment before taking his arm.

Joshua led her away from the house, choosing where best to begin. "If you recall, a week ago, I believed my brother to be dead." She nodded. "When I encountered Mrs. Lewis and her son, and recognized the connection, I also saw that her circumstances were less than affluent. I believed it fitting to provide for my nephew and spoke to my estate manager, Mr. Newson, about it."

Miss Emerson bowed her head, watching the ground before herself as they walked, hiding her reactions from Joshua. He took encouragement from the fact that she listened at all.

"Mr. Newson confided that Gerald and my father had argued about the lady. Gerald had been determined to wed her, and my father had disapproved. Though Newson was disinclined to share all the details, by dint of a pledge of confidence made to my father, I can only conclude that this relationship, deemed unsuitable by my father, was the reason my father bought Gerald's commission. I do not think my father knew about the child."

Miss Emerson looked up at this.

"There can be no denying it," Joshua said. "He is so like Gerald at that age. And I could not in good conscience allow Gerald's son to grow up in poverty. I arranged for the annuity, over the objections of Mr. Newson, and when I learned the boy—Francis is his name—had an ambition to become a smith, I offered to pay for his apprenticeship if the smith was willing to take him on. He cannot be responsible for his parentage, but I can give him an opportunity to create a respectable life for himself."

"You did not have to do as much," Miss Emerson breathed, admiration in her tone.

"I believe I did, for it was right, but Mr. Newson is inclined to share your view."

"Oh," she said softly and he dared to smile at her. She smiled in return and flushed in the most becoming way. Her eyes were sparkling now. "I thought she was your mistress and he was your son."

"No," Joshua said flatly. "Ten years ago, I was betrothed, and afterward I mourned Miss Havilland's loss. I have no mistress and no by-blows." He leaned a little closer to her and spoke sternly. "I would have confessed to them before making an offer of marriage, Miss Emerson, as any man of honor would have done."

"Yes," she said with evident relief. "You would have. I am sorry that I believed idle gossip."

"I am sorry that I spoke harshly to you yesterday."

She flushed again. "I understand, for I did not heed your advice." She raised her gaze to his. "I was afraid for you."

Joshua could not find fault with that explanation. "And I appreciate your concern." Their gazes clung in a most satisfying way. Truly, Joshua might have wished for Gerald's return and intervention earlier, even to the point of the bruises he had sustained, had he guessed that his brother would lend such speed to Joshua's suit.

Miss Emerson averted her gaze, and was clearly puzzling through some detail. "Is this Mrs. Lewis why your father sent your brother away?"

"Possibly. There is a tale that they argued about my brother's inclination to wed the lady. Of course, I had no notion of his survival when I arranged for the annuity."

"You simply acted as you believed was right," she said with undisguised approval.

"Indeed."

"Do you think he might have taken refuge with her?"

"It is possible," Joshua acknowledged. "The duke may have suggestions. He must know those in Haynesdale Hollow far better than I do."

"But it is a long way from Addersley Manor to Haynesdale Hollow without a horse."

"The road is the longer route, Miss Emerson. It runs south to Bramble Cottage, east to Southpoint, then north to Haynesdale. When we were boys, we ran to the east to reach Haynesdale Hollow much more quickly. The route is uneven, though we did not mind the brambles or the creek in those days."

"So, it can be travelled quickly on foot."

"Indeed, it can."

"Still I cannot understand why he did not write to you."

"He says he wrote to my father and was rebuffed." Joshua shook his head. "I cannot credit the tale, though. Why would my father not be relieved to learn that his son was alive?"

Miss Emerson nodded agreement and they strolled a little further together, the harmony between them more complete than ever it had been. Joshua felt no desire to hasten this interval. Indeed, he would have walked to London with her thus and been content.

"Was it you who came last night then?" she asked finally.

Joshua looked toward her with alarm. "Last night? No. Who came last night?"

"The rider in the cloak, on the great horse. I saw him from my window and he beckoned to me."

Joshua caught his breath. So that was why Specter had been abandoned in a lather. "But you did not heed him?"

She shook her head. "I did not think it was you. There was something amiss, perhaps in his posture." She slanted a glance at him, a twinkle lighting her eyes. "Of course, you have never proven that my champion was you."

"I have confessed my deception."

"But I think that only a kiss would convince me of the truth," she said lightly.

"Miss Emerson, you are most audacious."

She laughed then and he could find no fault with her at all. "If you disapprove of my nature, sir, you should cease to call upon me."

"But I do not disapprove, Miss Emerson," he confessed quietly. "Indeed, I find you utterly enchanting."

She turned to face him then, her expression so welcoming that he nearly did claim that kiss—though offending Lady Dalhousie would only hamper his progress. She laid a hand upon his arm, and met his gaze again. "And I, sir, realize that my impulsiveness led me astray for the last time." She swallowed. "I could only wish…"

He dropped a fingertip to her lips to silence her. "It is possible that I divine your wish, Miss Emerson," he murmured, watching her smile. "May I be so bold as to continue to call upon you?"

"I should like that very much, sir."

"Then we are agreed, as amiable acquaintances should be."

"I believe an amiable acquaintance has its limits, though, my lord. It must always become more or less in time."

"True enough, Miss Emerson. I for one shall hope for more."

"Oh, Lord Addersley. So shall I." She granted him a smile that could not be mistaken for anything other than her complete approval. Joshua, much encouraged, dropped his own gaze to her ripe lips and considered the merit of removing the last of her supposed doubts, regardless of Lady Dalhousie's possible response. He bent a little closer. Miss Emerson, to his satisfaction, rose to her toes.

Then Lady Dalhousie's cry echoed across the garden, ending all such happy possibilities in an instant. "Viscount Addersley!" she cried. "Whatever brings you to Bramble Cottage?"

AUNT HAD the most wretched ability to sense an event of interest, and worse, to ensure it never occurred. Aunt Fanny charged across the garden with her cane, showing an agility that Helena had not known she possessed. Helena kept her hand upon the viscount's arm, a detail that she watched her aunt note. Aunt's lips tightened and she glared at Helena, who did not change her posture.

Aunt exhaled noisily, striving to catch her breath. "Helena! What is the meaning of this encounter?"

"Lord Addersley was telling me about the unfortunate situation of his brother's mistress and son. It seems he just learned of them last week and has since ensured that their futures will be more comfortable. Is that not a kind gesture?"

"Your brother?" Aunt echoed, looking between the two of them.

"It seems that my younger brother and this Mrs. Lewis had a liaison before my father bought him a commission. I knew nothing of it, and I suspect my father knew nothing of the child. Perhaps my brother did not either."

Helena realized that he did not intend to reveal the detail of his brother's survival. She would not do as much either.

"Well!"

"I halted here on my way to meet with Lady Haynesdale, at her request. I am hoping the duke is returned that we might consult upon the situation with these ruffians who have taken up residence in the ruins."

"Who do you imagine them to be?"

"There are many decommissioned soldiers in need, and others yet unwelcome in their own homes now that they are returned."

"How wicked," Helena said.

"Many a wife is not glad of an injured or addled husband's return," he told her politely and Helena nodded understanding. He turned to Aunt again. "I had promised to escort Miss Emerson to the dressmaker's to collect her slippers before the ball, and would not let so minor an injury as my own to interfere with her pleasure."

He was so gallant!

Aunt softened slightly. "But sir, you must know what is being said of you."

"And we cannot place our trust in rumor and gossip,

Lady Dalhousie. I will defend your niece with my life, I pledge it to you."

"Becky could accompany us, Aunt," Helena suggested, for she saw that her aunt was disinclined to relent.

Aunt's resistance faded. "That is an excellent notion. I know you want your slippers but without carriage or horse, there is no way for us to fetch them." Aunt took the viscount's other elbow and turned him toward the cottage. "You must change your dress, Helena, to go to town, and in the meantime, Lord Addersley, I wonder if you might regale us with the tale of your battle with the ruffians yesterday. It might put rumor to rest for once and for all…"

~

LORD ADDERSLEY WAS NOT VEXING.

Nor did he have a mistress or a son.

By every accounting, he was perfect.

Helena spun in her room in her delight before she changed. Only her favorite blue dress would do.

By the time she descended to the kitchen again, Becky fast upon her heels, the butcher, his wife, Aunt and the Nixons were enthralled by the viscount's tale and clearly convinced of his merit. Aunt beamed, gratified to have proven her own merit as a provider of local news and the other women exchanged glances as the viscount rose to his feet at Helena's appearance.

He bowed over her hand and Helena hoped she was not the only one to see his admiration.

He looked very handsome himself in his navy jacket and she did not fail to note the fine embroidery on his silken waistcoat. It suited him well to dress a little more finely than had been his custom when they first arrived. Truly, she was certain there was no more handsome man in Nottinghamshire, if not in all of England.

He led her to the gig that was just inside the rhododendron hedge. It had no roof, and she guessed he had chosen it because the day was fine. The horse was a glossy chestnut mare with white socks and a white mark on her brow. Her mane and tail were darker and braided neatly, and she watched their approach with interest.

Aunt followed them, still chattering. "Thank you kindly for the fullness of the tale, my lord. We are most gratified that you were not more seriously injured than you were."

"I took a pummeling, Lady Dalhousie, but granted one in return." He touched his eye. "This is the worst of it, and the bruise will fade quickly enough."

"But to confront the villain alone! That is an act of bravery, sir. You might have faced a dozen brutes!"

"I knew there was but one, Lady Dalhousie." The viscount's eyes glinted as his gaze slid to Helena and she knew he would not reveal her part in events of the day before.

How had she ever imagined him to be inscrutable? She saw the way he inhaled sharply when she smiled at him. His eyes had darkened to that sensual hue and there was the barest curve of a smile upon his lips.

"But they say…"

"People say a great many foolish things, Lady Dalhousie. I am sufficiently hale to see this matter resolved today. You need have no fear of Miss Emerson's safety in my company."

"Oh, I do not, sir, and I did not mean to imply otherwise!"

"Of course not. Come, Miss Emerson, your slippers await, as does the dowager duchess." He offered his hand to her and Helena let him guide her toward the gig. He halted beside the horse. "Perhaps you would like to make the acquaintance of Molly before we depart." The horse nickered then nuzzled Helena's outstretched and gloved hand. "She knows the way to Haynesdale Hollow as well as I do."

Helena smiled at this assertion, then stroked Molly's nose. "I wish I had an apple for her."

"She will have one when she is home again," he said, leading her toward the gig. He considered the height to the bench, then spoke in a murmur. "If you will permit the familiarity, Miss Emerson," he said, then fitted his hands around her waist and lifted her before she could reply.

It was glorious to feel his hands close tightly around her, to catch the scent of his skin, to feel his heat so close. Helena felt almost faint, but she strove to hide her reaction from all but the viscount. She watched through her lashes as he gave Becky his hand, helping her to the seat at the back of the gig. Then he climbed in the seat with ease and settled beside Helena. She was delighted that his thigh was so close to her own.

"We will return as quickly as possible, Lady Dalhousie," he assured Aunt who nodded agreement. He clicked his tongue and flicked the reins, so that Molly turned and trotted through the hedge. Mischief barked from the kitchen behind them, but Helena could not have been happier.

"I am most relieved that we are to be friends again, sir," she said when they were clear of the rhododendron hedge.

He was visibly biting back a smile. "Miss Emerson, you are as forthright as ever."

"I think you do not mind," she said, his manner making her doubt his statements of the day before.

"I believe you are correct." He cast her a glance that was all simmering humor and she thought her heart might burst with satisfaction. "I do have a proposition for you, Miss Emerson."

Helena's heart leapt.

"As mentioned the other day, a curricle is not ideal as the first conveyance one commands. Two horses can be more challenging than one, and the vehicle itself is more prone to mishap." He flicked a glance her way. "A gig is a more sensible place to begin, particularly with a horse such as Molly, who does not truly need much guidance."

Helena felt her eyes widen as she understood his meaning. "You mean to let me take the reins!"

"Miss!" Becky whispered from behind her.

"One must learn sometime, in my view, and it is prudent to do as much before one is under duress." The viscount was firm and Helena took courage from his confidence in her. "First, consider how I hold the reins. They are neither slack nor taut. I can pull on one or the other to guide Molly's path–she will turn in the direction of the pressure. When I pull on them equally, but gently, Molly will halt." He did as much and Molly halted. The horse blew out her lips, apparently seeing no cause to stop on the road to Southpoint, and stamped a hoof.

The viscount flicked the reins and clicked his tongue. "Walk on, Molly," he said and she did. He encouraged the horse to a trot and then a canter as Helena watched, then slowed and halted the horse again.

"Take the reins," he said to Helena.

"But I..."

"You can rely upon me to intervene if necessary," he assured her.

Of course, she could. Helena cast him a triumphant smile, watched his eyes darken, then took the reins. Their gloved hands brushed in the transaction and her heart skipped, then all of her attention was upon Molly and the road ahead.

She meant to prove that his trust in her was deserved.

~

MISS EMERSON WAS as sensible and careful as Joshua had expected. She watched the horse more keenly than most people were inclined to do, but perhaps that was the influence of her brother. She surveyed her surroundings constantly and paid heed to the road ahead.

A rabbit emerged suddenly to bound across the road, an incident that might have spooked a horse less steady than Molly. Becky had scarcely gasped in alarm by the time Miss Emerson saw it and slowed their progress. The rabbit was long gone by the time they reached the point where it had appeared and Molly did not so much as flick her ears. Joshua sat back, having been braced to intervene, and simply watched his companion.

It was clear that she both welcomed the opportunity and enjoyed the challenge of learning a new skill. "You must correct me when I err, sir," she said, sparing him only a fleeting glance.

"I would not hesitate to do as much, Miss Emerson, but it appears that you already know how to do this."

She laughed. "I do not. I suspect that you have contrived my success."

"Do not fail to grant Molly her due," he said and she laughed again. Then she sobered and slowed Molly to pass Southpoint, taking the bend in the road at a sedate pace. Joshua saw Captain Emerson emerge from his stable and look after them, shading his eyes from the sun with one hand as he took a better look. Joshua raised a hand to wave and saw surprise on the other man's face before he grinned. Then Miss Emerson completed the turn and Southpoint was lost behind them, Molly being urged to a trot once more.

Joshua watched Miss Emerson, his admiration of her growing with every meeting. She was audacious and bold, but not overly so. She enjoyed whatever opportunity presented, and he was convinced that she was not as foolish as her aunt and relations might believe.

She had need of a husband and protector, in his view, no more than that, and he believed that matter would shortly be resolved.

"I do not think I can manage Haynesdale Hollow just yet," Miss Emerson confided as that village drew nearer.

"You have done very well for a first attempt," Joshua acknowledged.

She urged Molly to a halt, then returned the reins to him, her exultation clear.

"Miss, you might have been driving all your life!" Becky said.

"Indeed, you may have a curricle in hand by the end of the year." Joshua clicked his tongue to Molly.

"Only if someone is so kind as to let me take the reins again and again. I should like to be more confident before attempting a curricle. I thank you, sir. That was—" she took a deep breath "—most wondrous."

What was wondrous was the glow in the lady's eyes.

Joshua considered the influence of this lady upon his own perspective in just a few days, and could not begin to imagine how she might change his life once she was truly a part of it. He lifted her down to the ground at Mrs. Jameson's establishment, savoring the fleeting contact, then left her there with Becky and his promise to return as expediently as possible.

He was assured that she could happily spend all the day perusing ribbons and lengths of silk.

Joshua tipped his hat and rode for Haynesdale House, thinking less of the dowager duchess, the duke and his brother than of the lady he had just left.

Perhaps he might propose to Miss Emerson again this very day.

Doubtless she would demand a kiss to prove his identity before she agreed, a prospect that made Joshua Hargood smile.

~

THE DOWAGER WAS WAITING for Joshua before her teapot. She looked lovely in hues of pink and there was a touch of color in her cheeks, as if she was pleased about some tidings. An open letter reposed on the table beside the tea tray.

"I have had a letter from my son," she said immediately, then poured for them both. "He will return for the ball."

"What splendid news," Joshua said. He had wanted to speak to the duke, but had no reason to expect the duchess to be so concerned in providing him with the news of his pending arrival. "I had hoped he might have arrived already as I have a matter to discuss with him."

"I expect him on the morrow," the lady confided, much to Joshua's disappointment. "He asked me to speak to you in advance about a certain confidential matter."

"Indeed?" Joshua said.

Her lips tightened briefly and he sensed that she was not entirely pleased by whatever she had learned. "My son, evidently, is bringing his ward."

"I did not realize His Grace had a ward."

"Nor did I," that man's mother said, her tone arch. "And yet, she will be arriving here within days."

This might not have been welcome news, by the lady's reaction.

Joshua waited.

"Damien has specifically asked me to encourage your interest in the young lady. He believes, if I may be blunt, that she would make you an excellent wife."

Joshua blinked. "Indeed," he managed to say. "How kind of him."

"It may be kind," the older lady ceded. "Or he may wish to undermine any speculation about his own intentions before they begin. At any rate, you are in need of a wife, by all appearances, and Mlle. Sylvie LaFleur is evidently both young and pretty. She has no dowry of her own, but my son declares that he will make a settlement upon her when she is married." She sipped her tea and met his gaze, her manner expectant.

"I am greatly honored by the consideration, Lady Haynesdale."

She smiled a little. "But not enticed, even by the very logical nature of the proposal?"

Joshua opened his mouth and closed it again. He frowned and took a sip of hot tea before speaking. "I do have inclinations of my own, Lady Haynesdale."

"You are smitten with Miss Emerson," she said with complete authority. "I saw it myself on the day I introduced you and to be sure, I thought you might make a match there. I do not mean to belabor a point, but she has declined you, sir, and I would not have you persist in a suit that shows no promise. Your mother would chastise me greatly if I did not encourage you to be sensible."

"I am always sensible, Lady Haynesdale."

She smiled. "Then we are agreed. Of course, you likely wish to see the lady before making the arrangements but let us assume you to be interested. I will instruct Mlle. Sylvie to save her first three dances for you at the ball, and during that interval, you should be able to ascertain for yourself her many charms."

"But Lady Haynesdale…"

"Tut tut," she said, silencing him with a wagging finger. "Damien says she is a beauty beyond compare. You will be pleased, sir, rely upon it."

But Joshua knew he would not be pleased, regardless of how many charms Mlle. Sylvie LaFleur possessed. There was only one lady he desired to take to wife.

Rather than resolving a challenge, this visit had added another. The sole way he could see to politely circumvent the dowager's suggestion was to propose to Miss Emerson this very day and gain her consent. At the very least, he would have to prepare her for his newfound obligation of dancing first with the duke's ward.

As the duke was expected at any hour, he asked to leave a message for that man and wrote a note in the duke's study. "I entreat you, my lady, to surrender this to his Grace upon his arrival," he said when he granted it to her. "It involves a matter of urgency."

"You may rely upon me to place it in his hand the moment he arrives."

"I thank you." Joshua bowed and departed, checking his watch with a wince. Writing the letter had taken more time than he had intended, and Miss Emerson might be growing impatient. The last thing he wanted was to lose her goodwill at this moment.

He strode to the gig and Molly, unaware that the dowager watched his departure. No sooner was Molly trotting toward the village than the dowager broke the seal and opened his message to the duke. He would have been gratified to see her astonishment to learn that Gerald was alive.

FAMILY WAS a man's bulwark against the world, in the view of William Jones. If there were people one could rely upon, in good times and bad, it should be one's relations. Had he not stood by his sister when she found herself unwed and with child? Had he not given both her and her babe a home? He had, indeed, because she was his family, and the last of it, too.

Had he not repaired her situation once he had finally learned the name of the father? Truly, William had. Written to the man's brother, he had, saying as all should be made right. He had been in his cups when the viscount called with Darney and the tale of the annuity, and he had doubted the truth of it all. But Viscount Addersley was a better man than his brother, to be sure, for he had made matters aright, taking a responsibility his brother had not. William was inclined to think that he and the fine gentleman shared a similar view of the world.

There remained, however, the question of the babe in Alice's belly, another child of the viscount's brother. If he should provide for one, why not the other?

When William saw the viscount leave that new lady at the dressmaker's, he had a notion that he would make another appeal.

No doubt, the viscount would return for the pretty miss. William had no pressing obligations on this fine day, and he would wait for the chance to yet again improve his sister's circumstance.

He took his leisure, imagining a better future for all of them. Perhaps the viscount might be inclined to find Alice a husband. Moving to Addersley village would be good for Alice, get her and Francis away from the temptations of Haynesdale Hollow.

Aye, William would wait and speak to the viscount.

HELENA BEGAN to wonder what delayed the viscount. She had collected her slippers and reviewed nigh every item in Mrs. Jameson's shop, lingering over some particularly lovely silk. She had expected him to appear at the door at any time, amused by her fascination.

But he had not come.

They had exhausted their welcome in the shop, Helena having no resources to make an acquisition and had finally left the establishment.

The viscount was not there, nor was there any sign of him approaching.

They stood before the shop, looking up and down the main thoroughfare of Haynesdale Hollow. A heavy-set man seemed to take note of them and settled against a wall some twenty feet away, his gaze fixed upon them. Helena strove to ignore him.

"We cannot go to the tavern, miss," Becky said. "Though I should love a cup of tea."

"As would I," Helena agreed. "But we must wait here, lest we miss the viscount."

"I hope no ill has befallen him, miss," Becky said long moments later.

Helena held fast to her parcel and hoped the same. Where could he be?

A throat was abruptly cleared behind them.

"Begging your pardon, my lady, but they say you are the one Viscount Addersley is courting." Helena turned to find a young boy addressing her. His expression was earnest and she could not escape how strongly he favored the viscount.

"I could not say," Helena said, then made a guess. "Would you be the son of Mrs. Lewis?"

He smiled. "Aye, my lady. Francis is my name. My mum says as there are details you should know of his lordship and she is the best to tell you of them." Could there have been an assertion better designed to pique Helena's curiosity? "Will you come to her, my lady? It is not far."

Helena hesitated.

"My mistress is not interested in gossip," Becky began, but Helena raised a hand to silence her maid.

"What manner of details?"

"My mum has known that family all her life. She knows *secrets*, my lady."

Secrets.

As mistress of the viscount's brother, Mrs. Lewis might well be privy to secrets, either known within the family or told of them. She might, for example, know where the viscount's brother had his refuge. Was it possible that Helena could learn some detail that would be of aid to the viscount?

"We will both come," she said, giving Becky a glance to silence her.

"Miss! Are you sure?"

"We may be able to assist the viscount," Helena replied in a whisper.

"I am not certain as it is your place to do as much, miss," Becky whispered back.

Helena was quite certain that it was not her place, but she would strive to learn more anyway.

The boy bobbed his head, then turned to lead them onward. They walked a short distance along the main avenue of Haynesdale Hollow, then the boy turned into a smaller lane. Helena hesitated, considering the darkened and narrow path. Once again, she looked for the viscount, but there was no indication of his return. The lane appeared to be deserted.

The heavy-set man was still watching them, his interest more than disconcerting.

"Down here, my lady," the boy called, his manner encouraging.

Helena had to learn what she could. It was broad daylight in a busy town. What could befall them? And the viscount would return momentarily, she was certain.

Helena squared her shoulders and followed. The boy remained just ahead of them, and was good to his word. They had not gone thirty steps down the lane before he halted and indicated a door.

It was not a promising entry. The paint was faded and peeling, and the threshold had not been swept. Did anyone live in this abode? If so, their habits were not tidy ones.

"We will not be here long," the boy supplied. "Mum says that since the viscount provided for us, we will have finer quarters." He lowered his voice. "This is my uncle's home." His manner was so furtive that Helena guessed the uncle was not kindly disposed toward his sister and her son.

"I understand the viscount bought your mother an annuity?"

The boy beamed as he nodded. "And I am to have an apprenticeship if the smith is willing. I should like ever so much to be a smith."

Helena could not halt her answering smile. "You will have to work hard to learn such skills."

"But it is all I ever wanted. I cannot wait to begin."

He was so enthused that Helena found herself wishing him well. She liked the boy, and the viscount was right—his conception could scarce be held against him. She would have knocked upon the door, but he seemed to recall himself. He opened it and ushered her and Becky inside, then closed the door behind them. It took a moment for Helena's eyes to adjust to the dimly lit interior, then she took a step back.

There was a man leaning against the opposite wall, a familiar man whose gaze burned with hatred. "How delightful to encounter you again," Gerald Hargood said with a bow that seemed slightly mocking. He also moved stiffly as if he had been injured even more than his brother the day before.

Helena supposed she should not have been so glad of that.

"I should never have come if I had known you were waiting," she said.

"Which is precisely why I ensured you did not know," he said, gesturing to a bench.

"I will return to Mrs. Jameson's, thank you."

"You will not depart without my leave," he said, his voice hard. "Lock the door, Francis."

Helena realized that a woman sat beside the hearth, mending in her lap, her gaze locked adoringly upon Gerald. The bolt was shot loudly and Helena's heart sank. She gripped her parcel tightly, wondering what she could do to ensure their safety. Once again, she had followed impulse – admittedly in a desire to help – and erred mightily. Would the viscount follow them? If he did, he would come to their aid, of that she was certain, but would he know where to look?

The best strategy she could contrive was to keep everyone talking. Perhaps she might discern a solution then.

Helena could only hope.

CHAPTER 13

"Is it true that you are Lord Addersley's brother?" Helena asked the man before her, as if she had just encountered him at tea in her aunt's drawing room. "I had understood that Gerald Hargood was among the casualties at Waterloo."

"I ensured that all believed as much," Gerald said. "It suited my plans best."

Helena did not think she would like his plans, but delayed asking about them for the moment.

"Francis then must be your son," she said, gesturing to the boy who had brought them to this place.

"He saw us last week," the woman said, her tone rising as if she expected to be challenged. "He arranged it all." There was a hint of admiration in her tone but Gerald gave her such a look that she flinched.

"He gave me a ha-penny, too," Francis said with satisfaction.

"Then why did you fight with him yesterday?" Helena demanded of Gerald. "Surely you had no argument with him ensuring the welfare of your family?"

"He spends a few pounds and I am to fall on my knees before him?" Gerald sneered. "Lord of the manor.

Casting alms to the poor. Perhaps he thinks it pearls before swine."

Helena felt her indignation rise. "The viscount ensured the welfare of your mistress and son, which evidently you had never done! He had no obligation to do as much."

"And I had no coin to do as much," Gerald snarled.

"I do not believe it. You wasted what you were granted."

"What do you know of it?"

"I know that your brother is a fine and honorable man, a respectable man worthy of anyone's trust and respect."

Gerald snorted.

"And I know that you strove to assault me yesterday, which is no good indication of your character."

"He has taken everything from me," Gerald retorted. "Now I shall take everything from him."

Helena did not like the sound of that. "But why? Were you not raised with every advantage?"

"All advantages save the important ones. The title. The legacy. The fortune."

"But he is the older son."

"And he is the lesser son!" Gerald declared, jabbing a thumb at his own chest. His manner became so agitated that Helena tried to ease closer to the door. "*I* should have been viscount. *I* should have been Father's favorite. I should never have been sent to war, and I should have been welcomed when I returned. Even Joshua's betrothed recognized that I was the better man. Charlotte adored me, not him!"

"I hardly think it a testament to your character that you courted the lady who was betrothed to your brother." In other circumstance, Helena might have been surprised to find herself sounding so prim. As it was, her fear was rising and she knew only that she had to keep

Gerald talking. "Nor does it say much of hers that she chose to welcome your advances."

"I took her, just as I will take you."

"I am not yours to claim, sir," Helena said, though her fear was mounting.

"And Francis will be a viscount," Mrs. Lewis contributed.

Helena looked between the two of them. "But Francis can only inherit the title if Mr. Hargood claims the title, and that can only happen if the viscount dies first."

Gerald smiled at her. "Finally, you understand. I must say, Joshua does have an affection for foolish women. Charlotte took months to comprehend that Joshua's close calls were not accidental."

Helena bristled on that lady's behalf. "What close calls?"

Gerald laughed. "Do you truly believe that I could not fight my own duels? No, I convinced Joshua that I could not duel, that he must take my place, then challenged every marksman I could find."

"And you courted Miss Havilland."

"I seduced her."

"Yet you did not love her."

He laughed. "Love? Of course not. It was the principle of the matter. No one would have found me such a wealthy wife. No one would have arranged my match. No one cared if I did not wed at all. Why should I not have Joshua's wife first? I would seduce her better than he ever could." He took a step closer. "Why should I not have you first?"

"Gerald!" Mrs. Lewis protested.

"I will have you first, and he will see it before he dies." Gerald shed his jacket. "He will follow you here and find you despoiled, a fitting reward for both of you, then he will die."

"Miss!" Becky whispered.

Truly, Helena had nothing to lose in speaking the truth.

"You are despicable!" she said, her words low and hot. "You are all foul beyond compare. Your brother has treated you with honor and dignity and you would insult him, rob him and injure him after his kindness to you." Knowing that Gerald's heart could not be reached – indeed, she doubted he possessed one – she spun to face Francis. "A fortnight ago, did you have any prospect of an apprenticeship?" The boy shook his head, eyes wide. "So, you show your gratitude for this opportunity, which the viscount was under no obligation to provide, by betraying his trust? You tempt me here, at this man's bidding, knowing full well that my fate will not be good?"

"I did not know, my lady…" the boy protested but he dropped his gaze.

"I do not believe it. By participating in this scheme, you show that a foul nature can be inherited. I am ashamed of you, Francis."

Francis looked as if he might cry. He hastily unbolted the door and lunged through it, his footsteps echoing on the street. Helena gave Becky a shove and the maid tried to follow.

Before she could reach the door, Gerald lunged forward. He was between Becky and the door, then closed it with a savage gesture and bolted it. "We have need of a witness," he whispered and Becky retreated even as she shivered.

Helena took a breath, determined to hide her fear.

"And you," she turned her attention to Mrs. Lewis. "An annuity is given to you, yet you contrive the downfall of the man who has graciously provided it."

"I will be a viscountess," she said proudly. "I will have no need of a little annuity. I will have all the wealth of Addersley Manor to call my own, and my son will inherit the title."

"You are assuming that the viscount will die."

"He will die," Gerald said. "He has been fortunate time and again, but this time, he will die."

"You have tried to kill him before," Helena said, wanting him to declare as much. Gerald was not the only one who could make use of a witness.

Gerald smiled, an expression so cold that she shivered. His confidence was such that she understood another detail.

"It was not Miss Havilland who was supposed to die that night," she suggested and his grin widened.

"I should have told her we were changing places," he said. "She heard that I had challenged Michaels and everyone knew that Michaels never missed. I even started a wager that he would miss this time, the better to goad him into taking that shot. Then I pretended to be uncertain so Joshua would fight in my stead. He always has to step in to save matters." Gerald spat on the floor. "Charlotte had to ruin it all by interfering. Stupid woman."

"Maybe not so stupid as that," Helena said, wanting only to shake his confidence. There was a small knife on the table closest to her and to seize it, she would have to distract Gerald. "I find it easy to tell the two of you apart, though the resemblance is strong," she said, daring to provoke him. "I am certain Miss Havilland knew the duelist was your brother, and that as he held her heart, she strove to save him."

"You lie!" Gerald said, his eyes flashing, and reached back for his knife.

Helena, undaunted, stepped quickly toward the table and claimed the small knife, hiding it in her skirts by the time he looked up. "Did she refuse your advances? Did she favor your brother over you, and remain loyal to her betrothed?"

"You know nothing!"

"I will guess that your father bought you a commission because he knew the truth. He knew you meant to kill your brother. He knew you had tried. So, he did the only thing a father could do to defend his heir without scandal, he sent you to war."

Gerald's expression hardened.

"That's why you knew he wouldn't be glad of your survival," she continued easing away from Becky and toward a corner. "That's why he didn't welcome your return. He knew that you would try again."

"He always preferred Joshua. I deserve the title!"

"Murderers don't inherit titles."

Gerald laughed. "I'm not such a fool as to do it myself."

"He will die, and I will be viscountess," Mrs. Lewis insisted.

Helena saw the pitying glance that Gerald granted her.

"He is not going to marry you," she said to the other woman. "He will never marry you. He is here because he needs you for the moment, perhaps to have a refuge. He cares only for his own advantage, and if he ever inherits the title, his association with you would bring him nothing. He will dismiss and forget you."

"He would not…"

"He *will*," Helena said. "I knew a man just like him. He was all grace and courtesy, so long as he believed I was heiress to a fortune. Once he learned otherwise, the truth of his nature was revealed." She smiled coolly at Gerald. "This man would spend every penny of an inheritance, then he would wed an heiress to ensure his own comfort. He will take your annuity and he will claim the funds allocated for that apprenticeship, he will sell everything he can and he will spend only on his own comfort. He will not ensure the welfare of any of you. It is his brother who has done as much to date, and his brother who is the finer man."

"I heard as you declined him," Mrs. Lewis said, her tone snide.

"Because I was a fool who did not see his merit."

"You are still the one he wants," Gerald said. "And that, you must see, is why I must take you away from him." He raised the knife and stepped closer, his intention more than clear. Helena found the wall behind her back and could not summon another word to her lips. She had no more questions, no more means of stalling, and Gerald knew it. There was a kind of glee in his eyes, a focus on his scheme that ignored all other details.

He did not hear the running footsteps in the lane.

He glanced toward the door at the sound of the viscount's shout. "Miss Emerson!"

"I am here!" she cried, even as Gerald lunged toward her.

There was a crash of splintering wood as the door was forced open. Helena saw Gerald glance over his shoulder, then was blinded by the sudden glare of daylight. A shadow moved across the opening and Mrs. Lewis screamed. There was a crack, a clatter and a thump.

Then such stillness that she opened her eyes to look.

JOSHUA STOOD in front of Mrs. Jameson's shop, unable to fathom what had happened to Miss Emerson and her maid. There was no sign of them. They were not in the shop, though they were not long departed, by the dressmaker's word. Where could they have gone? Surely she would not have ventured into the tavern?

Joshua found himself uncertain what Miss Emerson might do, which to be sure, was a measure of her appeal.

He noticed Mrs. Lewis' brother leaning against a nearby building, looking as if he summoned his nerve for some deed. Joshua looked down the street for Miss Emerson, not wanting to have another discussion about him owing for Mrs. Lewis' next child. He was resolving to walk toward the inn in search of Miss Emerson as a young boy raced up to him.

It was Francis Lewis.

"Sir!" he said. "You must come. The lady who awaited you here is in danger."

Joshua was immediately alarmed. "Where has she gone?"

The boy pointed, then led the way. Joshua strode after him, his fear rising at the boy's manner. Why had Miss Emerson left this spot? He prayed her impulse did not steer her false.

He did not like that they turned down a lane, nor did he like that Mrs. Lewis' brother followed behind him. Joshua had the sense of a trap closing around him, but he could not abandon Miss Emerson if she was in need.

The boy went to a door and tried to open it, without success. Joshua could hear an argument within and a woman's voice that might be that of his lady. "Miss Emerson?" he roared, and was relieved when she replied. Her voice was high and he knew she was fearful. He shook the door, which was more doughty than it looked at first, and took a step back with the intention of forcing it.

Instead, a dark shadow barreled past him and collided heavily with the door, splintering it and sending it crashing inward on its hinges. Mrs. Lewis' brother William had shattered the door. More importantly, the beam of sunlight revealed Gerald within, a knife held high as he threatened someone. Mrs. Lewis screamed as the door fell in. Gerald lunged forward even as William roared with fury and seized a stool, bringing it down upon Gerald's head with a crash.

"I told you never to come here again," he growled as Gerald crumpled to the floor, a pool of blood spreading rapidly around him. "You would leave my sister soiled once more."

"My lord!" Mrs. Lewis shrieked and fell to her knees beside Gerald.

His brother did not move. Given the rapidly growing pool of blood around him, Joshua suspected he might never move again.

"God in heaven," whispered Becky, who looked as if her knees might fold beneath her.

And then there was Miss Emerson, pale with fear but defiant, a small knife clutched in her hand. She was backed into the corner, her parcel from the dressmaker clutched against her chest. "I had to come, my lord," she whispered. "I had to discover whether she knew your brother's refuge."

And she had found it, almost at her own expense.

"I fetched him, my lady, I fetched him," Francis said to Miss Emerson. "You were right, my lady, so I fetched him."

Miss Emerson smiled at the boy. "You did well, Francis," she said quietly, the tremor in her voice revealing her own fear.

William let the last leg of the stool slip from his grasp, even as he stared down at Gerald. "I did not mean to do it," he whispered. "But I could not let him betray her again." He appealed to Joshua. "He lied to my sister and she believed him. You made it all right after I wrote to you, though," he said to Joshua, then eyed Gerald and Mrs. Lewis. "You made it right." His sigh came from his very toes. "That wrong had to be righted." He pushed his hand through his hair and sat on the floor beside Gerald.

So, it had been Mrs. Lewis' brother behind the notes, and Gerald's seduction of Mrs. Lewis had been the crime.

"Find the magistrate," Joshua told Francis, who pivoted and ran to do his bidding.

He stepped across the threshold himself and paused beside Gerald only long enough to ascertain that his brother was dead. Then he went directly to Miss Emerson. She trembled but did not falter.

"He confessed," she said. "And Becky heard as much, too. You were supposed to die in that duel, not Miss Havilland. That was why your father sent him away. He *knew*. Your father knew and he wanted only to protect you." Joshua was astonished. Miss Emerson took a shaking breath, pity lighting her gaze as she considered Gerald. "He meant to kill you now," she added. "That was why Mrs. Lewis expected to become a viscountess."

It made a treacherous sense. Joshua could scarce believe that his brother had hated him so very much. All the same, he could not doubt Miss Emerson. He was awed that she had sought out this confession, that she had taken such a risk so he might know the truth. Even as he considered the revelation, though, a hundred little details fell into place. Finally the puzzle was complete.

"It is true, sir," Becky said. "Every word of it."

But Joshua had already recognized as much.

And the lady who had solved the riddle stood before him. He offered Miss Emerson his hand. She placed the knife carefully on the edge of a table, then seized his hand, her grip so tight that he knew she was deeply shaken. Her valor impressed him mightily, but when he felt how she was shaking, Joshua swept her into his arms, wanting only to see her away from this scene.

He heard her sigh with a contentment that warmed his heart. He felt her lean against him, utterly confident in his protection, and knew he would do anything to defend her.

For he loved this lady, heart and soul, and she alone could make his life complete.

~

ONCE THE VISCOUNT ARRIVED, Helena knew that all would be resolved. Though she did not wish to be apart from him, he took her and Becky to Haynesdale House, where the dowager duchess poured them tea and demanded the entire tale.

The viscount returned to what was apparently the home of William Jones, Mrs. Lewis' brother, and ensured that the magistrate's task was fulfilled. He returned an hour or so later, grim and inscrutable, then returned them to Bramble Cottage. Helena knew that he was shocked by his brother's animosity, for once again, he might have been made of stone.

They had just arrived at Bramble Cottage when a covered cart passed, on its way to Addersley Manor. Helena saw the shadow cross the viscount's features and knew his brother was being taken home for the last time.

"I am so sorry," she whispered.

"As am I, Miss Emerson," he said in his lovely deep voice. "As am I."

"You must feel it more greatly, having lost him twice."

But a week ago, she knew he would have turned away, but he hesitated, then spoke again. "I feel I lost him thrice, Miss Emerson, each time more painful than the one before. I only wished that we might one day be reconciled."

She smiled at him and pressed his hand. He looked down at her hand resting upon his, and when he spoke, his voice was hoarse. "I do not know when our paths will cross again, Miss Emerson. My house will be in mourning, as is right and proper."

Helena understood. He would not attend the ball at Haynesdale House.

"Of course," she said softly and he kissed her hand, his gaze rising to lock with hers.

"I trust you will find a plethora of willing partners," he said, but Helena knew that she wanted only one. He turned then and strode to the gig, as crisp and composed as ever. She stood in the yard and watched him go, yearning for what might never be.

IF EVER ADDERSLEY MANOR had seemed quiet and lonely, that had been nothing compared to its echoing emptiness on this night. Joshua knew he would never sleep, his thoughts still spinning at the depth of Gerald's malice.

His brother, his own brother, had despised him—and he had never guessed the truth. Oh, he knew that Gerald often made jests at his expense, and he was aware that Gerald had courted the attentions of his betrothed...and he knew that Gerald had stolen from the house, and he knew that Gerald had threatened Miss Emerson, simply because Joshua admired her.

The truth was that he had often suspected this truth, but had refused to believe it.

He recalled the night of that last duel and saw a dozen little hints and signs that he had overlooked before. Perhaps he had deliberately overlooked them. Perhaps he had been unwilling to believe that he and Gerald were not as close as brothers might be.

He went through the entire house, seeing it as Gerald must have done, not as an obligation or a responsibility or even a gift, but as the possession of another. As an injustice. As a goal. The realization saddened him as much as Gerald's death.

William Jones awaited the duke's return and the justice he so admired. Mrs. Lewis would raise another child without a father, though the annuity would mean that she did not starve. Joshua dared to hope that Francis would make a good smith. Gerald would be buried in the family cemetery and mourned yet again, but this time, he would not rise from the dead to return.

Did Specter know that Gerald was gone? It seemed the horse did, for he was unusually calm on this night. Joshua went through the stables, spoke with Hoskins, accepted the condolences of his staff, and took two dogs into the house for company. He could not face the meal that Mrs. Baird prepared for him, or the vast emptiness of the dining room, despite Fairfax's encouragement. He left the dogs snoring before the fire in the library, amused to think that Miss Emerson would approve.

Miss Emerson. He could not think of her, of the peril she had faced, of the possibility that she could have been injured.

In his chambers, Reed was buffing the tall black boots that had been in storage. "I thought as they would be fitting for the funeral, sir," he said, and Joshua nodded agreement. They reviewed together the clothing that Reed had laid out for the service the following day. It would be small and private, Gerald having been mourned once already.

"Not this waistcoat," Joshua said, noticing the green

and gold striped one with the embroidery. "It is too decorative for such services."

"But not for a ball, my lord."

"I cannot attend Lady Haynesdale's ball, Reed, not after my brother's funeral. It would not be fitting."

Reed cleared his throat. "But you have been in mourning for your brother's loss over a year, sir. I believe an exception could be made."

Joshua considered the waistcoat, the one he had worn the night he had carried Miss Emerson home, the garment that had filled him with such a welcome sense of possibilities. "You are right, Reed," he said, his mood improving with the choice. "I will order the coach, in case the ladies from Bramble Cottage have need of conveyance home afterward. Fairfax did say there might be rain tomorrow night."

"A wise choice, sir. It is an admirable trait for a gentleman to be prepared to be of service to ladies." He gestured. "The black trousers for the service, then, and the buff breeches for the ball?"

IT WAS a glorious night for a ball. The skies were clear and the moon was just a whisker past half full. It hung silvery overhead, the stars glittering all around it. Helena peered out the window of Nicholas' carriage as they drew near Haynesdale House. Torches flared before the house, footmen hastening to open coach and carriage doors as the guests arrived. Everything, it seemed to Helena, glittered and the night might have been made for magic.

She wore a new dress, a white confection that shimmered with gold embroidery upon the hem. She wore her new ivory slippers and there were golden leaves twined into her hair. Aunt Fanny had been distraught that she possessed no gems, but Helena did not care. She wore the little gold chain that she had from her mother, with its tiny pendant of a rose carved from coral. Her gloves were glorious, borrowed from Eliza, made of gleaming white satin that extended past her elbows. She felt like a queen and wished only that there was a prospect of the viscount attending. Even if he did not dance, even if he spoke to her in his wondrous deep voice, even if he merely looked at her, his eyes glimmering and a little smile curving his lips, her evening would have been complete.

Only a day had passed and she missed him utterly.

Nicholas had sent the carriage to Bramble Cottage for herself and Aunt Fanny, then he and Eliza had joined them when the carriage passed Southpoint. All of them were most handsome, to Helena's view, though she preferred her brother in regimentals. Eliza was attractive in silver and pale blue, while Aunt Fanny wore her favored pewter and silver gown and a small tiara graced with pearls.

They had to wait in a line of arriving carriages, but finally reached the base of the steps. A footman opened the door and another offered his hand to Aunt Fanny. All the windows of Haynesdale House were alight, a sight most festive and welcoming. Nicholas and Eliza led their small party up the stairs to the open door. Footmen took the ladies' cloaks and they continued up the sweeping staircase to the ballroom, where their arrival was announced.

In truth, the room was so crowded and the noise so great that no one could hear the names of the new arrivals. The orchestra was playing a jig, though there were few dancers so early in the evening. Footmen moved through the crowd of chattering guests with trays of glasses. Aunt Fanny spied Lady Haynesdale and ensured they made their way to their hostess to make their compliments.

"Is your son returned?" Nicholas asked, just as Helena had hoped he might.

"Yes!" Lady Haynesdale declared. "Damien only just returned this afternoon, though there is no telling whether he will come to dance. He is exhausted from his errand, poor lamb, and was most disgruntled to learn that there would be a ball on this night. I cannot believe he had forgotten."

Nicholas seemed to be fighting a smile. "I can imagine his response."

Lady Haynesdale's gaze rising to another guest and she smiled a greeting. "Why, the judge did manage to come!"

Helena watched Lady Haynesdale move to greet a gentleman so elderly that he could scarce walk, let alone dance, then turned to survey the room herself. There were no less than three chandeliers, ablaze with candles, and already the room was becoming warm.

One wall of the ballroom looked over a stone terrace, offering a view of the shadowed gardens below. Several of the doors to the terrace were open, admitting the beguiling scent of fresh flowers and the tinkle of fountains. The small orchestra played with finesse and the floor was crowded with dancers.

Nicholas ensured that Helena was introduced to a number of young men and she soon was dancing without pause. She could not keep herself from stealing glances toward the doors, in hope of a glimpse of the viscount, even though she knew he did not plan to attend.

In truth, it was difficult to recall how much she had anticipated this event. In the viscount's absence, it was very nice, but already the time drew as long as her current companion's tale of a hunting expedition. He was the son of a country squire and most attentive, though Helena had no more than a polite interest in his tales of his prowess at the hunt.

She thought to ask him why he hunted at all, turned to do as much, and fell silent in astonishment.

Lord Addersley had just entered the ballroom and was speaking to the dowager duchess. He was taller than that lady and looked down at her, smiling slightly at whatever she confided in him. His hair was a little tousled and he wore a splendid silk waistcoat of green and gold that was achingly familiar. Helena caught her breath at the sight of him, her heart fluttering.

He had come!

When he glanced over the ballroom, his gaze collided with hers and her heart stopped.

Did he smile? Just a little? She thought he did, but then he stepped out of view.

The duke had arrived.

Helena wished he would move, for he blocked her view of the viscount.

"His Grace, Damien DeVries, the Duke of Haynesdale, and his ward, Mlle. Sylvie Lafleur!"

The duke was a familiar figure with his limp and his cane, but it seemed to Helena that he leaned less upon it than had previously been the case. He seemed younger and straighter, with greater vigor in his manner since she had last seen him.

He still was impossibly ancient, but Helena doubted she was alone in wondering whether the young lady by his side should be credited with the change. She was blonde and lovely, perhaps even younger than Helena, her gaze downcast modestly as the duke beamed at her with pride. His manner was protective and Helena knew she could not be the only one who suspected this must be his intended duchess.

And yet, she was not disappointed to find her own

ambitions thwarted. She wished him joy. She wished both of them joy.

Indeed, she could not recall why she had imagined the duke to be so alluring.

The orchestra began to play and the guests cleared the floor. A few couples moved to take their positions for the dance to begin, and Helena gripped her hands together in anticipation when she caught sight of the viscount again. The squire's son cleared his throat pointedly, but her gaze was fixed on Lord Addersley.

Would he dance?

Had she persuaded him?

Would he dance with her? Helena hoped with all her heart that he might.

But the man in question turned, bowed, and invited the duke's ward to dance.

This could not be!

Helena stared, knowing her shock and dismay would be evident to all, and not caring a whit. He led the lady to the dance floor and turned her elegantly, then they began to dance. That he danced beautifully was no consolation when he danced with another.

Helena had convinced him to compromise his vow, yet he had done as much for someone else, someone he did not even know.

"You did refuse him, my dear," Aunt murmured from beside her and Helena knew she flushed crimson.

"Refuse who?" the squire's son asked, looking between Helena and the dancers.

That folly had been before, before she saw the viscount's merit, before she fell in love with him, before she knew that he was the only man who would satisfy her.

But her realization had come too late. She flung herself through the doors to the terrace, not caring who saw her distress or how scandalous her behavior might be considered.

~

"Miss Emerson?"

Helena spun at the sound of a familiar voice. The viscount was silhouetted in the lights of the ballroom, and she hated that she could not see his features.

His expression would be inscrutable, though, she knew that much and the realization made her smile. The truth of his thoughts was in his voice and his manner, and she could hear that he was uncertain of his welcome. Her mouth was dry but she turned to face him, striving to hide her own uncertainty.

"I thought you did not dance," she said, then feared it sounded like an accusation.

He stepped toward her, apparently undeterred. "I have been assured of the merit of seizing what opportunity presents itself."

"I thought you did not plan to attend this evening."

"And so I did not, but again, I was reminded of the risk of lost opportunity." He stood before her now, his features shadowed but his eyes glinting. "Dare I hope that my presence is not unwelcome?"

"Of course not," Helena said, feeling flustered by his scrutiny.

"And what of my companionship here?"

"I am honored by your attentions," she managed to say.

"I would have you know, Miss Emerson, the reason why Lady Haynesdale summoned me yesterday. I meant to confide it in you afterward, but..." A frown touched his brow and she longed to smooth it away with a fingertip.

"But matters went awry," she provided and he nodded agreement.

"They did, indeed. Lady Haynesdale is possessed of a notion that I am in need of a bride, and convinced that the duke's ward would be the ideal choice. She would not be readily dissuaded from her view, and insisted I claim the first three dances with Mlle. LaFleur." His gaze met hers and Helena's heart leapt with hope.

"You danced only one," she noted.

"Indeed." He captured her hand in his and lifted it, entwining their fingers and watching their hands. That gave Helena the opportunity to watch him closely and admire, not just his attractiveness but his very nature. Of course, he kept a promise that he made. He was reliable in all things. It was part of what she loved about him. "I confess that when I was obliged to make that promise, it was my hope that I would be otherwise committed by this evening. In being thus, no one would be able to fault me for letting another man take Mlle. LaFleur to the floor first." His gaze slid to hers again, his manner so intent that Helena felt hot to her toes.

"How might you be otherwise committed, sir?" she managed to ask.

"By already having chosen a bride, and having won that lady's agreement, of course." He caught her other hand in his as Helena's heart thundered. "I meant to renew my addresses to you yesterday, Miss Emerson, and dared to hope that my second offer might be accepted."

"Oh!"

"Oh," he echoed and she saw his smile. "I do recognize, though, that you have conditions upon the nature of any man you might choose to wed." A waltz began to play and he met her gaze steadily. "Might I have this dance, Miss Emerson?"

"Here?" Helena caught her breath. "In the moonlight?" The very prospect was exciting beyond all and she knew that such a dance would be one she would long remember.

"Where else?"

"It would be scandalous indeed to waltz without supervision, sir."

The viscount nodded as he considered this. "That is true, Miss Emerson. Would it not be unfortunate, though, to never know what it is like to waltz on a terrace like this, on a night like this, beneath the stars?"

Helena could not suppress her smile. "You read my own thoughts, sir."

His smile flashed. "Perhaps the sole solution is to do as much with a man you are pledged to marry."

"I think that would be far less scandalous. It might even be appropriate to share such an experience with that man."

"Indeed. Will you do me the honor of accepting this dance, Miss Emerson, with the understanding that I will make an offer of marriage if the dance is deemed acceptable?"

Helena laughed. "I will." She moved into his arms with contentment. As anticipated, he was an elegant dancer and they moved across the terrace smoothly, the weight of his hand on the back of her waist. He was close, so deliciously close, and she was excited beyond all. She wanted the dance to last forever.

As they turned, she saw the gold and green stripes of his waistcoat and the embroidery she would never forget. Her champion. How could she have doubted that he was the man for her?

She looked up to find him smiling down at her. "I must confess that I have another condition, my lord."

"I have no doubt of it. You are a lady of firm convictions."

"And you do not find that a flaw?"

"I find it most admirable to encounter a lady who knows her own desires." He leaned closer, his lips brushing her ear. "I invite you to confide them in me, Miss Emerson."

Helena closed her eyes in delight. "I thought, sir, that you abandoned all the pleasures of your rakehell days."

"It is true that I did, but now I consider that such experiences had a purpose."

"Truly?"

"Truly. For I have realized that such temptations can be savored in smaller measure, that a man can be wicked, for example, for only his lady wife, to ensure their mutual satisfaction, but be sober and reliable in all other facets of his life."

"What a notion, sir."

"I did not mean to scandalize you, Miss Emerson."

"No, sir, I find the suggestion most compelling."

He chuckled, a lovely sound that Helena wanted to hear again and again. "Now, what of your next condition, Miss Emerson?"

"I must be certain that the man I wed is the same man who captured my heart the day that I turned my ankle."

His brows rose. "A man captured your heart and you are unaware of his identity?"

"He was disguised, but no hood could hide his merit."

The viscount smiled, his eyes fairly glowing. "And how would you be sure of his identity, Miss Emerson, if he was disguised?"

"His kiss will reveal his true identity. I am quite certain of it."

He feigned astonishment so that she laughed again. "His kiss? Miss Emerson, are you in the habit of kissing strangers in disguise?"

"Only when such a man captures my heart."

"And how frequent an occurrence might this be?"

"It has occurred only once, sir, and my heart remains in the keeping of my champion."

"If only you knew who he was."

"If only." Helena smiled up at him as the music changed and he spun her to a halt. She remained in the circle of his arms, happier than she had ever anticipated she might be in Nottinghamshire.

"Then let me make a case in my own favor," Lord Addersley murmured, his hand sliding into her hair as he pulled her closer. "And hope against hope that you might be convinced to accept me this time." His mouth closed over hers with all the assurance and power that she recalled, his kiss deepening with satisfaction as she wound her arms around his neck and kissed him back.

Long moments later, there was the sound of a footfall on the terrace. "Helena!" Aunt cried and the viscount lifted his head, shielding her from view.

"Dare I hope my suit is accepted, Miss Emerson?" he whispered against her ear.

"You know it is, sir," she said, watching his smile broaden.

"Joshua," he murmured and she repeated his name with pleasure.

"Dare I hope you have a special license?"

"I have arranged to collect it tomorrow," he confessed. "For I have become convinced of the merit of haste in such opportunities as this one."

Helena laughed with delight, stretching to her toes to kiss her champion again.

CHAPTER 14

Mrs. Agnes Dawlish of Carting Corners was relieved.

In fact, she was delighted. Matters could not have resolved themselves in a more satisfactory manner for the young lady she had assisted just over a month before.

When the wedding invitation arrived from Addersley Manor, there was no question of whether she would accept. Mr. Dawlish had made a token protest over the inconvenience but, as was so often the case, his objections were immediately over-ruled. The entire family had taken themselves to the inn at Haynesdale Hollow, in order to attend the wedding of Lord Addersley and Miss Helena Emerson on the second Saturday in May.

To be sure, Mrs. D. – as she was known to her friends and close acquaintances – was initially inclined to fear that Miss Emerson had embroiled herself in some mischief. The girl was not wicked, but she was exuberant, and Mrs. D. had witnessed that she could be willful. Had Miss Emerson beguiled an elderly viscount into marrying her?

But no, the widowed Viscount Addersley who Mrs.

D. recalled had recently passed away. She had been able to ascertain that in Carting Corners, no less that his son and heir was said to be both young and handsome, if reserved in his nature.

Such a man, cool and composed, perhaps so devoid of emotion as to have ice in his veins as she heard by one account, seemed unlikely to have captured the attention of the lively lady Mrs. D. had met. Had Miss Emerson overwhelmed that man's restraint with her charms? To what purpose? Mrs. D. could not imagine Miss Emerson as one to wed a man for his fortune alone.

It was a puzzle. Mrs. D. had arrived at the church in Addersley village, husband and children in tow, with considerable reservations.

The day of the wedding was sunny and clear, and it seemed they were not the only ones making their way to the chapel in Addersley village. She recognized Captain Emerson immediately and that man's satisfaction with the situation could not be feigned.

He had greeted them heartily, introducing his wife – the sister of the Duke of Haynesdale! Goodness! – and his aunt, Lady Dalhousie. They were introduced to the groom, a man of impeccable manners and grace. He seemed to be a man of composure, but not an emotionless one.

The Dawlish family found themselves in quite exalted company, for the duke himself soon arrived, along with his mother and his ward, a very beautiful French girl. All of the village was in attendance, their joy in the match unmistakable.

Mrs. D. awaited the appearance of the bride to be certain.

Captain Emerson had departed to fetch his sister and all the guests were ushered into the church. It was a lovely small country church, with old stone walls. The air was cool inside and the whispers fell silent at the sound of the horses' hooves. They all turned to watch the door as the bride entered with her brother. Helena looked even prettier than Mrs. D. recalled her to be. She was, in fact, radiant with happiness, and not with the joy of having secured her ambition. No, she was a lady in love and the sight made Mrs. D. heave a sigh of relief.

Even better, the viscount beamed at her, his attention so rapt that she might have been the sun, the moon and the stars. Perhaps he was the one who saw his ambition achieved in the vows of this day. Mrs. D. could imagine him as a man who recognized his desire when he saw it. The quiet ones were often thus in her experience. Unswerving once their goal was viewed.

Captain Emerson escorted his sister to the altar, then placed his sister's hand upon that of the viscount. The pair appeared to be lost in each other's eyes, their mutual adoration so potent that Mrs. D. felt a lump rise to her throat. There was more than one damp eye in her vicinity and even Mr. Dawlish gave her a gruff nod. Flora, close by her side, was transfixed by the sight and Mrs. D. could only hope for similar happiness for her oldest daughter.

Who might have imagined that the betrayed maiden would find a worthy man so soon? Not Mrs. D., but then love was a mystery, appearing unannounced and making sudden conquest of the hearts of those unprepared for such sudden good fortune. She knew it had claimed these two hearts, and brought this couple together forever.

As a result, Mrs. D. found herself not just satisfied but very happy indeed.

~

Fairfax was determined that all should be prepared. He wanted nothing less than perfection for this day's event. Mrs. Baird had been baking with a vengeance. They had taken on half a dozen new servants in the house and that many more simply for the day. It was more than the event of the viscount finally taking a bride—Fairfax wanted all to be precisely as the new viscountess desired. He wanted her first event at Addersley House to be a complete triumph.

He liked the lady very much, though he would have done his best even if he hadn't liked her. But she was lively and cheerful, reminding him of the old viscountess in a satisfying way. He sensed that she would be good both for Addersley and for the viscount himself, and Mrs. Baird was already anticipating that the nursery would be needed within the year.

Best of all, the new viscountess had ideas. This day was a perfect example. Why not combine the strawberry social once held annually with the wedding breakfast? Why not invite everyone to celebrate the joy of the day together? That it had never been done did not mean it could not be done, and in fact, once the idea was expressed, Fairfax would have moved heaven and earth to make it happen.

Even the weather was perfect for the day. It was sunny, the skies clear, yet there was a light breeze. Awnings had been set up across the lawn, and there were clusters of chairs and tables, in either sun or shade. There were more chairs upon the terrace, by the viscountess' own artful arrangement. Fairfax admired how the casual dispersion of the chairs contrasted with the formality of the garden itself.

When Lady Haynesdale had buckets of cut roses delivered that morning, Fairfax had taken the liberty of ordering flower arrangements to be added to the tables.

The blooms were all shades of pink and white, spilling from their vases with abundance.

In addition to the roses, he could smell strawberries, plucked from Addersley's own field. They had been prepared in dozens of ways, as tarts and sliced fruit, in fools and crumbles and atop cakes. There was strawberry jam or preserves, thick cream, scones and crumpets. There was tea and there was wine, as well as a veritable army of servants to pour and deliver such refreshments. He heard the carriages arriving from the church in the village and surveyed it all one last time, pronouncing himself content with arrangements.

His lord and lady were first to step onto the terrace, the eyes of the new viscountess lighting with pleasure. His lordship's ring was upon her finger and that man's contentment was clear. Fairfax bit back a smile himself.

"Fairfax!" the lady declared. "It is perfect. It is beautiful!" She took his hand and smiled up at him, her expression such that he thought she might grant him a kiss, of all things. "Thank you ever so much. Everyone will remember this day forever."

He rather wagered they would. "The planning was yours, my lady."

"But the details, Fairfax, are all yours. I never thought of the roses, but they are the perfect touch. Thank you."

"You might thank Lady Haynesdale. She had them cut and delivered from her own gardens this morning."

"How very thoughtful." The bride smiled with genuine pleasure. "I will thank her, as well."

The first of the guests arrived, their expressions a mix of awe and delight as they looked upon the preparations. The viscount offered his arm to his bride, sparing an intent glance for his butler. "I thank you, Fairfax, for ensuring all was prepared so well."

Fairfax gave a little bow. "I had to do all within my powers to ensure my lady's success," he said, watching the viscount smile. "May I offer my congratulations, sir?"

"Thank you, Fairfax. I trust you have arranged for punch in the hall tonight, as well as a fine supper."

"Of course, sir. We are all pleased to celebrate your nuptials."

"Mrs. D. came," the bride said to her husband. "I must welcome her." As the viscountess crossed the terrace, it seemed to Fairfax that joy emanated from her, infecting everyone she encountered. She laughed and embraced the lady in question, prompting both butler and viscount to smile.

"Your lady is a veritable breath of fresh air, my lord," Fairfax dared to say.

That man smiled as seldom he had in recent years. "She is, Fairfax. She is, indeed, and I knew the first moment I saw her."

Fairfax bowed as the viscount strode toward his lady wife. He had great anticipation for the future of Addersley and might have savored the sight of the new couple together in other circumstance. As it was, Lady Dalhousie was without a cup of tea and such a situation had to be addressed with haste.

COULD SHE BE ANY HAPPIER? Helena was quite certain it was not possible. The past fortnight had been a whirlwind of arrangements, each day ending with a long slow kiss from Joshua that left her simmering all night long. She had wished more than once that Eliza might yet have some of that book by Mrs. Oliver, but could not find a single page of it at Southpoint.

She had looked, repeatedly.

Although Helena had little doubt that Joshua would

make their wedding night memorable. She spoke to their guests, sometimes by his side and sometimes on her own, moving across the lawn and terrace as if she had been hostess of such functions a hundred times before. It was quite satisfying to organize matters, and the servants at Addersley Manor had been both helpful and welcoming.

How could she have imagined a liaison with the duke? She looked at him, certain he was of an age and infirmity to be her grandfather. Then she looked at Joshua and her heart skipped with joy. There could be no comparison between them.

There was an older woman alone on the terrace, one who might have been the duke's grandmother. She leaned on her cane, a plethora of veils draped around her crooked figure, and Helena thought she had never seen such an unfortunate collection of fabrics and colors on one person at one time. Her voice carried over the company, rising and falling as she complained about the sunlight. Other guests moved away from her, which only encouraged her to increase her volume.

Who was she?

A footman brought a chair for the lady and placed as she instructed, then she fell into it like a sack of potatoes. Helena was both appalled and fascinated when the woman pointed at her, then beckoned. "You," she said in her hoarse voice. "You, girl. Come here."

Helena exchanged a glance with Joshua, then followed the older woman's bidding. She was looked up and down, then the woman harrumphed and thumped her cane on the terrace. It was difficult to discern her features through the layers of veils, but what Helena could see confirmed her sense that she spoke to an ancient crone.

"Do you know who I am?" the woman demanded, her voice so deep that she croaked like a toad.

"I fear I do not. Perhaps you accompany one of our guests, or are visiting in the village."

"Ha! I am a guest of the Duke of Haynesdale," the woman said, almost crowing in her triumph. "What do you make of that?"

"Only that you are welcome, as the duke's guest."

The older woman laughed. She leaned closer. "And would you not even ask my name, my lady?" Her question might have been a dare. Of what import was this woman's name?

"It seems you wish to confide it in me."

The older woman fixed her with a surprisingly intent look. "I am Mrs. Delilah Oliver."

"Oh!" Surely this could not be the same Mrs. Oliver who had written those pages of amorous advice that had been in Eliza's possession?

"Oh!" Mrs. Oliver mimicked, then chuckled. She poked her cane at Helena. "I believe you recognize my name," she said.

Helena glanced toward Joshua, who spoke with the duke, then Eliza, who conferred with Nicholas and Aunt Fanny. "I did hear of a Mrs. Oliver who had written a book," she said carefully. "Might you be that same Mrs. Oliver?"

"What do you know of this Mrs. Oliver's book?"

Helena found herself as crimson as a strawberry herself, but she could not lie. "My brother's wife had some pages of advice from it." She took a fortifying breath and glanced about to ensure that no one was watching. "*Upon the merit of a forthright touch,*" she whispered, quoting the pages in question as her cheeks heated yet more.

Mrs. Oliver cackled. "How unsuitable a choice of reading for an unwed lady." She seemed to be more inclined to be amused than scandalized. "I am indeed the author of a volume about the amorous arts. It is as yet in the writing."

"I found it fascinating," Helena confessed. "I do not suppose there are any copies of your book available for interested individuals to read?"

The older woman cackled, thumping her cane so that people turned to look. "I knew it," she said in a gleeful whisper. "I knew you would want to see it." She dropped her voice. "They say you are a bold one, my lady, and I see no cause to dissuade audacity in a young wife." Her voice dropped yet lower. "You received a parcel in the post here this very morning, though you may not be aware of it as yet. It is of a goodly size." She marked the dimensions with her hands. "It contains copies of some of the newest pages. I should appreciate your comments upon the contents when you return those pages to me, shall we say in a fortnight or so?"

"Then it is not a wedding gift."

"The opportunity to read it is the gift, my lady, and it is not a small one. How scandalous it would be for you to own such a volume." She tut-tutted, her eyes glinting. Then she leaned back to survey Helena. "I believe you might appreciate it a good deal."

Helena smiled, having a very good idea of what to expect. "I believe I might, if the pages I read earlier were any indication. Thank you, Mrs. Oliver." The older woman inclined her head. "Would you like a cup of tea?"

"I would prefer a glass of wine, if you are not saving it all for the christening," Mrs. Oliver retorted. "And do not make it a small one. There is no cause for compelling the footman to appear at my elbow every few moments."

Helena beckoned to Fairfax and passed along the instruction, then dropped her voice. "Was a large parcel delivered by post today, Fairfax?" she asked, marking the dimensions as Mrs. Oliver had done.

"It was, my lady. I placed it in your bedchamber as we have not yet resolved where you will open your letters."

"That will be fine, Fairfax. Thank you."

Helena could barely restrain her delight. She had a copy of the book, or some part of it, for a fortnight. She intended to make use of every page, every day and night.

~

FINALLY.

They had chatted and eaten strawberries, gossiped and drunk wine, accepted congratulations and dined quietly. Joshua had enjoyed the day and its festivities, particularly Helena's triumph as a hostess, but he was not sorry to climb the stairs that night to his chamber. Helena had sparkled beside him all day, flitting from guest to guest like a butterfly, enchanting him with her laughter and her smile.

Tonight, there would be more.

She was a madness he could not deny and one from which he had no desire of recovery. She kindled impulses within Joshua that should have never been stirred to life again. She tempted and provoked him. She teased and tested him.

He opened the door to his own bedroom and was not truly surprised to find her already in his bed. Her hair was unbound and she wore only a silken dressing gown, her feet bare and her smile welcoming. "I dismissed Reed," she confessed. "I said I would assist you."

Joshua sighed in mock disappointment as he closed the door and leaned back against it. Several candles burned, filling the room with their golden glow, and the heavy velvet drapes were closed against the night. The room had been decorated in hues of midnight blue and gold, a combination that might have been specifically chosen to favor this lady. "And I had so hoped to assist you."

"Perhaps on the morrow, sir." She rose from the bed, opening the robe and letting it slide from her shoulders as she approached him. He could not help but survey her, so smooth and rosy, so delightfully curved and soft. He reached out to cup her breast in one hand and felt her catch her breath as he slid his thumb slowly across the nipple, watching it tighten at his caress. Her hand landed on his chest and she whispered his name, even as he bent and captured her lips beneath his own. He slid his hand into the loose ebony tresses of her hair, feeling it engulf his fingers like a silken web, and lifted her to her toes to deepen his kiss.

Of course, his bold bride was undaunted by his hunger for her touch. She slid her hands up his chest and around his neck, twining them in his hair as she opened her mouth to him, surrendering to his embrace with a trust that humbled and thrilled him. She was in his arms in an instant and he carried her toward the bed without breaking his kiss. En route, he reconsidered his choice, knowing she would welcome a less conventional choice. He took a seat before the fire on the settee there, holding her in his lap. She laid back in his arms, the firelight gilding her, and smiled. He kept one hand beneath her nape and slid the other up her thigh, returning to tease that nipple again.

"And what do you know of what will happen this night?" he asked, watching her smile broaden.

"That it will be wondrous," she said. Her own hand swept down his chest to touch him through his breeches. "That your greatest sensitivity is here." She moved her hand and he caught his breath, a reaction that seemed to please her. "That the darkness of your eyes and the intensity of your attention can only be a good portent."

He eased his hand between her thighs and claimed a kiss even as his fingertips moved ever higher. She felt like a goddess in his arms, so trusting, so soft and so willing, and yet she was his wife for this night and all others. There was only his bride and her delight in his touch, only this lady and the cultivation of her pleasure. He kissed her slowly, caressing her breast, mouthing the nipple to a turgid peak as she writhed beneath him. He eased his fingers up her silken thighs. Her lips parted in a silent gasp of surprise when he touched her, the dampness he found there casting his own reservations to the winds.

This was right.

This was true.

This was what he had been seeking, unaware of what he needed.

With Helena was where he belonged.

Joshua eased her to the settee, slipped between her thighs and closed his mouth over her sweet heat. She moaned as he teased her with his tongue and his teeth, and he felt the storm gathering within her. He kissed her and caressed her, building the storm and letting it ebb again, wanting her pleasure to be greater. He felt her skin heat and watched her flush. Her pulse leapt beneath his hands, she arched her back and moved with a vigor that fired his own desire.

But the lady would find her satisfaction first, even if the delay nigh killed him.

She was his lady and would be thus forever.

~

JOSHUA TOUCHED her with a reverence that Helena found irresistible. He was both strong and gentle, protective of even her pleasure, that she trusted him completely. His fingers swept across her like an invitation to sensation, one she could not decline any more readily than his kiss. He kissed her lips, her ear, her throat, his mouth conjuring a response beyond anything she had ever felt—and Helena wanted only more.

She was startled when he moved to kiss her there, but then the sensation was so splendid that she did not want him to stop. His hands roved over her, the warmth and crackle of the fire made her feel that they two were alone in all the world. They had a haven in this chamber, one where they could explore each other and do whatsoever they desired. She trusted him completely to guide her on this journey, and loved the sound of her own unwilling moans.

She felt a tide rising within herself as Joshua caressed her, his touch so sure that she followed him willingly. Her body knew more of this dance than she, but Helena already found it enticing beyond all. His mouth moved against her and she felt her body respond to each stroke. Her fingers were in his hair, his touch making her melt with need. The spark awakened by him was stoked to a flame, then coaxed to a blaze that threatened to consume her. She found herself entreating him for a release, desperate for whatever pleasure he meant to give, though she did not know what it might be.

And when the tumult came, she was astonished by its power. It swept through her from head to toe in a majestic torrent, an unstoppable tempest that left her both trembling with satisfaction and wanting more.

She opened her eyes to find Joshua watching her, his eyes darker than she had ever seen them, his fixation upon her complete.

"Oh, Joshua," she whispered in awe. "Tell me there is more."

And he laughed aloud for the first time she had ever heard him do as much. He stood and unfastened his cravat, casting it aside with impatience. The waistcoat she would always associate with him as a highwayman was next, followed by his boots and his breeches. He unfastened his shirt, his gaze fixed upon her, and Helena rose to her knees, no longer content with just the sight of him.

"I must touch you," she whispered.

"You are incorrigible," he murmured, but he let her lift his hands away. He smiled down at her as she unfastened his shirt then opened it wide. She bit her lip as she surveyed his broad chest, then ran her hand through the thicket of hair she found there. She looked up to meet his gaze, letting her hand slide ever lower, watching as he grew taut with need. She explored him gently, closing her hand around him, noting how he caught his breath and what caresses he appeared to favor.

"Helena," he whispered, his voice hoarse.

"I am yours, my lord," she replied and he caught her face in his hands, framing it as he kissed her with a hunger that set her very soul afire. She kissed him back, feeling the heat rise between them, and she found herself caught up against his chest again. She kicked her feet and he gripped her closer, then lowered her to the settee again. This time, he followed her, bracing his weight atop her, staring into her eyes as he moved between her thighs. She gasped at the first feel of him then arched her back as she welcomed him within her.

He whispered her name again, pressing a kiss to her shoulder, then met her gaze once more, a question in his own.

Helena smiled. "I am full of you," she whispered,

then rolled her hips. She laughed at the way he caught his breath, then he moved deeper and she was the one who gasped in wonder. At his gesture, she wrapped her knees around his waist, feeling cossetted and cherished. And when he moved, she felt her lips part in awe, for the storm was conjured again, mustering with every stroke and every caress. It built within her steadily, as natural as a rising tide, as unstoppable as a great wave. She gripped his shoulders and reached to kiss him, loving the sense that they two became one, that this was but the first of many such unions, that an exile from what she thought she loved best had brought her precisely where she was meant to be.

With Joshua.

Forever.

He moved more quickly then, the tumult rising with greater and greater urgency, until Helena was certain she could stand it no longer. Suddenly the tide cascaded over her in torrents and she laughed aloud as he held her close and roared in his own release.

"Again," she said into his shoulder. "Again and again and again." And the breath of his laugher swept over her skin, his eyes filled with stars as he pulled back to survey her.

"You are a marvel, Mrs. Hargood." He pushed a hand through her hair and kissed her roughly, his mouth open and his need undisguised. She kissed him back with equal passion to his own. "I love you, Helena," he murmured in her ear, his confession making her heart leap.

"And I love you, sir, with all my heart." It was a long while before she had the opportunity to say so much again.

~

JOSHUA AWAKENED on his first day as a married man with a contented smile. He had not slept overmuch the night before, but he had no regrets.

There was much to be said for an audacious wife.

He eased his hand across the sheets without opening his eyes, glad yet again that Helena had shown no inclination to retreat to her own chamber to sleep. He liked having her soft heat beside him, her scent filling his dreams.

His eyes flew open at the realization that she was no longer in the bed beside him. He sat up, wincing a little at the sunlight shining into his chamber, and smiled at the sight of his lady seated by the window. She wore his shirt from the day before, the front open, the crisp white fabric contrasting beautifully with the soft rosiness of her skin. Her hair hung in dark curls down her back and she bit the fullness of her bottom lip as she read some volume with great concentration. He rose from the bed and strolled toward her, choosing where he would kiss her first.

She glanced up at him with a contented smile and lowered the book to her lap. Joshua bent to kiss her sweetly, then tilted his head to read the title of the book. "What so fascinates you this morning?" he said, then felt his eyes widen.

The Ladies' Essential Guide to the Art of Seduction.

He blinked but Helena only smiled. "It is most instructive. I had read some of it earlier, which was how I knew to be encouraged by the hue of your eyes."

He scooped her up and took her seat, with her in his lap, then kissed her again. "How did you come to read any of such a scandalous volume?"

"I wasn't intended to, of course, but I was curious. And it was useful to know." She opened the book to the frontispiece and displayed it to him.

Joshua read.

It cannot be denied that in matters of intimacy between husband and wife, a gently-bred lady has no recourse to information, save her spouse's counsel. Many men decline to provide any tutelage, leaving their wives dissatisfied or discontent though they cannot clearly identify the cause. Such is the result of a lack of education in matters of intimacy. This volume intends to fill the deficit by ensuring that ladies of merit know not only what to expect in the marital bed, but also how to induce their husbands to join them there frequently and with enthusiasm.

"One can scarce argue with such good sense," Helena said.

Joshua could find no cause to protest frequent and enthusiastic unions himself.

Helena turned the pages, evidently seeking the one she had been reading. "I found this most apt," she said, turning the book for his consideration.

Upon the matter of gentlemanly restraint...

There is a notion commonly held that women are fragile and delicate, that we fear passion and cannot be expected to enjoy the sensual pleasures of the bedroom. Those who hold this view believe that women endure intimate relations—while, in my experience, ladies may not only savor such intervals, but welcome them and incite them.

Consider the merit of surprising one's husband, lover, or partner. If the man in question believes that he must initiate all sensual encounters, his ardor may be stirred by an unexpected seduction. I encourage you to embrace the unexpected—in both timing, location, and posture. Challenge his expectations by your willingness for congress at times other than those which have become your custom. Does he come to you in darkness at night? Go to him in sunlight, in the morning. There is much to be said for surprising a man in his bath, and no opportunity for him to disguise any enthusiasm for the interruption.

There are men, as well, inclined to hide their emotions and passions from view, presenting the world with an austere countenance and a rigid upholding of expectations. I assure you that there is a delicious pleasure to be found in conquering the reticence of such a man. Those hidden desires may be tumultuous and, when coaxed forth, may overwhelm his restraint with such abandon that the resulting encounter becomes most memorable.

Indeed, releasing the passion of a man who appears to have none is among the most rewarding of all sensory pleasures, and one that will forever change the balance of a relationship. To hold such a man in thrall to the satisfaction that only you can offer is a power that is to be welcomed, yet one that should be wielded with grace...

Joshua was well aware that Helena was watching him closely. He looked up to find her eyes sparkling with mischief. "A delicious pleasure?" he repeated and she laughed.

"A most satisfying one," she said, stealing a kiss he was only too willing to surrender.

He sighed with mock forbearance. "And now I suppose you mean to hold me in thrall." In truth, he suspected she already did.

"I take it as a challenge," she said, fanning the pages. "After all, I have this incomparable resource, though only a fortnight to take advantage of its counsel."

"How so?"

"It was lent to me, though I will not confess by who."

He might have argued that point, but she turned the pages again. "Does this not bring you and I to mind?"

Upon the matter of feminine capitulation...

It is the expectation of many men, and indeed of society at large, that women should be biddable and docile, always taking the counsel of men with regards to their behavior. I would suggest to you, gentle reader, that there is a delight to be found in challenging such expectations, particularly in matters of intimacy.

In the bedroom, in privacy with one's lover, a lady can reveal her own urges as nowhere else in the world. Be bold in your caresses, and forthright in your demands. Instead of lying back and accepting whatsoever your partner deigns to offer, tell him what you wish of him. Make the first address. Touch him as you wish—or touch yourself as he watches. I have written of boldness before, but the combined power of audacity and surprise cannot be underestimated, nor can its ability to change the foundation of a relationship be overlooked...

Joshua found himself grinning. "I have never expected you to be biddable, Helena, and certainly not docile."

Her pleasure in his approval was most clear, for she rewarded him with a kiss. He deepened it slowly, ensuring that it would be a memorable one. She was flushed when he raised his head but turned again to the wretched book. "I read this part this morning and could only wonder, Joshua, just how wicked you were inclined to be for me?"

Upon the merit of secret pleasures...

Joshua lifted the book from her hands and dropped it to the floor without needing to read more. "I vow to be as wicked as you desire me to be, my Helena."

"I think you will find, sir, that might be very wicked indeed," she managed to say before he kissed her to silence. He was prepared to take the better part of the morning to show her that he had no need of a book to discover ways to please her—much less of how to be wicked.

A lady's desire should always be fulfilled, after all.

ABOUT THE AUTHOR

Deborah Cooke sold her first book in 1992, a medieval romance called **Romance of the Rose** published under her pseudonym Claire Delacroix. Since then, she has published over ninety novels in a wide variety of sub-genres, including historical romance, contemporary romance, paranormal romance, fantasy romance, time-travel romance, women's fiction, paranormal young adult and fantasy with romantic elements. She has published under the names Claire Delacroix, Claire Cross and Deborah Cooke. **The Beauty**, part of her successful Bride Quest series of historical romances, was her first title to land on the *New York Times* List of Bestselling Books. Her books routinely appear on other bestseller lists and have won numerous awards. In 2009, she was the writer-in-residence at the Toronto Public Library, the first time the library has hosted a residency focused on the romance genre. In 2012, she was honored to receive the Romance Writers of America's Mentor of the Year Award.

Currently, she writes paranormal romances featuring dragon shape shifter heroes under the name Deborah Cooke. She also writes medieval romances as Claire Delacroix. Deborah lives in Canada with her husband and family, as well as far too many unfinished knitting projects.

Visit Deborah's websites to learn more about her books:

DeborahCooke.com

Delacroix.net

THE CRUSADER'S HEART
THE CRUSADER'S KISS
THE CRUSADER'S VOW
THE CRUSADER'S HANDFAST

The Rogues of Ravensmuir
THE ROGUE
THE SCOUNDREL
THE WARRIOR

The Jewels of Kinfairlie
THE BEAUTY BRIDE
THE ROSE RED BRIDE
THE SNOW WHITE BRIDE
The Ballad of Rosamunde

The True Love Brides
THE RENEGADE'S HEART
THE HIGHLANDER'S CURSE
THE FROST MAIDEN'S KISS
THE WARRIOR'S PRIZE

The Brides of Inverfyre
THE MERCENARY'S BRIDE
THE RUNAWAY BRIDE
<u>THE STOLEN BRIDE</u>

The Bride Quest
THE PRINCESS
THE DAMSEL
THE HEIRESS
THE COUNTESS

THE BEAUTY

THE TEMPTRESS

Christmas at Tullymullagh

Easter at Airdfinnan

Harlequin Historicals

UNICORN BRIDE

PEARL BEYOND PRICE

Time Travel Romance

ONCE UPON A KISS

THE LAST HIGHLANDER

THE MOONSTONE

LOVE POTION #9

Short Stories and Novellas

BEGUILED

An Elegy for Melusine

❧

To learn more about Deborah's contemporary and
paranormal romances,

please visit

DeborahCooke.com

❧